DADDY'S PRECIOUS JEWEL

Claimed by Daddy - Book One

POLLY CARTER

Published by Blushing Books
An Imprint of
ABCD Graphics and Design, Inc.
A Virginia Corporation
977 Seminole Trail #233
Charlottesville, VA 22901

Polly Carter
Daddy's Precious Jewel

EBook ISBN: 978-1-64563-281-8
Print ISBN: 978-1-64563-315-0
Audio ISBN: 978-1-64563-316-7
v2

Chapter 1

Pearl

Under the bright fluorescent lights, the jewels glistened and sparkled in their glass display cabinets. While Pearl didn't expect to ever own any such expensive treasures herself, her job as sales assistant at the high-end, exclusive jewellery shop, Mon Addi, afforded her the opportunity to gaze entranced at the colours sparkling off the diamonds, the fires crackling in the opals and the creamy translucence oozing from the pearls and moonstones. When she was rearranging the displays or serving clients, as the customers were called, she could hold the beautiful objects in her hands or against her skin, and occasionally try on a necklace or bracelet when asked to model one.

In the few months she'd been working at Mon Addi, she had, however, saved up to buy a pair of diamond studs. She wore them every day, and sometimes when she was gazing into the display cabinets, her hand would reach up to touch one to remind herself they were there, tiny but beautiful and sparkling.

It was a quiet morning in the brightly lit, elegantly decorated store, but Pearl didn't mind. She was equally as content admiring the treasures in the display cabinets while she polished the glass or as she was laying them on a black velvet cloth for clients to consider. She couldn't explain why she was so drawn to objects that glittered, flashed and shimmered in the light; all she knew was that they fascinated her and she wanted to learn everything she could about them.

She glanced up as the door tinkled to herald a client entering. In case she was called upon to be of service to the tall, expensively-dressed man coming in, she quickly returned to the main counter and hid her cleaning equipment behind it, then straightened her black skirt and primped her short, thick ash-blonde hair.

"No you don't, Pearl. Marcus Holding is mine. Stay away," her boss, Marcie Jones, hissed as she glided past on her way to greet the client. "Marcus!" she called in a decidedly friendlier tone. "What a nice surprise. It's been far, far too long."

Her voice dropped seductively as she reached him, took hold of his arm and gazed up with her most inviting bedroom eyes.

"Hey, Marcie," the dark-haired man greeted her, bending to exchange cheek kisses. As he did so, he glanced beyond her and caught sight of Pearl. Their eyes met and Pearl gasped as a bolt shot through her. She quickly dropped her eyes to the ground, peeked up, then lowered them again when she saw he was still watching. Her whole body was trembling for reasons she couldn't explain. She'd seen enough to know Marcus Holding was, without doubt, the most gorgeous man she'd ever seen but, as he was so far out of her league, there was no reason for her pulse to be racing as it currently was. He must be wealthy if he shopped here, and everything about him oozed confidence and sophistication while she was a simple country girl and retail assistant.

Giving herself a silent dressing-down for her ridiculous reaction to his handsome face, dark hair, muscular body and dominant air, she retrieved her cleaning equipment and moved to the farthest end of the store, facing away from her boss and the unsettling client. She wanted to have a better look at him. Who wouldn't? But brazenness was not in her nature so she kept her eyes averted and minded her own business as she dusted and polished the glass display cabinets attached to the wall, and lost herself in admiring the shiny gold chains hanging within them.

"Pearl." She started at her boss's voice directly behind her, and swung around to find herself being glared at by a pair of angry eyes.

"Yes, Miss Jones?" she replied, quickly casting her eyes down, wondering what she'd done wrong but certain she would find out soon enough.

"Mr Holding has requested you serve him. I warned him that you have practically no experience and are ignorant of fine jewellery, but I think he feels it is his duty to at least let you try."

"Yes, Miss," Pearl replied obediently.

"But," Marcie went on in a low voice, "don't get any ideas about flirting with Marcus Holding. If I see any inappropriate behaviour from you at all, it will result in your instant dismissal. Are you absolutely clear about that?"

Pearl's eyes stayed staring at the floor. "Yes, Miss."

"Right, well, I shall be watching you closely. Mr Holding is not only a VIP as far as Mon Addi is concerned, he is also my, shall we say, special friend? So don't go making a fool of yourself and embarrassing the good name of this store. Do what you can and call me when you are out of your depth. I will stay close enough to keep an eye on you."

"Yes, Miss." Pearl glanced over to see the handsome Mr Holding waiting for her by the main display cabinet. She quickly went to him and replaced her duster and spray bottle behind the cabinet.

"Good morning, Mr Holding," she said as professionally as she could, ignoring the unnerving thumping of her heart which kicked in the minute her soft brown eyes met his piercing blue ones.

"Hello. Marcie tells me your name is Pearl Sinclair. Is that right?" His voice was deep but gentle.

"Yes, sir. That's right," Pearl replied, demurely keeping her eyes down, all too aware she was being watched.

"Well, I'd like to call you Pearl, if I may."

"Of course, sir. Thank you." She nodded shyly, thinking she'd never heard her own name sound as pretty as when he said it.

"Right, Pearl. Then perhaps you can help me choose something for my mother for her birthday today. I'm on my way to meet her for lunch and, as usual, have left buying her gift until the last minute. It has to be expensive, I'm afraid, or she will accuse me of not loving her. She's rather inclined to value love with a dollar sign. And don't be embarrassed about the price tag. I have an obscene amount of money." He grinned a charming lop-sided grin to take some of the sting out of his words and Pearl had to exert all her control to prevent her knees from buckling.

"Of course, sir." Pearl's hands fluttered with eagerness and she had to clasp them together as her cheeks deepened to a rosy pink at the prospect of showing off her lovely treasures. "Do you have something in mind?" she asked as Marcie had taught her.

"To be honest, I didn't, but now I think pearls might be just the thing."

"Oh, yes. We have lots of lovely pearls. Come and see!" Well aware she was being watched by her boss, Pearl forced herself to walk calmly as she led Marcus to a floor cabinet containing an array of pearl jewellery behind which was a wall cabinet holding strings of pearls of all sizes and colours. She took the display board from behind the cabinet and placed it on the glass top.

"We'll be fine, Marcie," Marcus said firmly, dismissing Pearl's boss who had followed them and was hovering nearby. Pearl heard a small grunt of annoyance behind her and inwardly flinched. Marcie was not impressed and would no doubt take it out on her once they were alone in the shop. Pushing those thoughts aside, she assumed her most professional smile and focused her full attention on her client.

"Why don't you pick something out?" he was saying to her.

Pearl clasped her hands in front of her chest as she ran her eyes over the cabinet's contents. Having quickly made her choices, she opened the sliding door and removed the first piece.

"This is perfect for a woman who prefers traditional, understated jewellery," she said, mimicking the voice and words she heard Marcie use when talking to clients. She placed a delicate brooch consisting of a small clump of pearls set in the centre of a gold spray on the cloth. "Or perhaps she would prefer something that makes a slightly bolder statement? These are so lovely, aren't they?" she asked, fetching a single strand of gold South Sea cultured pearls from the wall cabinet behind her and draping them on the cloth. "And for a woman with flair and her own unique style, we also have these exquisite earrings." She took a box containing a pair of pearl drop earrings from the floor cabinet, and laid them on the cloth. Each one had four chains of black mother-of-pearl falling like rain drops from a single pearl set in gold and diamonds. Her treasures displayed, she clasped her hands under her chin and gazed in awe.

Marcus immediately reached for the earrings.

"Oh, I do like the black on these. I think that suits my mother perfectly. And she does rather fancy herself as avant-garde. Yes, I think these will do nicely, thank you."

Pearl looked up to see him smiling down at her. Her heart did another crazy thump and she had to drop her eyes afraid of what he would think and worried Marcie, who was watching like a hawk, would notice the slight trembling of her hands.

"Well, Marcie told me you were new—and you can't have been here long because I haven't seen you before, and I generally come in at least a couple of times a year. She said you wouldn't know what you were talking about, but I'm very impressed with the small selection you showed me."

"Thank you, Mr Holding." Pearl's outward demeanour remained calm and professional but she was inwardly thrilled by his praise as she returned the unwanted brooch and strand to their cabinets, and then put the earrings in their box. Marcus reached out and took her hand.

"You don't wear much jewellery yourself, I see. No rings? No symbol of you belonging to any man anywhere." He'd said it all casually, almost disinterestedly, but Pearl felt her heart race out of the blocks again, and this time her palms grew damp with dread that Marcie might have noticed.

"That's right, sir," she said coolly, withdrawing her hand and ducking her head to hide a blush as she finished packaging the earrings. "If there's nothing else, I can show you…"

"Actually, there is. I've just realised I do need one other piece of jewellery, but have no idea what. I will need your advice. Perhaps we could start with you showing me your favourite piece. If you have a favourite piece, that is; I rather get the impression you like most of them."

"I do love them all," she admitted bashfully. "But," she went on, her face lighting up, "I do have a favourite piece. I think it's the most beautiful thing I've ever seen. Although, it may not be to every woman's taste." She paused for a moment and wrinkled her nose. "I'm sorry, I assumed it was for a woman, but perhaps it is for you, or another man?"

"No," he said with a chuckle. "You were right first time. It is for a woman. In fact, it's a surprise gift for an exceedingly lovely and quite delightful woman, so I'd like the most special and beautiful thing you have. I'm sure if you love it, she will too."

Pearl led him to the main cabinet, laid the display board on top, unlocked the sliding door at the rear and removed a choker.

"I don't know what your lady friend will think of it, but I love this more than any other jewellery I've ever seen."

Marcus picked it up and turned it around in his hand, studying it minutely. It had a big heart made of champagne diamonds in the centre at the front, and smaller filigree hearts tessellated three up then three down made up the band. The first three hearts were white diamonds, the next three champagne, the next three white, then champagne and so on.

After studying it for a moment, he turned to Pearl, his eyes burning into hers. The casualness of before had gone. His muscular body was taut under his business shirt, and Pearl noticed a small pulse in his neck. Impaled by his eyes, she couldn't move and the air between them was suddenly so thick it would have been like walking through molasses if she'd tried to get away.

When Marcus finally broke the spell, his voice had a

gruffness she'd not noticed before.

"This is your favourite?"

She nodded, her eyes shining. "Oh, yes, sir. I love how it fits around the neck, like a beautiful collar. And how it has love hearts all the way around. And how all the beautiful diamonds sparkle and throw off flashes of colour, like tiny fairies, when it moves. And see how beautiful these champagne diamonds are!" Suddenly realising she had been enthusing perhaps too eagerly, she blushed and lowered her gaze.

"Look at me, Pearl," he said softly.

She obeyed, feeling herself falling into his fathomless eyes.

A tiny smile hovered around his lips.

"It's perfect," he said quietly. "It couldn't be more so. I'll take it."

"Pearl!" Pearl jumped at the sound of Marcie's angry voice right behind her. "What are you doing? Don't just stand there. I believe Mr Holding is in rather a hurry. Isn't that right, Marcus? You're having lunch with Linda, aren't you? His mother," she explained proprietorially to Pearl.

Marcus gave Pearl an exaggerated sigh and another heart-stopping grin. "She's right, unfortunately. I must get a move on. Mother awaits and," he glanced briefly at Marcie, "we both know she hates being kept waiting, don't we? But I think my business here is very satisfactorily concluded... for the moment."

"Shall I gift wrap these for you?" Pearl asked quickly.

"Just the earrings, thanks. The other doesn't need wrapping." She hurried off but could overhear him telling Marcie how pleased he'd been with the service.

He left with his purchases shortly after without saying anything else to Pearl except another 'thank you' and a 'goodbye'; Marcie made certain of that.

"May I go to the bathroom, please?" Pearl asked quickly when Marcie returned from showing Marcus out. Sensing she was about to receive a dressing-down, she raced off before she could be stopped, desperate for a moment to herself.

Once locked safely behind the bathroom door, she couldn't hold herself together a moment longer. Collapsing on a stool, she shivered as cold perspiration formed beads on her upper lip and her thoughts scrambled as they tried to make sense of what had just happened. She had made the biggest sale of her short career, almost a six-figure sum, and yet it wasn't that achievement, exciting as it was, that was uppermost in her mind.

Marcus Holding. She whispered the name to herself, feeling her whole being resonate with the music it created. It was ridiculous. She was being ridiculous. But for this brief moment, she was giving her imagination permission to go wherever it wanted, and it wanted only to conjure that handsome face in front of her, those blue eyes staring deeply into hers, those lips kissing her softly, and those strong arms wrapping around her and keeping her safe.

She pictured him holding that beautiful diamond collar and trembled. How she envied the woman around whose neck he would place it. She was sad the beautiful thing was gone, but glad it was Marcus Holding who had purchased it, and gladder still she didn't know the woman who would wear it. There was nothing stopping her imagining that she was the woman in front of him, and hers the neck around which he was fastening it.

Pulling herself together, she prepared to face her boss. She knew she hadn't done anything unprofessional but Marcie had seemed angry anyway. Time to stop dreaming, accept whatever reprimand was coming, forget about Marcus Holding and get back to work.

Chapter 2

Marcus

Marcie carried the small gift bag containing Marcus's purchases as she escorted him to the door and out onto the street.

"Call me, Marcus," she whispered as he took the bag from her and she leaned up to kiss him.

"It's not going to happen, Marcie," he replied firmly. "I've told you that a dozen times. Friends we've been and friends we'll stay."

"We have been more than friends though," Marcie wheedled petulantly.

"It was a long time ago, and it was a one off," Marcus stated matter-of-factly. "We both agreed that at the time. Now I must go. I don't want to upset Mother." And with a quick nod of his head, he strode down the street towards his car. Marcie's eyes followed him, narrowing with annoyance and bitter determination. She wasn't ready to give up on all that money, especially when it came attached to such an attractive man. As she re-entered the shop, she caught sight of Pearl inside. She'd definitely have to do something about her.

Striding towards his Jaguar F-type sports car, a thirtieth birthday present from his mother two years previously, Marcus's thoughts were not on Marcie. She was an attractive woman and they'd had one night of hot sex together. Apart from that, though, the chemistry wasn't there for him, and he suspected she would also be far less keen were it not for his considerable wealth, or at least his mother's considerable wealth, some of which would likely be his one day.

Climbing into the driver's seat, he put his bag on the passenger seat and took his phone from his pocket. "Hey," he called to it. "Send Mother a text. *I'm on my way*," he dictated when the phone had responded.

As he manoeuvred his car through the city streets and onto the freeway, he was tingling with excitement. He loved his car and driving it, but that wasn't the only reason for his present feeling of exhilaration, which was translating into a semi-erection. He was consumed by a heady feeling of discovery and anticipation such as an explorer, preparing to open the door to a hidden treasure trove, might feel.

Pearl. How that name suited her. Small. Perfect. Milky-white translucent skin, pale blonde hair, and such a sweet face with its big, soft, brown doe-eyes, dinky button nose and full lips. And she clearly was completely unaware of how beautiful she was; she had not an ounce of artifice.

Marcus was a man on a quest. He had enjoyed being single and playing around. Attractive and rich as he was, he had had no trouble finding women willing to keep him company and act out whatever sexual fantasy he asked of them, but always behind their willingness to submit to his sexual desires was the agenda of his money. He'd yet to find a woman who genuinely complemented him, or a woman who would be as interested in him were he a poor man instead of a fabulously wealthy one.

Pearl, though… Efficient and professional, she had a mature confidence when showing off the shop's wares that he was sure would put any customer at ease, and yet there was something else about her: a genuine child-like innocence and joy that suggested vulnerability and playfulness at the same time. It had instantly aroused his protective instincts. He grinned to himself thinking how he'd half expected her to skip about the shop, and he couldn't help but picture her in short skirts, tiny tops, frilly socks and laced-up shoes, and pigtails.

Then his eyelids lowered slightly and his mouth pursed as he lingeringly recalled how she'd lowered her gaze so demurely, and then raised it when he'd asked her to. She wasn't being flirtatiously coy; it was so natural he doubted she was even aware of the effect it had on him. He wondered what else she would do if he asked, and the thought of exploring how far she would go hardened his erection further. His face broke into a broad grin as he pressed down on the accelerator, the additional surge of power causing a rush of adrenaline. He banged his fist gently on the steering wheel and laughed aloud.

"Goodness! You have excelled yourself, my darling," Linda Holding purred a short time later as she took the earrings out of their box with a perfectly manicured hand. "Don't tell me these were Marcie's idea? I must have misjudged her. I thought her much too dull for something as exotic and wicked as these. I love them."

Her son leaned back in his chair and took a mouthful of the wine his mother had ordered before his arrival. "You're right in thinking it wasn't Marcie's idea. Her assistant showed me around today."

"Oh?" Linda flashed Marcus a questioning look, her

maternal antennae suddenly on high alert. "Her assistant?" she probed. "You mean Leah?"

Marcus shrugged as casually as possible, but he was aware the battle was on. Somehow, and it was a complete mystery to him how she did it, his mother had picked up on some nebulous thing in his apparently unimportant observation.

"Leah's gone," he answered. "There's a new girl. Who apparently did a good job. I'm pleased you like them, Mother. I thought they were perfect for you the moment I saw them. Why don't you try them on? They will go perfectly with your black top. Come on."

For a brief second, Linda hesitated. Then she removed the earrings she was wearing and replaced them with her new ones.

"What do you think, darling?" she asked.

"They look good off but you absolutely bring them to life," he answered flatteringly. "Don't be surprised if every woman in here is eyeing you enviously and every man lustfully."

"Oh, stop it." She waved her hand dismissively, but he could see she was pleased. "Well, like I said, they were an inspired choice. Perhaps I should go and thank this new assistant myself. What did you say her name was?"

Marcus grinned and shook his head. "I don't think I did. I believe it is Miss Sinclair."

"Miss? Exactly how old is this *Miss* Sinclair?"

"Really, Mother?" Marcus rolled his eyes and exhaled sarcastically. "I clean forgot to ask her that, what with the buying of the earrings and her being the shop assistant and all. I'm going to order." He nodded to a nearby waiter who came over.

Unfortunately, true to form, his mother was not yet ready to give up on her quest for information. Once the waiter had been dispatched, she brought the bone out for another chew.

"Young? Old? Pretty? Plain? This Miss Sinclair."

"I have no idea." Marcus saw no way out of this but to stick to his story no matter what sort of barrage his mother threw at him. "My eyes and attention were on the jewellery." *And she was the most stunning jewel of all.* "I was choosing something for you, after all, but let's say she is young and passably pretty. I mean Marcie must have hired her and she likes to have attractive women as her assistants so they can seduce their rich male clients into spending pots of money." *She certainly did that, albeit quite innocently.* The choker he had impulsively bought was waiting for him in the glove box of his car. He pictured it, and how those sparkling golden-brown, champagne diamonds would be set off by her blonde hair and brown eyes. It was a struggle to control an impulse to rush back to the shop and demand she put it on this instant. And it was reckless of him to leave such an expensive trinket in his car, but this bewitching, pocket-sized blonde had made him feel quite reckless. He mustn't frighten her, though. He had plans for her. Big plans. And it would require patience and care to bring them to fruition.

"Have you organised a date with this young, passably pretty shop assistant then?" his mother asked, cutting through his thoughts as if she could read them.

"No, of course not," he was able to answer truthfully and emphatically. "Our dealings were purely a commercial transaction." *This time.* "And now we have fully exhausted the topic of the shop assistant, shall we talk about other things? What are your plans for tonight?"

"Alan is taking me to dinner," she replied brusquely, not yet finished with her bone. "You're thirty-three, Marcus. Don't you think it's time you thought about settling down and finding a wife? I'd like some grandchildren before I'm too old to enjoy them."

"I'm thirty-two," he corrected her. "And I have no objection to settling down with one woman, when I find the right one but I have to find her first, no?" *And maybe I have.*

"I worry that you might fall for someone entirely unsuitable." Her eyes narrowed and she wagged a finger at him. "Like a passably pretty, young shop assistant."

Marcus rolled his eyes. "Ah, thank goodness, here's your lunch. How about we eat and I promise I shan't run off and get married on your birthday."

"You can joke about it," Linda replied, shaking out her napkin and laying it in her lap, "but I am deadly serious. You are nearly thirty-three, and you have a responsibility, not only to yourself and your own selfish wants, but to the family and the business. I shan't be letting any pretty, young, gold-digger lead you by the dick to the altar so she can get her conniving hands on your money."

"No? How charming of you, Mother," Marcus answered calmly as he speared a roast potato with his fork. He'd heard it too many times before to be in the least shocked.

Linda finished chewing and swallowed the small morsel of carrot she had in her mouth. "There are perfectly suitable girls amongst our friends you could marry. Some are bright and not ugly. All are wealthy and will bring their own money to a marriage. What about Tina Fielding? I've always thought she would be an eminently satisfactory daughter-in-law. She's not ugly and has wide-enough hips to produce healthy children. And she's been trying to marry you for years."

Marcus fixed the most exasperated expression he could on his face. "Enough! When I marry, *if* I marry, it will be to a woman I have chosen, who may or may not have wide, child-bearing hips. Either way, that won't be a deal-breaker."

"I've warned you, Marcus." Linda's voice had an ominous tone. "I shall not stand by and watch any gold-digging madam get her hands on our family fortune or our family business. Have you thought about Alan's daughter? Eileen?" The question was presented casually, but the underlying tension would have required a steak knife to saw through it. "All right," she said, holding her hand up before Marcus could speak, "She's a couple of years older than you and maybe has some past…"

"*Some* past? She's got more history than the British Empire."

"That's rather unkind, Marcus," Linda replied calmly. "Although she does have almost as much money as the British Empire."

"Ha!" Marcus snorted. "And that's a rather bigger exaggeration, but even if she was that loaded, it would make no difference. I have no interest in Eileen."

"You're an inverted snob."

"Call me what you like; the reality is I'm not marrying for money, and if and when I marry it will be to a woman I love and respect. And even her past won't matter. It's not who Eileen was in the past that turns me off; it's who she is now, and that's not anyone I am interested in spending any time with. She's…"

But Linda cut him off. "All right, all right. There's no need to go on about it." She shrugged. "Anyway, I'm planning for her to be your step-sister one day so perhaps it would be tacky for you to be married to her. Unless you two got married before Alan and I. I think that would be acceptable."

"It's not happening, Mother. Ever. And I shan't allow you to brow-beat me or meddle in my affairs," Marcus said calmly but firmly. "Truce. Let's not spoil your birthday by arguing. This conversation is closed."

Linda glared at him and opened her mouth, but realising he was in no mood to hear any more, changed the subject.

And, no matter how he tried, Marcus was unable to get the image of a petite blonde raising her eyes from the floor to meet his at his command, only in his mind's eye, she was naked and around her neck she wore a diamond-encrusted collar made of hearts.

Chapter 3

Pearl

What was that? Something. Just beyond reach. A feeling. A memory. Rising up from the veil of sleep, Pearl's mind groped for the thing, *that* thing, that niggling thing. She could feel it, but not yet identify it. All she had to do was open her eyes, but this was a lovely warm, safe feeling. She couldn't quite think where it came from and it might vanish like a dream if she didn't stay absolutely motionless, but her eyelids flickered. Sleep wouldn't stay.

Oh! There it was. There *he* was: Marcus Holding. Marcus Holding. Marcus Holding. She looped the music of his name over and over, stalling visualising the man himself, savouring the anticipation, like waiting for a lover to come around the corner. Exerting all her control, she forced her memory into linear mode, starting with the tinkle of the shop's bell. It was strange to think that, at that moment yesterday when the bell rang, she was utterly oblivious to even the existence of Marcus Holding. She was simply preparing to serve one of the usually nice and generally wealthy people who patronised Mon Addi as she had many times since starting there.

She relived in detail the first glimpse she had of him. He was dressed in business clothes, tall, well-built, older than her but not substantially, and with short, expensively-cut dark hair. It was only a glimpse and not quite enough information for her to fully appreciate the presence that was Marcus Holding. All that changed when he had looked past Marcie and seen her. *Seen her. Her!* The instant their eyes met, everything changed. If it had been a movie, her eyes would have become thumping cartoon hearts and invisible musicians would have played a serenade. It wasn't a movie, though, and he wasn't a movie star, which was a shame because, as it was, she couldn't be sure she'd ever see him again, whereas if he were in movies, she'd be able to see him there.

Wait! She sat bolt upright and grabbed her phone. So mesmerised by him had she been yesterday that she'd only relived the precious moments she'd actually spent in his company. His voice, his smile, his eyes, the way he treated her kindly, the way he'd praised her, the way he'd been firm with her. "Look at me, Pearl," he'd said, and she had raised her eyes to his. He'd said it kindly, but she couldn't imagine not obeying him, no matter what his command; he seemed so confident, so in control, so big and safe.

Desperate to see his face, she typed his name into her internet search bar. And there he was. Clutching her phone to her breast, she breathed a blissful sigh. He would be her secret pretend-celebrity crush. She picked a photo to have on her screen, then dressed for work. She wouldn't research him any further at the moment. It would give her something exciting to do this evening, but she wasn't going to be greedy; she would ration out photos and mentions. And then there was social media to explore as well. She picked up her phone and hugged it to her as though it were Marcus himself.

And he might return to Mon Addi one day. He did say he was a regular client. That was something to hope for as she made her way to work.

"Good morning, Miss Jones," she greeted her boss as she arrived the usual ten minutes before her official start time.

"Pearl." Marcie nodded perfunctorily. Pearl felt a chill as she put her bag away and prepared to start work. Marcie had never been particularly friendly but she seemed even less so this morning. Ignoring the chill in the air, she quickly fetched the vacuum cleaner and started running it over the carpet. The front door would not be unlocked for another fifteen minutes giving her time to ensure that, when it did open to the public, the shop would be as clean and sparkling as the treasures it housed. Determined to give Marcie no reason to find fault, she worked hard all morning without resting: attending to clients, and cleaning, tidying, and rearranging the displays whenever the shop was empty.

"Can you run these down to the post office," Marcie said around midday, handing her two letters. "It should only take you about twenty minutes and then I'll go to lunch."

On her own in the shop later, while Marcie was out, Pearl noticed the brooch she'd shown Marcus the day before was no longer in its place. She'd seen it earlier, so the only explanation was that it must have sold while she was posting Marcie's letters.

She was pleased. She wanted the shop to do well, and this week's takings had already been excellent with Marcus's shopping spree and the other pieces they'd sold, and now the beautiful, quite expensive brooch as well. Maybe it would even be a record week. The owners would surely be very pleased with their work.

She was totally unprepared then when Marcie, having returned from lunch, called her over to the display cabinet.

"Did you sell the pearl and gold brooch?" she asked. "I didn't see it on the sales record."

"No, I didn't sell it," a confused Pearl answered. "I noticed it was gone and assumed you had sold it when I went to the post office."

"Well, I didn't, and it was definitely here when I went to lunch. I checked all the cabinets before I left and it was there then. Did anyone come in while I was away?"

"Yes. A few people. I sold two gold chains, which I entered in the book, and a young couple paid a deposit on an engagement ring that I've locked in the safe. No one asked about the brooch. I didn't go near that cabinet for any reason the entire time you were at lunch."

"Well, if you didn't sell it, it must have been stolen, although I can't see how anyone could have stolen it without a key to the cabinet. Are you sure no one asked to see anything from in here? You had no reason to open it? Is that what you're saying?"

"Yes. I'm quite sure none of the clients asked to see anything in here."

"You do realise what sort of position that places you in, don't you, Pearl?" Marcie said grimly.

"Why?" Pearl asked, genuinely puzzled. Then she understood. "No! You can't think I stole it."

"Well, you certainly had plenty of opportunity, and you did like it. I've often seen you admiring it, and it was one of the pieces you chose to show Marcus yesterday. Perhaps you were hoping to pretend that he'd slipped it into his pocket."

"No!" Pearl's already fair skin paled further to a ghastly shade of white. "He wouldn't steal. I wouldn't do that. That's awful!"

"Well, the brooch is clearly not here, is it? And I can't think of any other explanation. Can you?"

Miserably, Pearl shook her head. "Perhaps I accidentally moved it to another display case. I'll check."

"Don't bother." Marcie held out her arm to stop Pearl going anywhere. "I have already done a thorough search. I'm afraid I can't have you in the shop any longer until the brooch is found or there is an acceptable explanation as to where it's gone. Fetch your bag, please."

With no choice but to obey, Pearl collected her bag.

"I have no idea where the brooch is, I promise. I didn't take it."

"Show me your bag," Marcie ordered, tipping the contents out when Pearl handed it over.

Even though there was no way Pearl could imagine how the brooch could have found its way into her bag, a wave of relief washed over her when there was no sign of it.

"Perhaps you had an accomplice come in while I was out," Marcie said grimly.

"I didn't take it. Honestly, Miss Jones," she pleaded. "Please, check the CCTV. You'll see I didn't go near the cabinet."

"Very well," Marcie agreed, but she quickly returned shaking her head. "Well, it seems the CCTV has been tampered with. The tape was removed, so it's not recording."

"No! I didn't!" Pearl said, shaking with disbelief that this could be happening.

"The jewellery in here is too valuable for me to take any risks. I am afraid I'm going to have to let you go. Should the brooch mysteriously reappear I shan't call the police, but I can no longer have you working here. I should not have trusted you. I gave you a wonderful opportunity by employing you, but that was obviously a mistake. I'm so disappointed. I think you should leave. I'll work out what is owed to you up until this time today and transfer it into your account."

"I'm not a thief," Pearl insisted. "Please don't fire me. I've done nothing wrong. I love my job."

"I'm sorry, Miss Sinclair. I love my job too, and I wouldn't keep it long if I failed to take action to protect the jewellery. I think you should just leave quietly. I'm already doing you a huge favour by not calling the police immediately. I'll give you forty-eight hours to return the brooch before informing head office, who will not hesitate to hand you over to the authorities and have you charged. If you are too embarrassed to bring it in yourself, you can put it in a white envelope and have a friend discreetly leave it behind the counter. If I find it there, I'm prepared to forget the whole matter. But I suggest you don't get another job in a jewellery shop if you can't avoid the temptation. Off you go. Forty-eight hours remember."

"I can't return the brooch in forty-eight hours or forty-eight years because I didn't take it," Pearl said, her sense of injustice giving her the courage to look her boss in the face despite having to fight against tears. "This is so unfair."

Marcie picked up her phone. "Leave, Miss Sinclair, and I don't want to ever see you in this shop again. Have someone else bring the brooch in. You are no longer welcome here. Leave, please, unless you'd prefer I call the police."

Pearl stared at her in utter disbelief. Without the slightest warning, her world had suddenly crumbled. Not only was she unfairly being accused of being a thief, she had lost the job she loved, and worst of all if she was no long working at Mon Addi there was no chance she would ever see Marcus Holding again. She could feel her lip begin to tremble, and the tears filling her eyes were dangerously close to spilling over and running down her cheeks, but there was no way Marcie Jones would see her cry. She quickly shoved her things into her bag, held her head up and walked out of the shop.

Chapter 4

M*arcus*

MARCUS DROVE through the huge iron gates that mysteriously opened as he approached and into the big, wide driveway of the mansion he shared with his mother. He parked his Jaguar in its garage, collected his bag and let himself into the self-contained, two-bedroom apartment situated across a large lawn from the rest of the house.

He was glad to be home at last. When his mother told him she needed him to sort out a problem at their logistics business's head office, it was supposed to be a three-day trip, a week at the absolute most, but as soon as he'd been ready to return, she'd called and asked him to sort out a problem at one of the Holding Corporation's mines first.

In both cases, Marcus could see no reason why the issues couldn't have been dealt with via conference call. He suspected it was a ploy to keep him out of the way for a while. Women's intuition and, especially his mother's intuition, never failed to amaze him. He'd barely mentioned Pearl and yet he was sure she had sensed danger and decided to meddle.

She couldn't keep him away from Pearl forever, though. He was planning a shower, a feed, a good night's sleep and then a visit to Mon Addi in the morning.

Laying on his bed after his shower, a towel across his groin and the diamond collar beside him, he grinned as he transformed the towel into a tent picturing himself standing in front of a kneeling, naked Pearl, her freshly-spanked bottom warm and rosy. It was only one of many scenarios he had in mind for the delectable jewel, and he was impatient to get started. That she wouldn't want to participate simply had not occurred to him. He knew in his heart that Pearl, whether she was aware of it or not, had a submissive Little girl inside and it wouldn't be long before she was calling him Daddy.

The following morning Linda seemed no less intent on controlling his time, no doubt to keep him away from Mon Addi, but he was having none of it.

"But I need you in the office," she said, when he joined her at breakfast to debrief from his trip and told her he was planning to have the day off.

"Do you though?" he retorted. "We are paying people millions of dollars. Why, if they can't attend to whatever you think needs doing so urgently?"

"For goodness' sake, Marcus!" she scolded him. "You're not a little boy. One day, and it won't be long, you will be in charge of the entire family business. The only way it will continue to grow is if you commit the necessary time and effort. Not taking days off like a schoolboy wagging school."

"Hardly fair, Mother. I just did over two weeks straight. Not even a Sunday off while I was traipsing about the country at your order. I think I've earned a day off, and I don't think the massive Holding conglomerate will collapse if I take one." His tone was light, but his eyes were glinting.

"Oh very well," she conceded, waving her hands in dramatic surrender. "How about we compromise and you come to the office with me now, but leave early? I do need to go through the Rambolan contracts with you. I was supposed to get them out by last Friday but you have to check them first."

It was Marcus's turn to admit defeat. "If you insist," he agreed ungraciously. "I'll come with you this morning, but I *am* leaving as soon as we're done."

"Of course, darling," his mother purred, sipping the cream off her coffee.

"NO, I'M LEAVING RIGHT NOW," Marcus told his mother firmly at half-past three, as she tried to get him to start a fresh task. Ignoring her pleas and demands, he tidied his desk and left. He'd been close to throttling his mother for deliberately delaying him all day. But she was wasting her time. He *was* going to see Pearl today, and no one and nothing was going to stop him!

He was as eager as a schoolboy with a first crush as he walked briskly up the pavement to Mon Addi. Pausing to collect himself before going in, he peered through the glass door, his eyes searching for a small blonde with big brown eyes and a soft, sweet expression. He didn't see her. He searched again, but he could still only see Marcie and a very pregnant Leah, the assistant before Pearl.

Barging in, his eyes swept the room for a third time, still sure he must have just missed seeing her.

"Marcus!" Marcie greeted him, taking hold of his arm. "What a nice surprise! Visiting us again so soon."

"Hey, Marcie." Marcus voice was cool and wary as he ignored her fluttering eyelashes. "Where's Pearl?"

"Pearl doesn't work here any longer," Marcie answered silkily.

"What do you mean? Why not? What happened? Did she resign? Where has she gone?"

Marcie's eyes narrowed and her brow furrowed further with each of his questions.

"She left. I have no idea where she is. Gone home to the farm in the small nowhere town she came from, I expect."

"Why did she leave? Did you have anything to do with it, Marcie?" Marcus had pulled himself up to his full height and was glaring down at Marcie with a thunderous face.

"Marcus, really," Marcie replied in a soothing voice as she patted his arm, "what on earth do you mean? Why would I have had anything to do with it? What *could* I have had to do with it?"

Pulling his arm away from her hand, Marcus glared at her. "She must have given a reason for resigning. And didn't she work out her notice? How long have you been back, Leah?" he called suddenly to the young lady who was watching them in surprise.

"Nearly two weeks, sir," she answered. "Marcie asked me if I could lend a hand until she could find a replacement for the girl who left."

"I see." He smiled at her, adding, "Oh, and congrats on the baby."

"Thanks," she replied, returning his smile and stroking her swollen belly.

"So, Pearl left pretty much immediately after I was here last?" His question was addressed to Marcie, who shrugged and moved away, but Marcus noticed her face blushing and her hands trembling. He moved in front of her and blocked her path so she had to face him.

"What happened, Marcie? Why did she leave? I got the distinct impression she was really enjoying her job."

"Come on, Marcus. My staff are my concern," she retorted angrily. "Miss Sinclair is no longer in the employ of Mon Addi. End of story."

"Give me her phone number then," he demanded.

Dipping her head so she could look up at him, she pursed her lips in feigned regret and shook her head. "You know I can't do that. Privacy laws and all."

"Damn!" He paused. "You call her then. Ask her if you can give me her phone number or give her mine."

"This is a jewellers, not a dating agency," Marcie said, shaking her head. "But how about I close the shop early, and we continue this over a drink somewhere? My treat," she offered.

"We're going nowhere until you tell me what happened and how I can contact her."

Marcie paused then held her hands up in mock surrender. "Okay, I wasn't going to say anything for the sake of the girl's dignity but as you are insisting, I had to let her go for stealing."

Marcus recoiled as though she'd struck him. "Stealing?" he barked. Then shook his head. "I don't believe it. What is she supposed to have stolen and what proof did you have that it was her?"

Marcie faced him squarely. "A brooch went missing. She was the only one who could have taken it. I fired her and told her that if she returned it in a white envelope within forty-eight hours I wouldn't call the police. The next day a white envelope appeared behind the counter and the brooch was in it."

"She brought it in?"

"Well, no. Not her personally. I didn't think she'd have the guts to do that. I suggested to her that she could get someone else to do it for her. That must have been what she did. I didn't see who it was. There was a period when we had a few clients in at the same time and, after they'd all left, I saw it behind the counter."

"Nope," Marcus said, shaking his head and frowning. "I don't believe it, and I don't know what game you're playing either, but I want to know where Pearl is. You will give me her address, or everyone at Holding Corporation will be moving their business to another jeweller. I've no doubt I can get at least as good a deal as we have with you elsewhere."

"You wouldn't," Marcie said defiantly but not without a tremor of insecurity. "Besides, I can't give you her address. Privacy."

"Right, well, I'll make a few phone calls then. I'll start with Rhinegold, shall I? They've been courting us for ages."

Marcus took out his phone and started searching for the number. Marcie blanched.

"All right. All right." Marcie fluttered her hands in surrender. "She's from Hicksville; Darling Flats, I believe it's called. Wherever that is. I guess she's gone there. I can't tell you more than that. I'll lose my job."

"You deserve to!"

She moved closer as he made to leave and lowered her voice to a sultry wheedle. "Come and have a drink, Marcus. We can have dinner and then take a bottle of wine to my place. Forget Miss Nobody. No doubt she realises she made a mistake coming to the city. She's probably already engaged to some neighbouring, similarly dim-witted, flannel-shirted yokel. She'll be much better off. She's a country bumpkin, Marcus. She's not sophisticated like you and me."

While she was talking, Marcus was backing in the direction of the front door, trying to extricate himself from her without making a scene. His expression was dark and angry.

"Thanks for the offer, but I fully intend to get Pearl's side of the story. And if I think you've done anything to deliberately harm her, you'd better worry about your job."

He strode off with a sense of urgency, leaving Marcie with a worried frown. She smoothed down her skirt and glared at Leah.

"Get a move on!" she barked and headed for the bathroom.

MARCUS DROVE STRAIGHT HOME, packed an overnight bag, jumped into his car and keyed the only address for 'Sinclair' he'd found in Darling Flats into his GPS. Heading out of town to begin his two-and-a-half-hour journey, he thanked landlines for still having at least one use. Without knowing the names of either Pearl's father or mother, he couldn't be sure he was headed for the right Sinclairs, but it would be a good place to start his search. He had briefly considered ringing, but he needed to see Pearl, not just hear her voice, and if it was the wrong house, he'd keep searching until he found her. That he had promised himself.

If all went well, he should arrive before eight o'clock; a not completely uncivilised time, he hoped, to knock on a stranger's door without fear of scaring them half to death. He had a full tank of fuel and could eat once he arrived, which meant he could drive straight through without stopping.

He was curious as to what his reaction would be when he saw Pearl. He'd been so taken with her when he'd met her at Mon Addi that he'd thought about her constantly since, but as every minute brought him closer, he wondered whether he had built her up into something in his mind that she could never live up to. Perhaps she was simply a pretty, dull, small-town girl with whom he had nothing in common, and with whom he would quickly grow bored should he spend any time with her.

He shook his head and increased the car's speed. No. He didn't believe that. There was something about her that called to him. He'd heard stories of people seeing someone for the first time and immediately being absolutely certain that that was the person they were destined to marry. Did he feel like that about Pearl? Maybe. Maybe not. But he did feel her calling to him in a way he'd not experienced with any woman before. So maybe it was destiny. His romantic heart wanted to believe so; his rational mind was counselling him to wait and see.

His thought's switched to Marcie and her story about having to fire Pearl because she'd stolen a brooch. He pictured Pearl's wide, innocent eyes and then Marcie's dark, calculating ones. He wouldn't trust Marcie not to try something underhand to get Pearl out of the picture if she saw her as a rival for the Holding Corporation fortune. Not that Marcie had any chance with Marcus; he wasn't the least bit interested in her romantically, but she hadn't accepted that.

As he swung the car off the road and into the Sinclair family farm's drive, his heart was pounding, no longer just from an expectant thrill at the possibility of seeing Pearl, but with anger. He was angry with Marcie for her disgusting treatment of Pearl, but he was also irrationally angry in general at a world, which would take so little care of his precious girl. The farm appeared to be quite poor and rundown, and her brave attempt to carve a life for herself in the city had cruelly ended in her being thrown out of work through no fault of her own. He shuddered to think how she was coping.

He tapped on the front door, his mind formulating a speech to explain his presence at a stranger's house in the dark. Even if Pearl did live here, she might not be in. His heart started thumping wildly in his chest as he heard the latch on the other side and the door opened. Then Pearl was standing there staring at him in utter astonishment.

"Hi, Pearl," he said, resisting an immediate and over-whelming urge to pull her into his arms and kiss her into oblivion. She was so adorable in a short pink dress, barefoot, her hair mussed as though he'd just woken her. "Remember me?"

"Oh," she gasped, leaning against the door as she collected herself. "Yes. Of course. Mr Holding. What are you doing here? Why…? How…?" Her expression changed to one of consternation. "Did I do something wrong? Is there a problem with your mother's earrings?" Before he had time to answer, she suddenly remembered her manners. "Oh, I'm sorry. Please come in."

Marcus grinned at her as he entered and waited for her to close the door behind them.

"Please, call me Marcus. And…"

"Is that a visitor?" A woman Marcus took to be Pearl's mother joined them interrupting what he was about to say.

"Yes," Pearl stammered, blushing. "This is Mr Holding, Marcus. Marcus, this is my mother, Mary Sinclair."

"Mr Holding," Mary said taking the hand he held out to her and shaking it firmly but briefly.

"Please call me, Marcus, Mrs Sinclair," he insisted, taking an immediate liking to her. She had the same guileless, open expression as her daughter but without the awkwardness of youth. He could see the likeness between mother and daughter: Mary was also petite and her hair was fair, albeit not as fair as her daughter's, but her eyes were blue, unlike Pearl's brown ones.

"Only if you call me, Mary," she agreed with a laugh. "Is this a social visit? Would you like a cup of tea? Coffee? A cold drink? Can I offer you dinner? We haven't had ours yet. We were waiting for Pearl's father to come in. He shouldn't be long."

"Thank you. That's very kind. It is a social visit," he said, smiling reassuringly at Pearl. "But if it would not be rude and if Pearl agrees," he went on, holding Pearl's eyes a second longer than necessary before looking at Mary. "I was rather hoping I might take her out for dinner. I'm assuming there is somewhere nearby we can get a feed?"

"The only place at this time of night would be the Chinese restaurant in town," Mary said. "They'll be open until nine o'clock, so you should have time. And I have no objection at all. It's up to Pearl."

"Would you have dinner with me, Pearl? I'm a big fan of Chinese."

Like a deer momentarily caught in the headlights and then startled into action, Pearl paused then nodded. "Yes, thank you. I'll be ready in a few minutes," she mumbled and fled into the darkness of the rest of the house.

Mary and Marcus talked about the drought and the urgent need for rain until Pearl reappeared, shoes on, a white bobbled cardigan over her dress, her hair brushed, and her lips pink and glossy.

Chapter 5

Pearl

As she slid into the passenger seat and waited for Marcus to close the door behind her, walk around and hop into the driver's seat, Pearl pinched herself. She must be dreaming. There was no other explanation. It hadn't occurred to her that Marcus would ever have given her a second thought.

How— Why had he found her? Why was he here? Was he aware that she had been so ignominiously dismissed? What would he say when he found out? Would he be angry he'd driven all this way for a thief?

"There's no need to look so apprehensive," he said as he started the car and drove down the drive and out onto the road. "After I saw you in Mon Addi a couple of weeks ago, I decided to ask you to dinner, but then I had to go out of town on business. I got home yesterday, so popped in to Mon Addi today and discovered you weren't there anymore. And why. Marcie told me you'd come here. I checked the phone directory online and found one Sinclair listed so took a chance on it being the right one, and fortunately it was."

"Oh." Pearl was relieved he appeared to already know she had been fired for allegedly stealing and had come anyway, but she still wasn't quite sure why. She stared at him with her mouth open and a puzzled expression.

He reached over and patted her hand. "I want to have dinner with you is all and, as you were here, I had to come here too. That's it. Relax. Okay?" He tilted his head and pretended to be stern. Pearl giggled.

"Okay."

"Good."

Even though driving in Marcus Holding's car might have been the last thing Pearl had been expecting to do this evening, it felt absolutely right, and he was such a gentleman: opening doors for her when they arrived, pulling her chair out in the restaurant, helping her with her order, and pouring her wine.

"To our first meal together," he said, smiling and raising his glass.

"Our first meal," she repeated, as a thrill skittered through her. *First.* He made it sound as though it wouldn't be their last.

"I want to know everything about you that you are willing to tell me," he said when she'd had a sip of her wine. "Do you have any brothers or sisters?"

"Yes, one brother. John. Four years older than me. He joined the army as soon as he turned eighteen, nearly ten years ago. He said it was too quiet and boring in the country and he couldn't see himself being a farmer. He's overseas at the moment but we get to see him sometimes."

"It's a shame for your dad, I guess, that he didn't want to stay and help on the farm."

"I think Dad was disappointed at first, but John seems to

have changed his mind. He's talking about coming home in a year or so when he can leave the army. He doesn't like being away from his family, and wants to start helping Dad on the farm."

"Family?"

"Yes. He has a wife, Debbie, and a son, Tom, who had his first birthday two months ago. Mum and Dad would love them to live closer so they could see more of their grandson."

"I guess they would," Marcus said. "Have you always lived in Darling Flats then?"

Pearl nodded. "Yep. Mum and Dad bought the farm when they got married. They both grew up around here and didn't want to leave. I hadn't ever lived anywhere else until I went to the city about eighteen months ago. I worked as a waitress until I got the job at Mon Addi. I was there a few months." She paused, not quite able to raise the topic of her dismissal. "Now I'm here. Not particularly interesting," she finished apologetically.

"It's interesting to me," Marcus reassured her.

"Really?" Her eyes opened wide in surprise.

"Yes, really." He winked, and she blushed. "What did you do between school and moving to the city then?"

Pearl shrugged. "I helped out around the farm mostly. Dad paid me whenever he could, but I didn't do it for the money. I knew he couldn't really afford to pay anyone else, and wanted to help him." She paused self-consciously. "Then I think Mum and Dad got worried I'd be living with them forever and I think Dad was feeling bad that I wasn't doing anything with my life but helping him, so they started encouraging me to move. They knew how much I wanted to work in a jewellery shop, so they helped me find a flat in the city. Mum was thrilled when I told her about the job at Mon Addi. Oh, did your mother like her earrings?"

"She did. She loved them."

"Oh, that's good."

"Her exact words were 'an inspired choice'. So, well done."

"I only pointed them out to you." Pearl dismissed his praise, but blushed with pleasure. "It was you who chose them."

"Well, you thought to point them out, so how about we agree it was a great team effort, eh?"

Pearl nodded as the soft feeling of pleasure seeped further through her like hot chocolate on a rainy day at the thought of her and Marcus Holding as a team.

The conversation was interrupted by the arrival of their meals.

"Mmmm. This smells good," Marcus said, as they both transferred spoonfuls of different dishes onto their own plates, and seemed pleased when she replied with a warm, slightly tremulous smile, "It's delicious. More inspired choices."

"Excellent. So," he added, his expression becoming serious. "I want you tell me what happened at Mon Addi. I think I can guess, but I want to hear your side."

"I didn't take that brooch!" Pearl said hotly, feeling anger burning her skin. "I'm not a thief."

"I know. I didn't think for a moment you had taken it. Do you have any idea who did though?"

"No. None at all. It was the day after you came in. The brooch was there in the morning; I saw it. Then Marcie asked me to go to the post office and, when I returned, she went to lunch. Then, while she was out, I noticed the brooch was gone and thought she must have sold it while I was at the post office, but when she got back she asked *me* if I'd sold it, and when I said I hadn't she accused me of stealing it and fired me."

Marcus nodded grimly. "When I spoke to her earlier, she said it was returned in a white envelope the following day."

Pearl clenched her fists. "Well, if it was, it wasn't by me because I didn't steal it. Why would I? I loved my job so much. I felt like all the precious jewels in the shop kind of belonged to me anyway," she said blushing and averting her eyes. "That probably sounds dumb, but I could admire them every day, and take care of them, and keep them polished, and show them off to clients."

She glanced at him and could see from his kind, understanding expression that he didn't think it was dumb at all. He reached out and covered her hand with his.

"I think I can guess what happened," he said. "And I know you didn't steal anything."

Pearl let out a long, sad sigh. "The worst part is, I wanted to work my way up to managing or even owning my own jewellery store. I wanted to learn everything about gems and buying them, and Mon Addi is such a prestigious store and it carries only fine jewellery, not like those chain stores that have mostly cheap synthetic stones. I was so lucky to get a job there in the first place. Now that I've been fired for stealing, no other jewellery store will want to hire me, so I don't know what I'm going to do."

"Have you got another job? How have you been managing?"

"I had some money saved, so I've just been helping Dad. The lack of water is making things harder and harder for the farmers around here, though. I've been trying to decide whether to try and get a job in town so I can help by giving Dad extra money, or whether it's better if I keep helping him so he doesn't have to pay wages. I was on quite a good wage at Mon Addi and could send some home. I can't earn as much here if I get a job in town. So, I haven't quite decided what to do yet." She clamped her teeth on her bottom lip to stop it trembling.

Marcus was quiet for moment. She could tell from his expression that he was thinking. Eventually he spoke.

"Tell me, Pearl, if you could work at Mon Addi again, would you want to? I mean, would you want to leave the farm and work with Marcie after her treatment of you? I'd understand totally if you'd rather never see her again."

Pearl's eyes opened wide in surprise. "Oh. I haven't thought about it because it never occurred to me it could ever happen."

"Well, think about it," he pressed her. "I might be able to organise it, but there's no point if that's not what you want."

"I do want to work in the jewellery industry, and I do want to manage a shop or have my own jewellery business one day. I haven't changed my mind about that."

"And Marcie? Could you bear to work with her, do you think? If she apologises? I'd keep an eye on her and ensure she treats you properly and with respect."

Pearl was overjoyed. She might be reinstated at Mon Addi, and Marcus Holding was promising to watch out for her which meant she'd keep seeing him. From grey and drab, her life was suddenly shining like the rarest of diamonds. Pure bliss bubbled in the centre of her being and she shut her eyes tight as though that might prevent it from escaping.

"Pearl?"

She had to open her eyes. She had to do whatever he said even if she didn't understand why. Her heart constricted as their eyes locked.

"Yes. I could. If you think it would be a good idea. But I don't know if I should leave my parents, or if I could afford another flat in the city."

"Fair enough." He nodded. "I realise it's not a simple decision, so I'm not going to press you for a quick answer, but at least we can both think about it and how we could make it work if that is what we want. Have your parents thought about selling the farm? I guess it's hard to get a good price for it in the middle of a drought."

Pearl nodded. "They want to sell eventually and buy a modest flat somewhere near the ocean. Not yet, but that's Mum's retirement dream, and Dad adores her and would do anything he could to give her whatever she wants. I don't think Dad plans to leave the farm for a little while yet, but if they don't keep the farm going, when they do come to sell, they might not be able to find a buyer at any price, never mind enough to buy an apartment by the sea."

Marcus nodded as he listened to her. "Well, that's something to think about," he said when she finished, "but for the moment I want to hear more about you. I think you told me you don't have a boyfriend at the moment; is that right? No local lad snapped you up? There must be dozens hanging around your door." He grinned, and she couldn't help a self-conscious giggle as she shook her head.

"Definitely not dozens. Not even one."

"Have you had many serious relationships? It's a personal question, but I am insatiably curious."

Pearl dropped her gaze, shook her head and blushed.

"Does that mean I'm being too nosy?" he asked.

She shook her head and whispered, "You'll probably think I'm an idiot."

"Why on earth would I think that?"

She shrugged but kept her eyes down. He felt her foot touch his as it poked at the floor.

"Look at me, Pearl," he ordered her gently when she didn't answer. "Pearl."

Slowly she raised her eyes to his, then quickly looked away.

"Have you ever had a boyfriend, Pearl?" he asked. She

shook her head. "You don't have to tell me if you don't want to. We can talk about something else."

"I don't mind," she said. "I've never had a proper boyfriend."

"How can that be?" Marcus asked, genuinely astonished. Pearl shrugged again, studying the table and drawing a circle with her finger.

"I never seemed to meet any boys around here apart from the ones I went to school with. My best friend at school was a boy, though. Tony. We hung out together all the time and everyone thought we were a couple but we weren't, at least not like that."

"How come? You're beautiful. I can't believe he wasn't attracted to you."

She blushed and giggled at being called beautiful. "And he is very nice looking. When we were seventeen and neither of us was interested in anyone else, we decided to be boyfriend and girlfriend. We held hands everywhere we went, and we kissed a few times." Her eyes still firmly on the table, she added quietly, "I'd had a crush on him for years so I wasn't interested in other boys anyway."

"What happened? Sex? You're not trying to tell me a seventeen-year-old boy was kissing you and didn't want to have sex?" Marcus squinted his eyes and tutted. "Unless, of course, your friend Tony is gay."

"We did, ah, you know, one day, we decided to…" she mumbled.

He grinned. "Go on. I get the picture."

"But it didn't work." She stopped and giggled, realising what she'd said and amazed she could be so open with a man she barely knew. "I didn't mean it quite like that. The whole thing was just wrong. Then Tony told me he had suspected he was gay when he was quite young, but he'd been pretending to himself that he wasn't and that probably all boys felt like he did. I suggested he talk to the school counsellor. He did and finally admitted to himself that he wasn't attracted to girls. I was a bit sad, but at least I didn't lose him as a friend. We're still close friends and he has a lovely partner now, Pierre. They live in the city, so I saw them quite often while I was there. You'd like them if you met them."

"I'd love to meet them, especially as Tony is your best friend. I'd best get in his good books, hey? And there hasn't been anyone else? How is that possible? There's no chance you're attracted to girls?"

Pearl's mouth opened and her brow furrowed in surprise. No one had ever asked her that before, and he wouldn't be asking either if he realised what a huge crush she had on him. "Um, no. No chance," she said squirming in her seat and scrutinising her fingers. "After I finished with school, I spent all my time at the farm and didn't meet anyone. I think that's part of the reason Mum and Dad were so keen for me to move to the city, but I didn't know anyone there apart from Tony and Pierre so I mostly stayed in my flat when I wasn't working. I guess I'm just not that outgoing or something. And I don't seem to have ever met any man I was interested in." *Until you.* "Or who was interested in me. But what about you? You're older than me. How come you're single? Have you ever been married?"

"I'm thirty-two, and you're…?"

"Twenty-four."

He nodded. "Okay. And to answer your question, no, I've never been married. I have had a few girlfriends, but no relationship ever lasted longer than a few months and none were serious. It's been a combination of things, I guess. My mother has very definite ideas of who are suitable potential Mrs Marcus Holdings." He grinned ruefully. "I'm not saying there might not be a perfectly nice young lady among them, but I'm afraid I have an intractably stubborn streak when it comes to having my wife selected by my mother. Plus, most of the women she has in mind come from wealthy backgrounds and are after a rich husband to take over from Daddy paying their bills. It's not a characteristic I find particularly attractive."

"Is that why you're here? Because my family doesn't have any money?"

"No, Pearl." He reached over and squeezed her hand. "I think that would make me as shallow as the women who come after me because I am rich, or at least my family is. It's knowing they are fluttering their eyelashes and offering their bodies because they find money arousing that is the turn off. I have dated wealthy women who weren't like that, and some of them were very nice and I'm also still friendly with a couple although none are my best friend," he said with a smile. "But I guess I've never met anyone I could envisage spending my whole life with either, and someone who would be my best friend as well as my wife." He caught her eyes with his and held them. "I don't know what this is, or why I couldn't rest until I'd found you. But I do know I want to spend more time with you and get to know you better. If that's agreeable to you, of course."

She nodded but didn't speak.

"That's a yes, it's okay with you?" he asked seriously.

She nodded again, and this time whispered, "Yes. It's okay with me."

"Excellent. Now, eat your dinner. You've barely touched it."

"I'm too full already to eat another thing." *Too full of happiness. He wants to spend more time with me!*

Marcus reached over and scooped up a spoonful of food and held it out to her.

"You don't have to eat it all. Just one more spoonful. Come on. Open up."

Pearl dropped her head and shook it. He was taking charge and taking care of her, and she was suddenly overcome as she realised how much she loved that he would do that. She kept her face hidden, embarrassed he might realise how she felt.

"Pearl," he said sternly. She glanced up, then quickly down. "Come on. Eat your dinner."

She raised her head and wriggled bashfully as she opened her mouth so he could push the spoon in.

"Good girl," he said, watching her chew. "Do you want to eat the rest yourself, or shall I feed you?"

I want you to feed me. Pearl took the spoon from him. "I can feed myself," she said, scooping up a small amount and putting it gingerly into her mouth. She chewed it and swallowed and put her spoon down. "I can't eat another bite. Honestly. I'm so full."

Marcus regarded her sternly and she thought he was cross, but then he smiled and her heart skipped with happiness.

"All right. Just one more mouthful of vegetables, and we can take the rest with us. I'm a bit concerned about you not eating properly, though. I will keep an eye on you. You don't have an eating disorder, do you? I'm not going to disappear if you do," he added quickly, "but it would be better if I know about it."

Pearl shook her head vigorously. "No. Promise. I usually eat plenty. I'm just not hungry." She quickly took another spoonful of food and ate it as quickly as she could, wishing her throat didn't feel so constricted. It was making it difficult to swallow.

"All right." Marcus said. "I don't want you to be sick." He called the waiter over and organised to take the leftovers with them.

Chapter 6

Marcus

Marcus paid the bill and escorted Pearl to his car feeling well pleased with the evening's events. He'd had no trouble finding her, she was as captivating and heart melting as he'd remembered, and she seemed as keen on him as he was on her. He smiled to himself remembering their conversation about previous relationships and sexual experience. She hadn't exactly said she was a virgin, but it sounded like she was or at least very inexperienced. He wouldn't have minded at all if she hadn't been, but she was so endearing the way she'd told him the story, and he would have to remember to go slowly and be gentle. The last thing he wanted to do was hurt or scare her.

He was particularly captivated by the way she seemed to automatically defer to him in so many situations. She was by no means incapable of taking care of herself; she'd proved that when she'd moved to the city, found and held down a job and lived alone. But she was more complex than that, he could feel it.

Watching her open her mouth when he'd told her to so he could feed her, and then feeding herself when he'd told her to had aroused both his heart and his cock. He loved the way she obeyed him. He'd been testing what she would do if he asked, but hadn't pushed too hard; it was too public and too early in their relationship, but he was more certain than ever that he wanted to have a relationship with her and more determined than ever to be careful not to frighten her away.

They didn't speak in the car, both lost in their own thoughts, then Pearl broke the silence as they neared their destination.

"Are you going home tonight? Or would you like to stay?" she asked breathlessly, inspecting her finger. "You can get a bed in town if you don't want to stay at our place, but we have a guest room you can use. I understand if you'd rather stay somewhere else though," she added quickly.

"Could I stay at yours?" He'd been trying to decide whether to try and find a bed in town or drive home. Staying at Pearl's was by far his preferred option even though he'd not considered inviting himself. "I'd rather not drive home tonight. Are you sure your folks won't mind?"

"They won't mind at all," she replied. "You saw Mum. She loves having people around to fuss over. As long as you don't mind that. And you haven't met Dad yet. He was outside when you came, but he loves having someone to have a good yarn with."

"Your mum certainly made me feel welcome, so if you reckon your dad will be okay, it sounds great."

"Come on, then," Pearl said as he brought the car to a stop outside the farmhouse. "We'll go and ask, but the answer will be yes."

Rusty, a black and white border collie dog, who'd still been out and about with his master when Marcus had arrived before, met them at the door, wagging his tail at Pearl and half raising his hackles and sniffing suspiciously when he saw a stranger.

"It's all right, Rusty," Pearl said. "Ignore him," she added to Marcus. "He's friendly really but he likes five minutes to pretend he's not. Come in."

As they entered the kitchen where Jack and Mary were chatting after dinner, Jack with a beer and Mary with a cup of tea, Marcus was once again struck by the warm, friendly, relaxed feel, so different to the starched atmosphere at his mother's house. Mary greeted them as they entered, and Jack stood up to be introduced. Marcus guessed he was late fifties. Like his wife and daughter, Jack was below average height. His hair was thinning on top and greying around the edges, and his skin showed the effects of a lifetime working outdoors. A few creases in his brow suggested he might not always have been free from worry, but there was a friendly twinkle in his eyes.

"Dad, this is Marcus Holding. Marcus, my dad, Jack Sinclair."

Marcus shook hands with Jack and immediately liked his firm, friendly grip and direct gaze as he said, "Pleased to meet you, Marcus. Pull up a chair. You might have to bring that one over," he added pointing to another chair. "I'm afraid this one is Moppy's personal throne." He bent and stroked a large ginger cat curled up on the chair at the end of the table. Moppy's only response was a brief deep purr. "Beer?" Jack offered Marcus.

"I'd like a beer. Thanks," Marcus said, putting the bag of leftover food he'd brought from the car onto the table and fetching the chair. Pearl had seated herself on the other side of the table next to her mother.

"How was it?" Mary asked.

"Excellent," Marcus said enthusiastically. "I like Chinese food and I reckon that was as good as I've had anywhere. We couldn't eat it all, so we brought the rest for you. If you'd like it."

Mary took the bag he pushed over to her, and licked her lips. "Oh, yum! Thank you! We can have this for lunch tomorrow… if you're sure you don't want to take it with you."

"I'm sure. Please, you keep it."

"Well, thank you again. We're pretty big fans, aren't we, love?"

"We are that," Jack replied handing Marcus a beer he'd fetched from the fridge. "It's a good cheap feed when we can't be bothered cooking, or if we feel like getting out of the house of an evening for a change. Not that that happens much."

Mary laughed. "No, generally we'd rather just put our feet up at the end of the day."

"Oh, Mum," Pearl said, suddenly remembering. "Would it be okay if Marcus uses the spare room so he doesn't have to drive in the dark?"

"Of course," Mary said warmly. "There's clean linen on the bed, and it's all made up. Did you bring a bag or anything? I'm sure we can find anything you need."

"Thank you," Marcus replied gratefully. "I really appreciate the bed, but I have everything else. I brought an overnight bag in case. I'll fetch it in."

"Bring your beer and come have a gander at the cars in the shed as well, eh?" Jack said getting up. "You like vintage cars?"

"Sure do. What have you got?" Marcus asked as he followed him out.

The two men disappeared, Jack telling him proudly

about the two old cars he was restoring, bit by bit whenever he had spare cash or came across a part he couldn't pass up.

When the men returned, Marcus found Pearl in the spare room, a duster in her hand, a clean towel, face cloth and soap on the bed.

"Is this okay?" Pearl asked. "Do you need anything else?"

"It's perfect," Marcus said, putting his bag down. "I can honestly say there's no room in the world I would rather be sleeping in tonight." *Except maybe yours.* "Are you tired?" he asked not ready to say goodnight to her yet. "Would you like to go for a walk outside? It's quite bright out there. I think the moon is full tonight."

"Yes," she replied, so eagerly he wanted to grab her and kiss her right there, but didn't. They would share their first kiss under the moonlight, he'd decided.

The night air was cool without being cold. Pearl had her cardigan on and Marcus had a jacket over his shirt. Once their eyes had adjusted, they could see quite well as they wandered around the garden and along the orchard fences. Marcus slipped an arm around her shoulders while they were walking and felt a tingle of excitement as she leant against him. With the moon in full view, he stopped to enjoy the quiet, broken only by the symphony of the cicadas, the call of a hunting owl, and the occasional bark of a dog in the distance which caused Rusty, who had accompanied them, to raise a half-interested ear.

"It's magic," he said softly, stopping to admire her, her hair and eyes shining in the moonlight. "It's so much more beautiful than in the city. The sound of nature instead of traffic. And a sky filled with stars. Must be a billion at least! And look how bright and shiny the moon is."

She gazed up at the moon and nodded. He could feel her leaning lightly against him, waiting, compliant, in his power.

He bent his head and brushed her lips with his. He felt her tremble and caught her to him so she couldn't fall. She felt so small and vulnerable as she hesitantly returned his kiss. Keeping his arms around her, he leaned back so he could see her face.

"Do you like me kissing you, Pearl?" he asked. She nodded but wouldn't look at him. "Look at me." She watched her foot as it poked at the ground. "Pearl?" She wriggled and her foot poked harder. "Pearl!" This time she looked up, slowly, her eyes darting away the moment they connected with his. He kissed her again, then released her with a chuckle and a muttered, "Naughty girl. Are you shy?" He took her hand in his and led her toward the outbuildings near the house.

She shivered as a cool evening breeze picked up, and he stopped, took off his jacket and draped it around her shoulders. Holding the inside of it, she pulled the jacket together across her chest, and Marcus put his arm around her. "Come in here for a moment. Out of the breeze," he said, leading her into a shed. Moonlight was pouring in through the window giving them enough light to see each other and so they wouldn't trip over anything. Marcus found a flat surface he could sit on and pulled her onto his lap. She snuggled against him laying her head on his chest, once again arousing both his heart and his cock. He closed his eyes savouring the feeling of being, for this brief moment, utterly complete.

"Hey, baby," he whispered. She raised her head enough so he could kiss her. Her lips were as soft and sweet as an old-fashioned flummery dessert. He pulled her close against him as his lips roamed over hers, and gradually he felt her moving her mouth against his. He pressed her lips with his tongue, and she opened hers, hesitantly at first but with growing confidence. He loved how she fitted perfectly into his lap. The kiss ended and she nestled her head on his shoulder.

"What is this shed?" he asked, peering around at the shapes visible in the semi-darkness. "It's not a woodshed, is it? Did you get spanked in here when you were a little girl?"

She wriggled and he heard a small muffled giggle as she shook her head.

"No?" he asked, grinning in the dark. She hadn't recoiled in horror. She'd giggled.

"No." She giggled louder.

"Come on, then," he said, gently stroking the nape of her neck. "We'd better go in. Your parents will be wondering where you are. It's getting late and time you were in bed. And I don't want your dad coming after me with a shotgun the first time I meet him."

This time she didn't stifle a fit of giggles as she jumped off his lap. He kissed her one last time, snuggled her against him with his arm around her and walked her to the house, only releasing her as they went inside. Mary smiled at them as they entered the kitchen and spoke to Marcus.

"I'm off to bed, but wanted to check you have everything you need first."

"Yes, thank you, Mary. I'm sure I shall be very comfortable. I think Pearl's going to bed, too."

"Yes," Pearl replied, aware of three pairs of eyes on her. "Goodnight, everyone."

"Would you like another beer before you turn in?" Jack asked Marcus, who rightly guessed Pearl's father was keen to find out who this man was who had come calling on his daughter.

"If you're having one, yes. Thanks. I'd be pleased to join you."

Jack fetched two open beers and handed one to Marcus. "Cheers," Marcus offered once Jack had sat down opposite him at the kitchen table. Both men raised their bottles and then took a swig.

"So, I can't say I remember Pearl mentioning you," Jack began. "Have you known each other long?"

Marcus settled in for a long chat and it was well past midnight before the two men shook hands with mutual respect and liking and headed off to their respective beds.

Chapter 7

Pearl

After she'd walked Marcus to his car the next morning and he'd kissed her goodbye and promised to be in touch, Pearl went inside to find her mother waiting for her, a big smile on her face.

"Marcus seems lovely," she said. "And he seems to be quite taken with you."

"He is lovely, isn't he?" Pearl replied as she hugged her mother, even happier, if that were possible, that her mother obviously liked Marcus too. "I can't believe he came to see me."

"Were you not expecting him at all?"

"No! We only met that once when he came in to Mon Addi and then I got fired the next day and I hadn't heard from him or seen him since. I honestly had no idea he'd even noticed me, let alone that he would come all the way here to see me. I'm glad he did, though," she added swinging from side to side looking at her feet to hide a wide, irrepressibly joyful, ear-to-ear grin.

"Did he say why he suddenly turned up?"

Pearl regained some control of her face. "He said he had to go out of town on business the day after we met and was away until the day before yesterday. He went to Mon Addi yesterday afternoon, found out I was here and," she said, clapping her hands together, "came straight here."

"Gosh! It sounds like he really wanted to see you, then."

Pearl wrapped her arms around her middle and squeezed. "I know. I can't believe it. He's so gorgeous and his family is fabulously wealthy so I never thought for a moment he would even notice me. Oh, Mum, I'm so happy."

"And I'm happy for you too, darling. He seems so nice and down-to-earth for someone with so much money. He's not at all snobby, is he? I mean, you'd never guess just from looking at him and talking to him."

"Apart from his fancy car," Pearl said, giggling and wriggling. "And, oh Mum, he's going to try and get me my old job at Mon Addi."

"Is he?" Mary's eyes widened in surprise. "Can he?"

Pearl shrugged. "He said his company is Mon Addi's top customer; Mon Addi gives discounts not only to the company but to the staff, too, so lots of them shop there. Mon Addi would lose a lot of business if they all decided to go elsewhere. That wouldn't look good for Marcie."

"It would serve her right! Would you want to work there again, though, after what she did to you? And where would you live? Is the apartment you had before still available, do you think?"

A small frown creased Pearl's brow. "I don't know. It might have already been re-let. I could try, though." Her face cleared. "But Marcus said he would make sure Marcie treats me properly and that he'll help me find a flat. How will you and Dad manage here without me?"

"We'll manage like we always do," her mother told her firmly. "If you want to work in a jewellery store in the city, that's what you must do. That's been your dream since, well, forever, I suppose. If you've got the opportunity, you should take it. Now I must get on, but I am happy for you, darling. And so far I like Marcus very much."

As Pearl started helping her father around the farm, she wondered if she would ever hear from Marcus. But then, less than two hours later, he sent her a text: *I've stopped for petrol. Thinking of you xx.* Her heart flipped; she'd been half expecting to wake up and find she'd dreamt the whole thing: his visit to the farm, having dinner with him, his feeding her, their walk in the moonlight, and him kissing her as she sat on his lap. When she'd relived it all in her mind after he left, it had seemed impossible that it could actually have happened, and yet here was a text from him the minute he could send one. *Thinking of you xx.* Her lips tingled as she looked at the kisses on the end of his message, and her fingers trembled as she replied: *Thinking of you too xx (blushing smiley face emoji).*

From then on, he contacted her multiple times a day, sending her 'Good morning' and 'Good night' texts, and ones during the day if anything interesting happened like when the woman in front of him in the cafe queue had a tiny, teacup dog in her handbag and it growled at him, or when he got a flat tyre and had to change it in the rain.

He rang her every evening as well and they chatted about nothing much. Then on Friday evening he told her he'd been to see her old boss, Marcie Jones, earlier that day.

"What did you say? What did she say?" Pearl asked, anxious that Marcie might still be claiming Pearl had taken the brooch. Marcus dispelled her fear immediately.

"Don't worry. She's admitted knowing you didn't steal anything, and has agreed to rehire you. Leah, the assistant she had before you, has been helping while Marcie was going through the recruitment process to replace you, but she doesn't want to stay, so the sooner you start the better. If that's what you want. You mustn't feel pressured either way, though. It's your choice."

"I do want to go. I do," Pearl said jumping up and down so Marcus could barely hear her.

"All right, then, sweetness. I'll have another talk with Marcie and let you know when she's expecting you."

Marcus rang at eleven o'clock on Sunday morning. "It's all organised," he told her. "Marcie is expecting you at ten tomorrow morning for a chat, and you can start Tuesday morning. I've found somewhere you can stay, so all you need do is pack and I'll be there in a couple of hours to pick you up."

Pearl gasped. "Today? But what about Mum and Dad?"

"I understand, baby. You need to talk to them. Why not do that and I'll call back in a few minutes."

"Of course you must go," Mary said when Pearl told her about Marcus's phone call. "If that's what you want, and it is, isn't it? You'd better get packed and, when Marcus calls, tell him you'll be ready and waiting. I'll make some snacks to take with you."

Pearl was ready and pacing up and down the front verandah when Marcus's Jaguar drove up.

"He's here! Mum. He's here!" she called through the front door.

Mary joined her as the car pulled up, the boot opened, and Marcus got out.

"I'm sorry there wasn't more notice," Marcus apologised as he collected Pearl's bags from the verandah. "I only found out this morning that everything was in place, so I immediately called Pearl, jumped in my car and drove here. It is what you want, isn't it, Pearl?" he asked gently. "You're not obliged to if you've changed your mind. It's entirely up to you, but I will help you all I can if you want to give it another go. Do you want to work at Mon Addi again?"

Pearl nodded, her head down, but when she raised it enough to glance up at him, her eyes were shining.

"Don't worry, Marcus," Mary assured him. "She does. She's been fascinated with shiny objects since she was a tiny wee thing, haven't you, Pearly? I'm not sure if that was because we called you Pearl, or whether somehow we knew that was how you were going to be and it was why we called you Pearl." She shook her head, as amazed as ever at the coincidence. "Have you time for a quick cuppa and piece of carrot cake before you head off?"

"We have," Marcus replied with a grin. "There would never not be time for a piece of carrot cake. How did you guess it's my favourite?"

Pearl could barely keep still while Marcus had a cup of tea and piece of carrot cake with Mary.

Mary, seeing her bouncing around, laughed. "You look like you've got ants in your pants. She's so excited she can't sit still," she added to Marcus. "It was such a lovely thing for you to do—get her job back, I mean. You must have been able to pull some strings, but I can still hardly believe Marcie agreed. Or that she could do that to Pearl and get away with it."

"She's not quite getting away with it," Marcus said seriously. "I went in to see her personally at the first opportunity I had, and she was in no doubt about how angry I was. She was surprised. She hadn't expected any repercussions. It just hadn't occurred to her that anyone would stand up for Pearl. I told her I knew exactly what she'd done and why, and she didn't even bother trying to deny it. She was quite mortified at being called out and terrified it was going to cost her her job. She begged me not to get her fired, but to begin with I couldn't see she deserved anything else. Then I came up with a better punishment because one thing I know for sure about Marcie is that status is extremely important to her."

"Status?" Mary asked.

"Yes," Marcus nodded. "She wants to feel important and she gets at least a bit of that by being a manager and having an assistant to boss around, doesn't she, Pearl?"

Pearl rolled her eyes, pulled a face and nodded. Marcus and Mary laughed. "I think I get the picture," Mary said.

"Because we are such a big client, I could certainly get Marcie into a whole heap of trouble if I told her boss my company was going elsewhere because of her behavior," Marcus went on. "She'd be out on her ear in a flash. And she knows she has no more chances, so I pretty much have her over a barrel and she knows it. If she so much as glances at Pearl the wrong way, she'll be looking for a new job. For someone as naturally bossy as Marcie it is going to be hard and painful for her, firstly apologizing to Pearl and in effect admitting what she did, and then treating her as an equal in the shop and not as a junior. I know Marcie well and so does my mother, and Marcie does not want to upset us any more than she already has. I think Pearl will find it's quite a different experience this time, and although Marcie is not going to enjoy not being able to boss Pearl around, with a bit of luck she might learn a valuable lesson. We'll see."

"Well, it's a lovely thing you've done for Pearl, and I'm glad you will be looking out for her," Mary said when Marcus finished, drank the last of his tea and popped the last bit of cake in his mouth. "I guess you'll be wanting to get going then."

"I think we should, if Pearl's ready," Marcus agreed,

standing up and holding out his hand to Pearl who shyly put hers in it as she stood up as well.

The flat Pearl had rented before had been re-let, but Marcus had found her a much nicer one: brand new, better location, bigger, lighter, and with a lift as well as stairs.

"Oh my. It's gorgeous! But how could I ever afford something like this?" she asked in a tiny voice a couple of hours later when he opened the front door for her and she saw inside.

"Don't worry about that for the moment," he said, brushing aside her concerns. "You do like it, don't you?"

"I love it!" Pearl answered, gazing in awe out the window. "What a heavenly view! You can even see the river and there's a park." She spun around to face him. "And if it's on the bus route to Mon Addi, it will be so easy to get to and from work. It's perfect. But…"

"Nuh uh uh," Marcus interrupted, wagging his finger at her. "No buts. Just unpack and get settled. It's rather plain and boring right now," he added, glancing around at the carefully orchestrated neutral décor. "But we can go shopping for some things to brighten it up next weekend. Would you like that? You can choose whatever you want. Come on." He carried Pearl's suitcase into the master bedroom and put it on the king-size bed. "You don't have anywhere else to go, so you may as well stay here for the time being."

Pearl took some clothes from her case into the walk-in wardrobe. "There's some clothes already in here," she said, her nose scrunched in bemusement. "They must belong to whoever was here before—but they're all new. They all still have their labels."

"They're yours," Marcus told her with a casual shrug. "If you want them. I bought a few things I thought might be nice for you to wear when we are here together. What do you think? Do you like them? You don't have to wear them if you don't want to. I can return them and you can choose some other things."

Pearl flicked through the clothes hanging up and thought how they were exactly what she most loved to wear: lots of pretty colours, short skirts, sparkles, hearts and teddy bears.

"Well?" Marcus asked. His voice sounded different, tense.

"I love them," Pearl whispered. "I love the colours and rainbows and hearts and teddy bears and sparkles and… and everything."

"Good!" Marcus said, letting out his breath. "Would you like to change into something now? You don't have to wear them out if you don't feel comfortable, but I reckon you'll be cute as a button and, if you want to wear them, who cares what anybody else thinks? Just don't wear them to work." He touched the end of her nose with his finger, and she giggled. "I'll wait out here while you change."

"Okay." Pearl nodded, hopping from foot to foot. She chose a short denim skirt with a frayed hem and a rainbow embroidered on the back pocket, and a multi-coloured striped, short-sleeved jumper. She also found some short, white socks with lace around the top and a pair of pink sneakers covered in sparkles. She wriggled and squeaked with delight when the shoes fitted perfectly, and jumped up and down in front of the mirror. She loved the outfit so much, and she felt little and safe because Marcus had bought it for her.

She went out to show him and twirled around so he could see it from all angles and then stopped in front of him, her hands clasped together under her chin, worried he might not like it.

"Utterly adorable," he said and kissed her, ruffled her hair and patted her bottom. "Would you like to go to the shops like that?" he asked. She nodded and he grunted with pleasure.

By the time she'd finished unpacking and organising her clothes for the following day and they'd been shopping to stock her fridge for the week, it was already getting dark. It was too late to cook, so Marcus bought take-away pizza for them to share at the flat. When they'd finished, he got ready to leave.

"Are you going?" Pearl made a sad face.

"Yes," he answered gently, tipping her face up and kissing the end of her nose. "It's getting late and I have things I must do. I'll pick you up at nine-thirty tomorrow and take you to Mon Addi for your meeting with Marcie. And you need to get a good night's sleep. You've had a busy day. I want you in bed by nine." He glanced at his watch. "That gives you half an hour to get ready. You can read in bed if you'd like, but lights out no later than ten." He looked sternly at her from under his eyebrows. "I'll call at nine-thirty to say goodnight and I want you to be in bed. I've left some pyjamas under your pillow. Wear them so I can see what an angel you are. Now come here so I can give you a thorough kissing before I go."

The next morning, she felt very nervous about seeing Marcie. Wearing the pink and white pyjamas with teddy bears kissing on the front that Marcus had left for her, she admired all her new clothes again before dressing in a knee-length black skirt, white blouse and black jacket that she'd worn at the shop before.

"Definitely Mon Addi," Marcus said approvingly when he arrived, then wrapped his arms around her for a long kiss.

When they arrived at Mon Addi, Marcus went in with her and stood by her side as she faced Marcie.

"Ah, Pearl," Marcie began, her fists clenched at her side. "Thank you for coming. I wanted the opportunity to tell you in person that I know you had nothing to do with the brooch being temporarily mislaid, and I sincerely regret any hurt or inconvenience caused by our silly misunderstanding. Both myself and the company are exceedingly pleased you have agreed to accept our offer of further employment."

Behind her placatory words, Pearl could see that Marcie's eyes were dark and her mouth tight. It made her knees tremble, but Marcus held her hand out of Marcie's sight and squeezed it to give her courage. He let it go when Marcie finished speaking.

"So, Miss Sinclair," he said formally. "I trust you are reassured that everyone understands you were in no way to blame for the brooch being misplaced, and I hope you feel able to leave that unpleasantness behind you. I would understand if you felt you might like to take legal action against Mon Addi for wrongful dismissal, but I think Marcie has been given the authority to make you an offer which you might be prepared to accept instead. Go ahead, Marcie."

"Yes," Marcie said through gritted teeth. "Management has authorised me to offer you employment with Mon Addi as a..." she paused, having trouble getting the words out, "trainee manager on a salary fifty percent higher than you were getting previously."

"Oh!" Pearl's eyes popped open and she flashed a look of confused surprise at Marcus. "Really?" she whispered. He nodded at her, then at Marcie as a sign for Pearl to keep listening as Marcie continued.

"Additionally, on top of the salary increase for your new position, Mon Addi will pay you for the three weeks you have been away plus an extra one month for the inconvenience and mental anguish caused to you. All of this to be calculated at your new salary rate. The lump sum payment will be transferred into your bank at the close of business today if you accept the offer."

Pearl couldn't think what to say. This was all completely unexpected. Her eyes sought Marcus's again, and his crinkled at her even though his expression remained professional and business-like.

"What do you say, Pearl?" he prompted gently. "Would you like to be a trainee manager?"

"Oh, yes. Yes, please," she replied, clasping her hands together and squirming happily at this completely unexpected promotion. "Thank you, Miss Jones. I would love to be a trainee manager. When can I start?"

"Tomorrow," Marcie told her, and she did. Marcus had to go away on another business trip until the end of the week, but they talked on the phone every night and she told him all about being a trainee manager, and he made sure she was taking care of herself and eating properly.

Arriving home after work on Friday, Pearl let herself into her flat, kicked off her shoes, grabbed her teddy bear and hugged it to her chest, and threw herself happily onto her bed. Her first week had gone well, and Marcus was coming to pick her up to take her out for dinner. Kissing her teddy and sitting him on the pillow, she jumped up and went into her wardrobe to dress. She had already chosen what she would wear: a mini dress with short, flutter sleeves, made out of lovely, soft material with small, bright pink flowers on a green background, her pink, sparkly sneakers and the white, bobbled cardigan she'd worn the night Marcus visited her at her parents' farm.

Ping! Her phone signalled the arrival of a message. It was from Marcus. *Be there in 15.* She was dying to see him, but she was also feeling apprehensive. Although, it was a month since they'd first met, and they had talked and texted quite a lot on the phone so he didn't seem like a stranger, she hadn't spent a lot of time with him in person. He'd kissed her quite a few times, and his kisses were delicious, but they hadn't done anything other than that. She couldn't wait for more kisses, and couldn't stop thinking about whether he would go further tonight. Would he want to make love to her? Would he want to stay the night? She hoped he wanted all those things. Although it felt quite scary, she did, and she hoped with all her heart he did too.

Chapter 8

Marcus

Marcus parked his car and caught the lift up to Pearl's apartment. He couldn't get her out of his mind and was longing to see her. Miss Perfect. He grinned to himself. That was what he'd taken to calling her when he thought about her. She did seem to be perfect in every way. As fetching and dainty as a doll, warm-hearted, easy-going, and willing to defer to him and allow him to take charge. But she was also clearly smart and self-sufficient when she needed to be, but she didn't mind if he decided he wanted to take care of her instead. She was independent, but not fiercely so. And that was precisely what he wanted: his own Little girl to love, spoil and protect and be a Daddy to. He was trembling with anticipation and hope that Pearl was the Little girl for whom he'd been searching.

God, she was so perfect, Marcus thought when she opened the door to him. He'd been eager to see how she would dress for their date. It had been another small test – seeing which clothes she chose – and another she had passed with flying colours. She was wearing some of the cute, little girl clothes he'd bought for her, and she looked utterly enchanting. He nodded appreciatively as he took her hands.

"You're wearing your new dress."

"Yes," she cried gaily, freeing her hands, and twirling around so he could see how the skirt spun out as she did. "Isn't it pretty?"

"It is indeed," he replied, talking about the whole package. "Right then, little girl, shall we go and eat? What would you like?"

"Can I have anything at all?" she asked, very seriously.

"Anything you want. I spoke to Marcie and she said you've been an extra good girl at work, so you deserve a treat. What would you like?"

"Pancakes!" she cried, clapping her hands and giving a gleeful hop.

"Then pancakes it is," he said with a tut-tut as he ruffled her hair.

Marcus found a cafe with booths that served pancakes, and fed Pearl most of her dinner without anyone noticing. She obediently opened her mouth when he raised her fork to it, and he used a napkin to wipe away any mess on her face.

"Would you like to feed yourself?" he asked, handing her the fork. "Can you manage?" He knew she could.

Instead of barking *Of course I can*, she squirmed, nodded and stabbed some pancake onto her fork.

"Good girl, then Da... I can eat my dinner too. Shall I?"

She had her head to one side as she watched him take his knife and fork and cut some of his pancake and eat it. She giggled as he put it in his mouth and he grinned at her. While they ate, he asked her about her first four days as a trainee manager, enjoying her unbridled enthusiasm as she told him about everything she'd learned and the sales she'd made. He was charmed by her talking about each piece of jewellery as though it were a pet, and by how rapt she was when they went to someone who clearly loved them.

He thought about the diamond collar in his safe and imagined how it would fit around her milky throat. There was no hurry, though. The time, place, and occasion had to be as perfect as she was, and he had to be sure she was ready and certain it was what she wanted. He wasn't going to rush; he was going to enjoy each new experience with her, and savour each new discovery as she was slowly revealed to him like an oyster opening to reveal its own precious pearl, and he planned to continue his exploration of his delectable treasure trove that night.

"Shall we go back to your place?" he asked as soon as they'd finished eating.

Pearl nodded. "I'll make you a cup of tea, shall I?"

"That would be lovely."

When they got home, Marcus watched her busying herself in the kitchen. She was so precious, like a little girl playing house.

"Would you like a biscuit with it?"

Marcus patted his belly. "No, thanks. I'm full of pancakes."

She giggled as she brought their mugs of tea to the coffee table, sat on the couch next to him, took her shoes and socks off and wriggled her toes.

"Do you like your flat?" he asked.

"Of course. It's the loveliest apartment I've ever seen. But I still don't know how I can afford it. Or even what the rent is."

He pursed his lips, raised his eyebrows and shrugged. "It's whatever I want it to be."

Her brow furrowed, and her eyes half-closed and then suddenly popped open. "Oh. Is it yours?"

"It is." He grinned widely, enjoying her surprise. "But I

don't live here, of course. I have another place. And I'm totally fine with you not paying rent. I can afford it. I don't need the money. I'd rather you kept it for yourself or gave it to your folks to be honest. But I don't know how you feel about being a kept woman, so if that makes you uncomfortable, you can pay whatever you want."

"I should pay something, though, shouldn't I?" Pearl asked, needing time to think about this surprise.

"Only if you feel you want to," Marcus answered easily. "I don't care if you don't. And tomorrow," he went on, changing the conversation away from rent, "I'm going to take you shopping so you can buy whatever you want to decorate your new home. Okay?"

With her hands cupped around her mug and it pressed up against her lips, her big eyes stared at him over the rim.

"And you're not allowed to say 'no'," he warned her sternly.

Her head nodded almost imperceptibly.

"Good." He finished his tea and set his mug on the table. Pearl immediately jumped up, picked up the empty mug and took it with hers to the kitchen, rinsed them in the sink, dried them and put them away. Marcus stood up, watching her as she walked toward him. When she was close enough, he reached out and took her by the shoulders.

"I'm going to kiss you," he said. "Is that all right?"

Pearl nodded. He pulled her closer and bent down so he was inside her personal space. She shivered.

"And I'm going to ask you to do something for me," he said, his voice low, his eyes locked into hers. "I want you to keep perfectly still while I'm kissing you. Keep your arms at your side and don't move. Will you do that?"

Pearl nodded her compliance, her eyes shining expectantly despite a small cloud of surprised confusion.

Marcus's lips quivered in a tiny, pleased smile as he slowly bent down and brushed them ever so gently against hers, drawing from her the softest moan. He paused, then kissed her harder and longer.

Pearl was shaking; the intensity of the sexual tension magnified by her having to remain motionless thus rendering her unable to alleviate it even a tiny bit. She moaned and her arms involuntarily fluttered.

"Don't move," he murmured against her mouth, and her arms fell to her side. He grunted with satisfaction. He could see it wasn't easy for her to fight her desire to move, but she was. Without question or complaint. She was so exquisitely lovely, he was having to fight his own battle of restraint. All the blood had rushed to his groin leaving him light-headed and with an aching bulge in his pants. His lustful self wanted to tear her clothes off, press her to the ground and plunge into her, but as satisfying as that might be, he was playing a longer game, and he was determined not to damage that for a short-term thrill.

He needed to be sure his instincts were right. He was confident enough already to risk his own emotions. If he was wrong, he'd be disappointed, deeply disappointed, but not hurt or betrayed. But if he claimed Pearl now, then discovered he was wrong and let her go, if indeed he could, he feared she might be seriously wounded, especially as she had already been hurt by her ghastly experience at the hands of Marcie Jones.

She was waiting, silently, patiently to see what he would do next. His eyes met hers and, as he felt a tremor run through her, he bent and kissed her again. This time he allowed his mouth to linger, gently moving against the softness of her lips. He felt the tension leave her as desire melted her will and sapped her strength, and she slumped against his hands.

"Put your arms around me, Pearl," he muttered as he let

go of her shoulders and wrapped his arms around her waist, pulling her up and crushing her to him. Feeling her arms raise up and encircle his neck, he kissed her ardently, swamping her mouth with his. He lowered one hand to her bottom and pulled her in tighter, so her belly was pressed against his groin. She lifted herself higher on her tiptoes and pressed against him. For long, long seconds nothing else existed but the seeming attempt of two bodies trying to occupy the same space.

When breathing became a driving imperative, and the kiss reluctantly ended, Marcus took Pearl's hand and led her to a chair. Sitting himself down on it, he pulled her onto his knee, bending to kiss her as she curled herself in his lap without hesitation.

"Sweet, sweet Pearl," he murmured as he ended the kiss. "You are so lovely. I want to see your body. Will you show it to me?"

"Yes," she whispered, taking a deep breath, her eyes opening wide but her gaze not faltering. "Shall I take my dress off?"

"Not yet." His hand stopped hers, "but I want you to do whatever I ask. Will you do that for me?"

Pearl's nose scrunched. Marcus touched it gently and kissed her.

"It's all right. I shan't ask you to do anything you don't want to. And you can say no."

She took in a deep breath and nodded, totally unaware that he was using little tests to explore her submissiveness and natural willingness to defer to him, and she was passing them all.

"Stand up," he said. She obeyed and he stood too. "I want to see your bottom. Will you show me?" He paused and she nodded tentatively, her cheeks turning pink. "Bend forward and rest your hands on the chair." She did as he said.

His heart lurched, he licked his lips and had to wriggle to ease the discomfort of his rock-hard erection. "Good girl," he praised her, raising his hand to stroke the curve of her firm, plump bottom. "It's perfect," he said, lightly massaging both cheeks through her dress.

"Are you okay with this, Pearl?" he asked. She nodded. "I'm going to lift your dress up. Is that okay too?"

"Yes," she whispered.

He lifted the skirt of her dress up to her waist, and was gratified to see her respond by arching her back. She might be self-conscious and unsure, but she was keeping still for him and couldn't hide her own arousal. He ran his hands over her perfect pale globes, pushing her tiny bikini briefs up to reveal as much of them as possible as his hands stroked and squeezed her firm, spongy flesh, he heard her breathing becoming louder as her hips moved in his hands.

"Do you like that?" he asked, relishing the small bounce and jiggle of her cheeks.

"Yes," she answered with a giggle and a wiggle of her hips.

"Nice! What about if I pat your little wiggle bottom?" he asked, gently slapping her.

"Oh!" She flinched in surprise, but Marcus was careful to ensure his hand was not hard enough to hurt, all she could feel was the pressure and a delicious ripple it sent through to her front.

"Have you ever been spanked, Pearl?" he asked.

"No." She shook her head, but stayed in place as he continued to gently slap her bottom.

"Maybe I will spank your bottom one day if you are a naughty girl, eh? What do you think?" She didn't answer and he didn't press her. His hand came down slightly harder and she flinched but didn't move out of place. "Good girl," he said gently, readjusting her clothes and taking her hand to pull her up to him. "Come here, baby. I want to kiss your beautiful mouth."

Putting his hand under her chin, he tilted her face up. She tried to avert her eyes. "Pearl," he admonished her sternly. "Don't look away from me. I want to see you." Obediently, she looked at him. She was biting her lower lip but her eyes were wide open and shining. Her arousal was palpable as her shoulders pulled back to thrust her breasts forward.

She was divine, and he inwardly groaned with the heavy weight of his pleasure and desire. Gathering her gently into his arms as though she were a fragile doll he might break if he held her too tightly, he kissed her upturned face, over and over.

"It's time you went to bed," he said finally, pushing her gently away from him. "Do you want to bring your shoes?" She picked them up and then took the hand he held out to her and let him lead her to the bedroom. The room was spotlessly clean and tidy, and her teddy bear was waiting for her by the pillows along with a toy dog and cat.

She blushed when he saw them. "That's Rusty and Moppy, like my dog and cat at the farm," she explained. She put her shoes by her bed and picked the black and white dog up and cuddled it. "He's so soft. Much softer than the real Rusty." She put it down and stroked the ginger cat. "The real Moppy is very soft though."

"They're adorable," he said with a grin, pulling her into his arms and kissing her. "And so are you. Now, pyjamas." He lifted her pillow and removed the pyjamas he'd rightly guessed would be there, then led her by the hand into the bathroom.

"What are you doing?" she asked.

"Getting you into bed. You need a shower first, though."

"Are you going to stay?"

"For a while, but not all night. Not this time. Let's get your clothes off." He felt around behind her for the zip on her dress, pulled it down and took hold of the hem. "Hold your arms up." Pearl raised her arms as he slid the dress over her head. Left wearing nothing but her bra and panties, her arms went automatically to the front to protect her from his gaze. "Move your arms and look at me," he ordered. "I want to see you. You are beautiful. Be proud of your body."

Dropping her arms to her side, Pearl looked up at him as he'd asked, trembling at the raw desire in his eyes as he ran them over the curve of her breasts rising above the top of her bra, her gently rounded belly, the small mound hidden by her bikini briefs and the curve of her hips and thighs. He pursed his lips and grunted his appreciation. "Beautiful," he muttered. "Perfect. I want to see your breasts now." Holding her eyes with his, he reached behind and unhooked her bra, and Pearl allowed it to slip down over her arms so her naked breasts were revealed to him for the first time. They were exactly as he'd fantasised, like two delicious cupcakes, each tipped with a dainty pink cherry. He reached out to touch them, circling the base of each with a finger and then his hand closing over one while he bent to kiss the nipple on the other. He paused to check Pearl's expression. Her eyes were huge, her cheeks flushed, her pink tongue dabbing at dry lips, and the tendons in her neck strained.

"You okay, little girl?" he asked.

"Yes," she whispered.

"Do you want me to stop?"

"No." Her answer was quiet but emphatic, underlined with a shake of her head.

"Oh, baby," Marcus groaned. He bent his head and took

her nipple in his mouth, gently pulling on it and lapping it with his tongue.

"You are so beautiful," he said, raising his head, taking hold of her panties and lowering them, never taking his eyes from hers as he did so. She lifted each foot so he could slide them over and off, and then she was naked, her eyes like saucers. He bent his head and kissed her mouth, then raised his head and slowly lowered his eyes.

"Not even the biggest, brightest most valuable jewel in the whole world is anywhere near as exquisite as you," he said gruffly, raising his eyes. "Now, shower." He reached into the shower and turned the taps on, checking the water was the right temperature, then guided her in. "Wash yourself, baby. Don't draw the curtain. I want to watch, and then I'll dry you off when you're done."

Chapter 9

Pearl

Soaping herself in the shower, Pearl couldn't bring herself to look at the man watching her. She scarcely recognised herself. Two weeks ago, her life was in disarray, and then as though she'd unknowingly been visited by her fairy godmother, the man she'd been dreaming about had knocked on her door. Two weeks later, she was a trainee manager at Mon Addi, living in his apartment, and he had just undressed her and was outside the shower recess, watching her and waiting for her to finish so he could wrap her in a towel and dry her.

It was too much to take in, too much to think about. She wasn't always sure what to do, but then Marcus would tell her and praise her when she did it, and she wanted him to praise her, to kiss her, to touch her. If doing what he asked of her, pleased him, she was content to do that and not think about it.

"Are you ready to get out?" he asked.

"Yes," she replied, rinsing away the last of the soap, turning the taps off and stepping out.

He caught her in the towel, wrapping it around her and patting her dry, her face, down her back, her breasts, under her arms and her belly.

"Spread your legs," he said, and she did. He patted up from her ankles and then gently rubbed where they met. Satisfied she was quite dry, he picked up her pyjamas and helped her on with them. "Clean your teeth, then bring me your hairbrush," he said as he went into her bedroom.

When she appeared a few minutes later, he was sitting on her bed waiting for her. "Hop in." He patted next to him and held his hand out for the hairbrush. She sat down next to him while he brushed her hair.

"You all ready for bed then?"

"Yes."

He put his arm around her, and she cuddled up against him, laying her head on his chest, wishing somehow she could melt right through his skin and be held safe and warm inside. He tightened his hold on her as if he'd read her thoughts.

"Precious," he said quietly, bending his head to kiss her, a kiss that started off tantalisingly soft but deepened as they pressed against each other. He ran his tongue over the inside of her lips and against her teeth until she opened her mouth wider. She had the same feeling as she'd had earlier, of melting into liquid in his arms. He slipped his hand under her pyjama top and fondled her naked breast, gently stroking it and rubbing his thumb against her nipple until it grew and hardened. He moved his hand across to her other breast and she shifted to give him access. Taking his mouth from hers, he lifted her top higher and bent to kiss and suck her breasts. Her body was on fire with sensations she'd never felt before.

Laying her flat on the bed, he kissed her face, nipped,

licked and sucked her ear, then trailed kisses down her neck. He undid the buttons on her top and pushed it open to expose her breasts. He kissed them again, then kissed down her belly. He raised his head to look at her.

"I want to kiss your pussy, baby," he said thickly. "Would you like that?"

She sucked in a shaky breath and her teeth started chattering as she shivered despite the lack of cold. She nodded.

"Good girl," he smiled, melting her heart. Whatever he wanted, she would give him. Anything. She would never refuse him anything he ever asked of her. No matter what it was.

He stood up. "Lie right down," he directed her. When he'd helped her into a position that afforded him comfortable access, he slipped off her pyjama bottoms.

"Bend your knees and spread your legs, baby. I want you to open your pussy for me."

Her feet moved but then stopped. She was trying to do as he'd asked but her feet didn't seem to want to cooperate.

"Don't be shy," he encouraged her. "You are beautiful. Every part of you is beautiful. Your pussy is beautiful and I want you to show it to me so I can show you how good I can make it feel."

She brought her feet up so her knees were bent and then moved them apart. Would he think her beautiful when he could see everything? Could he?

"A little bit further, that's a good girl," he crooned, pushing her feet apart and up so at last he could see the treasure he sought. Watching her, he ran his fingers up her thigh, and then gently squeezed her labia together. She shuddered and sighed. It felt heavenly.

"Lie back, relax and enjoy it," he told her as his fingers found their way in amongst the folds and spread them apart. "If you want me to stop, say 'barlese' and I'll stop. You might say 'stop' or 'no' and then when I stop want me to start again and that's fine but, if you say barlese, it will mean you want me to stop altogether. Okay?"

She nodded, her body rigid with anticipation. She trusted him but wasn't sure what to expect. How could it be good for him if she didn't do it right? What if she couldn't do what she was supposed to do? Would he lose patience with her and want another woman who was good at sex?

"I don't know what I'm supposed to do," she cried.

"You're not supposed to do anything, baby, except lie there, relax and allow whatever happens to happen. Don't fight it. Just enjoy it. And remember, if you say barlese, I'll stop. All right?"

Pearl nodded and squeezed out a tiny whispered, "Yes."

"Good girl. Lay your head down and close your eyes."

Pearl did as she was told, eyes tightly shut, quivering with anticipation. She'd read about what Marcus was about to do. She'd even watched a few videos on the internet. And she'd touched herself quite a lot and it felt nice, but nothing magical had ever happened. What if she couldn't do it, whatever it was she was supposed to do? Marcus was so gorgeous. He could have any woman he wanted, elegant, sophisticated, successful, wealthy women. What did she have to offer him? And now she was going to disappoint him with sex.

"Oh!" Her catastrophising was stopped dead in its tracks as she felt his mouth nestle itself between her thighs, close over her soft, juicy cave, and gently suck and squeeze. New sensations skittered through her and she wriggled as if trying to get away. He raised his head immediately.

"You okay, baby girl? It's not hurting, is it?"

She raised her head just high enough so he could see her wide-open eyes and rosy cheeks. She shook her head.

"Do you want me to keep going?"

She nodded.

He dropped a kiss high on her inner thigh still looking at her. "Good. You're such a delicious little morsel. I want to gobble you all up."

Pearl giggled and felt snug, like he'd pulled a blanket over them and made a makeshift cubby-house. As he bent down and she felt his mouth on her, she lay back and closed her eyes, holding the image of Marcus's blue eyes looking at her over her belly. She loved that expression in his eyes. It made her feel warm and safe. His mouth gently sucking and nibbling her was making her feel something quite different. It was sort of like when she touched herself, but *so* much nicer. She gasped as his tongue gently probed at her entrance, then slid slowly in and out.

His hands reached under her, cupping her bottom and holding it up slightly off the bed so he could better reach his target. Then his tongue withdrew from her hot, wet channel, flattened and pressed its way up, pushing her apart until its tip reached the tiny ball of pleasure nerves hiding under its hood.

Pearl's eyes popped open and her body went rigid at that first contact, and she felt Marcus immediately halt his gentle assault until she settled. Then he began again, slowly. This time Pearl didn't pull away, but exhaled deeply with a low moan as voluptuous sensations she'd not felt before began to flood her body. Her breathing quickened as a deep hot ache ignited in her lowest depths and began to radiate out in waves. Her fists clenched and her hips began to involuntarily rise and fall to meet the pressure from his mouth. Her head began to roll from side to side as though she were trying to escape the exquisite torment. She was gasping for breath, her body was rigid, and she sensed a presence moving toward her, getting bigger, rising up and threatening to swallow her. She was slipping away, losing control, and that thing, that presence was getting ever nearer. She gasped and grabbed for Marcus as that thing arrived, swamping her, rushing through her body in a flood of warm liquid tingling.

She cried out as her muscles contracted in spasms and her clitoris switched suddenly from being a centre of pleasure to one of pain. There was no need for barlese; Marcus immediately stopped touching it and kissed her inner thighs before moving up the bed to her. Her body was so sensitive in the aftermath, she didn't want to be touched for the moment. She just wanted to surrender to the loveliness inhabiting every part of her. As her breathing slowed, she felt the sensuous bliss receding and her body returning to normal. Keeping her eyes tightly shut, she fought hard to make it stay longer, but when she accepted defeat, she opened her eyes to find Marcus gazing adoringly down on her. He bent and kissed her lips and she could smell and taste herself on his mouth.

"How are you, little girl?" he asked tenderly. "Was that nice?"

Pearl took in a long deep breath and then exhaled it in a big slow sigh. "Oh, yes. It was strange but wonderful. I had no idea I could do that."

"Well, beautiful," Marcus said, gently tapping the end of her nose with his finger, "I'm available to do it for you anytime you want."

Pearl stretched luxuriously and smiled. "I think I'd like it all the time."

As Marcus moved up the bed and put his head on the pillows, she wriggled up next to him laying her head on his shoulder and nestling in as she stifled a yawn.

"Are you a tired bunny?" he teased her, kissing her head.

She nodded and mumbled into his chest, "But don't you want to… I mean, you… you know…"

"I do want to. More than I can say, but I'm not going to.

If I take my clothes off, I shan't be able to leave, and I have business to attend to before we go shopping."

"But I don't want you to go," Pearl said a tad sulkily. "I want you to stay here."

"Not tonight, baby girl."

Pearl pulled away from him and rolled over so she was facing away.

"You're not going to get sulky are you?" he asked, patting her still naked bottom. "Be careful. Sulky girls get spanked."

A shiver ran down Pearl's spine.

"Big girls don't get spanked," she said, quickly rolling over so her bottom was out of reach.

"Big girls behaving like naughty little girls do, though," Marcus warned her sternly.

She squinted at his face, trying to decide if he were serious. Was he saying *he* would spank her if he thought she was being naughty? An image of her over his knee, skirt up, pants down, his big hand spanking her bare bottom popped into her mind sending a tremor through her. She liked the image, she realised with surprise. For some reason, it made her feel warm and tingly, but that didn't mean she actually wanted him to do it. Did it? And, anyway, he was only joking. Wasn't he? She had to know.

"You wouldn't though, would you?" she asked hesitantly, barely able to get the words out through her suddenly chattering teeth.

"Indeed I would. If I thought you deserved it. What do you say to that?"

Lying on her side against him, Pearl brought her knees up so she was curled into a ball.

"You wouldn't spank me hard, would you?" This was not something she'd ever considered. Neither her father nor her mother had spanked her when she was a child; in fact, they vehemently opposed corporal punishment. It wouldn't be the same as being spanked by a parent if Marcus spanked her, though, would it? And why did that thrill ripple through her every time she thought about it?

"What if I said I would?" he asked seriously. "Spank you, I mean, and maybe even spank you hard if I thought you were very, very naughty. How would you feel about it? Would you like it? Not necessarily like the spanking but like belonging to me, being mine and being taken care of even if that care was sometimes a spanking?"

Pearl chewed on her thumb and didn't answer.

Marcus wrapped his arms around her and pulled her to him.

"Don't worry your pretty little head about it for the moment. You've been such a good girl, not only do you not deserve a spanking, you deserve to be taken out tomorrow and spoiled rotten. And that's what we're going to do, but first you must have a good sleep. Don't think about spanking anymore. Think about the lovely thing that just happened to you – your first ever orgasm, and all the lovely things we'll do together tomorrow. Okay?"

"Okay," she whispered, her thumb almost entirely in her mouth. He gently pulled it out so he could kiss her.

"Come on. Let's put your pyjama bottoms on and get you into bed. I'll tuck you in and see myself out."

After he'd left, Pearl lay in her big bed, snuggled up with her teddy and Rusty and Moppy, and her nose scrunched as she thought about things. Marcus was wonderful. She adored him. She hadn't known him long but already she couldn't envisage him not being in her life. She felt safe with him and she truly believed he wanted to do everything he could to help her. He was loving and supportive and funny and kind. But... he wanted to spank her! Did that mean he didn't care about her as she'd thought he did, or that he was a cruel man who wanted to hurt her? But maybe his spankings wouldn't hurt. They would only be play ones. Maybe the only way she could truly see how she felt about him spanking her would be to let him do it. At least once. If he wanted to. Which he might not. What if she refused him and he decided to stop seeing her? That would be way worse than a spanking!

Her hand pressed between her thighs. He'd made her feel so wonderful; she definitely wanted him to do that again! And she was going to see him tomorrow, so maybe he would kiss her there again. And maybe he would make love to her properly too. What would that be like? And he was going to spoil her during the day and play with her, and kiss her and make her laugh.

With all those wonderful things and how much she loved him… Wait? Did she love him? Maybe she did. It kind of felt like she did. If she loved him and he wanted to spank her, then she would let him, wouldn't she? How bad could it be? Most likely it would be fun, and it did make her feel little and warm and safe to think of being over his knee. She pulled her teddy closer, her hands up near her mouth, and as her eyes closed and she drifted into sleep, her thumb slipped between her lips.

Chapter 10

Marcus

Marcus was feeling satisfied as he drove home after leaving Pearl tucked up in bed. Not sexually satisfied, of course; a dull uncomfortable ache was serving to remind him of that, but it wasn't enough to spoil his elation. He was revelling immensely in getting to know her. She was utterly bewitching and each new experience he had with her was an absolute joy and further convinced him that she was the woman for whom he'd been waiting. Or should that be Little girl for whom he'd been waiting? She was an exquisite combination of both which was exactly what he wanted: a woman with a Little girl hiding inside who would come out and play with him and let him be her Daddy.

And he was feeling rather smug about his success in gifting her her first orgasm. He hadn't been certain he would be able to bring her to orgasm the first time, but in the end she had been so responsive, it hadn't been at all difficult. It would likely be even easier next time, and next time he wouldn't stop at one. Ahh! The pain in his groin reappeared with a vengeance as his cock sprang to life, ready and eager to get on with the job. He wriggled in his seat trying to make himself as comfortable as he could for the drive home. Once there, he could fix himself for the night, and he was confident that in the not too distant future he would have Pearl to sate himself with.

He pulled into his garage and frowned when he saw a light on in his flat. Surely his mother wasn't waiting up for him? This was getting ridiculous and it needed to stop.

"Ah, Marcus. There you are. I was beginning to wonder if you were coming home tonight. I was about to text you to see where you were." Her voice was as smooth and cold as ice.

"Really, Mother? It's Friday night and I'm thirty-two years old. Does it not occur to you I might have things to do on Friday night? That I might be going out or something?"

Linda's eyes narrowed, but she made her question as light and disinterested as she could. "Date?"

"I can't see that's any of your business."

"Well, it is. I've told you before, a family doesn't get as rich as ours and stay that way without its members doing what's best for everyone, and that includes sometimes making sacrifices. If you're seeing someone, I need to meet her to see if she is suitable wife material for the Holding family."

"Who I'm seeing, *if* I'm seeing anyone, is my business until I decide I want her to meet the family, which, at the moment, is basically you. But it's my life and I will make my decisions."

"You don't seem to realise how much damage a person of the wrong ilk can do to a family such as ours."

"So was it a person of the wrong ilk joining the family that drove Father to suicide and Ray to disappear into drug dens on the other side of the world? Who was that person, Mother?"

Taking three brisk strides to reach him, Linda raised her hand and cracked it across his face. "How dare you!" she said without raising her voice. "Your father was a weak and pathetic man. He didn't have the guts to go on living. And don't forget I am as much a part of the Holding family as you are."

"Oh, I forgot," Marcus replied. He hadn't flinched when his mother slapped his face. He wouldn't give her the satisfaction. He stared at her, his eyes glinting and his face burning. "You and Father were kissing cousins."

"Don't be disgusting." Linda's voice had resumed its conversational tone. "Your father and I might have had common great-grandparents but we were distantly enough related to make our marriage more acceptable than you marrying some pretty gold-digger you picked up in a bar — or a shop. The family approved our marriage, and don't forget I brought my own considerable fortune into the match as well."

"I'd be hardly likely to forget that, would I? Considering your constant reminders."

"You can sneer at our money if you think it's fashionable, but I don't see you denying yourself the luxuries it affords. So why don't you stop being such a hypocrite and accept that your best future requires your marrying a wealthy woman and doing it quickly?"

Marcus noticed a change in his mother's voice.

"What's the sudden hurry?"

"Well, you don't suppose I waited up for you just to quarrel, do you?"

"Why then?"

"I had a phone call from your brother." She waited for his reaction.

"Ray? Huh! What did he want? Mummy to send him a cheque to stop him starving, or to bail him out of prison, or pay for his next bag of dope? I suppose a phone call at least means he's alive."

"Yes. He's alive. And he wants to come home. He wants to go into rehab, get his life on track and re-join the business. If you're not careful, he'll take the CEO position out from under your nose."

"What do you mean?" This time it was Marcus's eyes that narrowed. Last time he'd heard anything about his older brother, currently overseas, he was a couch-surfing, drug addict. There was no way the board would appoint someone like that as CEO. For nearly four years, nothing had been heard from Ray except for an occasional text saying where he was and asking for money, and the two times Marcus had been sent to try and talk him into coming home had been dismal failures. Suddenly, out of the blue, he was planning a reappearance and wanted the top job?

"Sit down, darling," Linda said, pointing to the couch. Sensing she had Marcus's complete attention, she had calmed down.

They both sat. "Well?" Marcus asked.

"Ray says, and I'm as surprised as you, that he has money and he wants to invest it in the company."

"What? How did that happen? Did he rob a bank?" Marcus asked sarcastically. "And he won't have it for long if he's still on the junk."

"No. He didn't rob a bank." Linda's voice was light with a weight lifted off her heart now her elder son wanted to come home to her. "I didn't catch all the details, but I gather he talked to some person who gave him some tip about a start-up and he managed to get his hands on some money. I didn't ask how and I don't care. Anyway, that was two years ago, and I gather the business was sold for a vast sum of money and he got a share of it. He rang to say he wants to use some of the money for rehab and, when he's out, come home and join the business. He will need to convince the board that he is completely rehabilitated before they would consider him for CEO, but I think they will be impressed by his initiative. And," she added, with a shrug and a sigh, "he was always a favourite with your father's friends on the board, particularly the old conservative ones who believe in the succession of the first-born son."

"Well, if the board decides to appoint him, there's not much I can do about it, is there?"

"There's always something that can be done, no matter the problem," Linda scolded him, reminding him of the epithet she'd taught him from a young age. "You just need to strategize. As a mother, I'm relieved and couldn't be happier that my prodigal son appears to be fixing his life and coming home, but while I'm quite prepared to slaughter a fattened cow for him, or at least have my butcher do it, you're my favourite son, Marcus. You know that." She reached out and stroked the cheek she'd moments ago slapped as hard as she could. "It's always been my intention that you would be CEO. Len is going soon and I've told the board it's time there was a Holding at the head again. While Ray was away, there was no contest, but that's changed, unless you can convince Len to leave early and get the board to appoint you before Ray gets here."

"So, the fact I've been working hard while Ray has been mooching around stoned off his face counts for nothing?"

"It might have counted for more except, as we recently found out, the company took a hit to its bottom-line last year and Ray is offering a much-needed injection of new capital."

"That's it then," Marcus said with a resigned shrug. "I don't have any money of my own to invest in the business."

"There is a way you can get your hands on a considerably bigger pot of money than Ray is bringing to the table."

Tilting his head away slightly, Marcus squinted his eyes at her. "What are you talking about?"

"Marriage, of course. I've told you, there are at least two young women from wealthy families who would leap at the chance to marry you. You're young, handsome, and wealthy. What woman wouldn't want to snap you up? If you choose a rich bride who will give you access to her fortune, you can stack that against Ray's. With your experience and Ray's past, if you also offer more money, you'll win comfortably. What? Why are you looking at me like that?"

"You are suggesting, *again*, that I marry a woman I don't love to get my hands on her money? I thought you despised gold-diggers."

"Oh, don't be such a romantic, Marcus. There's the Fielding girl, Tina, and if you won't consider Alan's daughter, there's Don and Louise's eldest, what's her name? The blonde with the big arse. Some strange name they saddled the poor child with. I have no idea what they were thinking. Wilma? Poplar? Something like that. Willow. That's it." She shook her head slowly in bewilderment, then gave it a quick toss to dismiss the issue. "Both are pretty enough. They've been brought up right, so they can behave in public. Neither of them seems unutterably stupid. And both are extremely wealthy in their own right. What's not to love?"

"Did you love, Father? Or was that a marriage of convenience? Convenient for you, that is."

"Don't make me slap you again, darling," Linda said easily. "Go to bed and think hard about your future. I'm leaving tomorrow to pick up Ray and then we're flying to London. He's booked into an excellent rehab centre, the very best money can buy, and he'll be there for a couple of months, I would imagine. I'm also going to see Bob in the

London office to organise for Ray to spend a month there once he's out of rehab. If he's as clean and keen as he claims, Bob will let me know and I'll talk to Len and get Ray a position here. Once he's here, I intend throwing a big welcome home party. You are to come and I will expect you to be married or engaged by then, or to announce your engagement to a wealthy girl that night at the latest. Do you understand? That gives you plenty of time to get used to the idea, to get whatever you need to out of your system, and to organise it. If you don't do this, Marcus, I shall wash my hands of you, and you will be penniless, then see how keen on you your little gold digger is."

Marcus didn't speak or move as Linda stood up and walked behind the couch. She bent and kissed the top of his head then let herself out. In the shower a few moments later, Marcus was scrubbing his body as hard as he could as if to wash out the bad feelings he'd got from the conversation. He'd been so elated driving home from Pearl; now he felt sick and angry. There was no way his mother would permit his relationship with Pearl considering her family's lack of money, and no way the board would consider him for the position of CEO without his marrying a wealthy wife.

He was aware his mother thought she had him in a corner. While he was paid a salary for his work at Holding Corporation, it was not a large one, and the relatively small amount of money he was allowed to have in his own name would not support the kind of lifestyle his mother and her associates enjoyed. If she found out about the ten million dollars he'd fortuitously made buying and selling bitcoin and had hidden away, and that he'd bought the apartment Pearl was currently living in with some of it, she might well literally explode. But he had no intention of telling her about his secret money or of investing it in Holding Corporation. He had his own, as yet vague, plans for the future, but it wouldn't even occur to Linda that her son might choose relative penury and the woman he loved over billionaire status. It was why she had manipulated him by ensuring nothing was in his name. He lived in her house and even his car, despite it being a birthday present, was leased by Holding Corporation and not in his name. Linda believed, as he would take nothing with him if he left, that was sufficient insurance against his ever going.

By the time he was out of the shower, he'd washed away most of his reaction to his mother's conversation, and as he fell naked into his bed and his hand moved to grip his growing erection, he was able to focus his thoughts on something far more appealing: his lovely Pearl, how satisfying it had been to use his lips and tongue to bring her to orgasm and how eagerly he was anticipating spending the following day with her.

Chapter 11

Pearl

When her eyes flickered open the next morning, Pearl was curled in a ball, wrapping her happiness up and holding it as close as she was snuggling her teddy bear. She squeezed one hand between her thighs remembering how Marcus had kissed her there and how lovely it had felt. Her phone beeped. She picked it up and read a message from him. *Good morning, beautiful girl. Pick you up at 11.* She replied *Okay*, and added five smiley emojis. She wanted to call him something nice, like he'd called her 'beautiful girl', but wasn't brave enough to use endearments. What should she call him anyway? Darling? She giggled. No, definitely not that. My love? No. That sounded funny too and, besides, she couldn't be the first one to use the 'L' word even though she was sure she did love him despite not having known him long. He wasn't just handsome enough to be a film star, he was nice and kind, and fun to be with. He filled her heart with joy and she never stopped thinking about him and wanting to be with him.

It was way too early to get ready, so she made herself a cup of tea and sat in bed with her tablet learning about diamonds: what carats are, the different types of cuts, the different coloured diamonds and where they are found, and what determines the price of a stone. She already knew much of it but wanted to learn every single thing she could. When she finished studying, despite it not yet being ten o'clock, she couldn't wait any longer to get ready.

Standing in her walk-in robe, she tried to think what outfit Marcus would like most. She went through the clothes he'd bought for her: the dress she'd worn the night before, three skirts, two pairs of tights, two blouses, a rainbow jumper, and a long, soft, grey cardigan. The clothes she'd brought with her from home were also hanging up but she wanted to wear something he'd chosen. She took them all out and laid them on her bed and then arranged them in different combinations. There was the denim skirt she'd worn before, a grey, pleated skirt, and a pink one with a pocket on the back with a white heart on it. The tights were both colourful: black ones with fairies, and red ones with flowers, and as well as the rainbow jumper she'd worn with the denim skirt, there was a white blouse with yellow stars and a blue blouse that was plain but had a red trim of hearts around the collar and sleeves.

It wasn't going to be very warm so she pulled on the black fairy tights and blue blouse, the long, grey cardigan and a pair of white runners she'd brought with her, and then looked in the mirror. It was such a darling outfit, she wiggled her bottom happily and skipped into the bathroom to darken her eyes with eye pencil and mascara. She brushed her jaw-length hair and straightened the fringe, but frowned as she inspected the finished result in the mirror. Somehow her hair didn't match her clothes or her mood. She pulled it up into pigtails, one high on each side of her head, which she held in place with elastic bands. Most of her hair was too short to be caught in them, so they stuck straight up. She giggled watching them bobbling as she jiggled her head up and down and side to side. She liked them but not the plain elastic bands holding them in place, so she found a piece of paper and wrote 'pretty hair ties' on it and put it in her bag.

She began to get quite shaky with nervous excitement as the time for Marcus to arrive drew closer. To distract herself, she searched for rubies on her tablet and discovered the word ruby is from the Latin word for red, and the stones get the red colour from their chromium content. Like diamonds, their value is also connected to their carat weight, colour, cut and clarity which she was beginning to have a good under-standing of from her previous research. But, no matter how much she loved shiny, sparkling gems, she couldn't concentrate properly with one ear listening for Marcus arriving. *Ping!* Her phone beeped. *Downstairs. Coming up x*

She jumped up and opened the door as soon as she heard him outside and before he'd even finished knocking.

"Hi, beautiful," he said. She giggled and covered her mouth with her hand. "Or should I say cute little pixie," he continued, admiring her outfit. "Or fairy, seeing you've got fairies all over your tights. Do you like those clothes, little fairy?"

Completely overcome now that he was finally here, Pearl squirmed and nodded but couldn't quite bring herself to look at him.

"Are you shy, baby?" he said with a chuckle, pulling her to him and kissing her on the top of her head between her pigtails. He gently flicked them so they bounced. "I love these."

"Yes, but I only had elastic bands to hold them." Pearl forgot her shyness for the moment as she remembered the rather ugly elastic bands holding her pigtails in place. "I wrote 'pretty hair ties' on my shopping list," she added, bowing her head and tilting it to one side so she could see him.

"Oh you've made a shopping list? That's a good idea. What else is on it?"

"Nothing," she whispered. "I couldn't think of anything else except... oh... new laces for my shoes. See these ones aren't pretty at all." She pointed the toe of one of her shoes so he could see how dirty and discoloured her once white shoelaces were. Marcus nodded.

"Why don't you add 'pretty shoelaces' to your list as well, then?" he suggested. "And what else? Would you like some cushions for the couch? Pictures for the walls? A rug for the floor? A prettier doona cover than that plain black one?"

Pearl surveyed the apartment, then shrugged and folded her arms with a heavy sigh.

"Never mind," he said. "We'll go exploring and see what we can find, shall we?"

Pearl nodded happily, picked up her bag and looked up at him, glad not to have to come up with any ideas or make any decisions right then. All she could think of was how handsome he was with his dark hair and blue eyes, and how his tight, dark olive-green jeans and long-sleeved T-shirt accentuated his muscular legs and chest.

By the time they'd finished, it took both of them two trips to carry their bags and parcels up in the lift. Pearl had never been on such a shopping trip before. She didn't like to ask for things, but Marcus seemed to enjoy buying them for her anyway. It was like going shopping with Santa Claus! The rug she'd chosen for the living room went straight onto the floor. Round and coloured in geometric cuts of white, grey, black, blue and brown, she had immediately recognised it.

"It's a diamond," she had cried delightedly. "And, look, when you stand here, it's sitting *on* the rug. It isn't flat at all. It's like magic." She'd walked around, checking it out from every angle, fascinated by the way the colours had been combined to replicate the facets of a cut diamond, and how from exactly the right angle the diamond appeared to become three-dimensional and rise up from the rug. Marcus had bought it for her straight away without caring about the exorbitant price.

A second rug, pink with a white horse standing beneath a giant full moon went onto her bedroom floor.

"No jewels?" Marcus had teased her when she'd chosen it.

"No," she said, shaking her head and making a sad face, then brightening immediately. "There weren't any rugs with jewels, but I like this one anyway and I think there's a castle just out of sight full of treasures."

She jumped up and down on it and then stared at the bed where the rest of their purchases were piled.

"Happy, bunny?" Marcus asked, wrapping his arms around her from behind.

She nodded and wriggled. He kissed her hair and neck and bobbled the red hair ties with cherries hanging off that she'd bought and immediately twisted around her pigtails, then he bent down so his head was level with hers. "Would you like to open all the parcels and put everything away?"

"Yes, please!" She did a happy jump almost bumping his chin with her shoulder. He laughed, squeezed her and then took his arms from around her and walked around so he could see her face.

"Where would you like to start? How about with these?" He handed her a large plastic bag and she ran to the couch and upended the bag onto it. Four cushions tumbled out, two bouncing and falling on the floor. Pearl bent down and picked them up, and then hugged their softness to her chest. She held one out to Marcus who was watching her. "This is my most favourite one of them all," she said.

"Which one is it?"

"The pink one that matches the doona cover with the pussy cat wearing a tiara covered in jewels and a rainbow. It's got, three, no four things I love: pink, pussycats, rainbows and jewels. And I love this one, and this one, and this one," she went on, arranging two of the cushions at one end of the couch and the other two at the other end, making sure the unicorn, the princess, the pussy cat and the puppy weren't hiding each other. She surveyed the finished effect. "There! They are the loveliest cushions ever," she decreed earnestly.

"Right then, what's next?" he asked.

"Can we put the pussycat on the bed, please?" she begged, running to him, taking his hands and shaking them.

"Well, we can but if we do that first, we'll have to move everything off."

"But I want to see what my bed looks like with it on and it matches the cushion."

"True, but you can't see the cushion on the couch from your bedroom, can you?"

Pearl picked up the cushion with the tiara-wearing cat. She paused to study the sparkling jewels in the tiara that were glued on. "Can I have this one on my bed?"

"Of course. They're your cushions and this is your home. You can have them wherever you like. Come on then," he added as Pearl stood holding the cushion without moving. "Let's do the bed." He went to the bedroom and started moving the shopping onto the floor. Pearl followed and stripped the pillowcases off the pillows, and put them on a chair and the pillows on the floor with the cushion. While

Marcus pulled the doona cover off, Pearl opened the packet containing the new pink set with the same tiara-wearing pussycat as the cushion, and shook it out. Together they put the doona in the new cover and the matching pillowcases on the pillows and arranged them on the bed. Pearl nestled the cushion between the pillows and sat her teddy bear, dog and cat around it, trying not to hide the bejewelled cat on the pillows and cushion, then sat on the bed and stroked the cat.

"Oh, it's so pretty, isn't it? I can't wait to sleep in it tonight," she said, lying down, closing her eyes and pretending to snore.

Marcus laughed and kissed her forehead. "Wake up, sleeping beauty. We haven't put everything away yet."

Pearl jumped up and found the bags containing the clothes they'd bought. She lay them out on the bed: a blue denim pinafore dress with a dark blue long-sleeved tee-shirt covered with stars and moons; another dress with sewn-on tiny rainbows and stuck-on sparkling jewels that Pearl had grabbed and hugged as soon as she'd seen it. She also brought home her first-ever onesies, a short white one with red and purple hearts and a frill and bow on the bottom, and a full-length grey, fleecy-cotton rabbit suit with a baby rabbit and carrot design. Pearl had loved it straight away, especially the hood with floppy ears, and the white fluffy bunny tail on the back flap. She hadn't been able to bring herself to say how much she loved it, so had been surprised but over the moon when Marcus picked it up and insisted she buy it even without her having said anything.

But then he'd teased her as they left the shop saying, "You'll wear this when I spank you before bed."

She'd had a fit of the giggles imagining wearing it with the flap down and Marcus spanking her. Of course, he'd been kidding. He wouldn't ever really spank her. At least, she was reasonably sure he wouldn't. She'd peeked up at him, and he'd smirked at her like he was joking, but he'd also been a bit stern, too, like maybe he wasn't joking. She'd been dying to know if he was serious or not but couldn't find the courage to ask. And what if he'd said he was?

Seeing it on the bed gave her butterflies in her tummy and a warm ache lower down that made her clench her muscles hard. She stole a glance at him, and then looked quickly away as his eyes went from her, to the bunny suit, to her and he raised his eyebrows. What did he mean? Was he teasing?

She hid her face from him while she took some socks with frilly tops out of the second last bag and put them with the other things.

When they were all laid out, Marcus stood by her side with his arm around her. He kissed her forehead and hugged her gently. "Cute little clothes for my cute Little girl."

Pearl wriggled her bottom happily. "Rainbows, rainbows, rainbows," she sung. "Unicorns, unicorns, unicorns. And jewels!" She clasped her hands in front of her, trembling with excitement.

Marcus chuckled. "Where are your new laces?"

"Oh, I nearly forgot them," Pearl said clapping her hand over her mouth. She found the bag she'd taken the socks from, retrieved a pair of pink laces with shimmery silver stars and handed them to Marcus.

"Why don't you take off your shoes and I'll replace the old laces with the new ones while you put your clothes away?"

Pearl dropped to the floor and pulled her shoes off, handed them to Marcus and set about clearing away her clothes.

That done and her feet encased once more in her now beautified shoes, she picked up the last bag and took it into the kitchen while Marcus collected the wrapping, stuffing the rubbish into one bag and folding the rest of the bags into a neat pile. In the kitchen, Pearl took two mugs from her bag, one with teddy bears which said *Happy Little Bear* that she put on the shelf with the other mugs, and another that said *Best Ever* in a big red heart that she'd bought for Marcus with her own money while he wasn't watching but didn't have the courage to show him. She hid it behind the others, and re-joined Marcus in the bedroom.

"Well, I think that was a successful shopping trip, eh, beautiful?"

"It was lovely. Thank you…" Pearl hesitated, blushed and hid her face.

Seeing her discomfort, Marcus sat on the bed and pulled her onto his lap. "What's the matter, little girl?"

She shook her head, unable to speak.

"Come." He regarded her with semi-mock sternness. "You shouldn't keep secrets from me. I want you to feel comfortable telling me anything. What is it? Maybe I can help. There's nothing I won't do for you, Pearl." The last was said in earnest.

"It's just… just…" Pearl stammered and stopped.

"Just what? Come on, sweetheart, tell me."

Pearl buried her face against him and mumbled into his chest.

"I don't know what to call you," she whispered, hoping he hadn't heard.

"Don't know what to call me?" He had.

She nodded, but wouldn't look at him.

"Don't you like Marcus?"

She nodded and buried her face deeper.

"What then? Does it sound too formal?"

This time Pearl nodded exaggeratedly. He was silent for so long she allowed herself a surreptitious glance up at him. He was watching her and her heart lurched. She quickly buried her face again. At least he hadn't scolded her for being silly. He did seem to understand even if he hadn't said anything. He made as if to say something, but then stopped. She peeked up. This time he seemed to be quite serious, as though he was thinking about something. Then, in an instant, the clouds lifted and he smiled, filling her heart with sunshine.

"I tell you what, my precious," he said, crushing her to him and kissing her forehead, "we'll have a think about it, shall we? Maybe we can think of something you'd like to call me that I would like too. It doesn't have to be right away. You can call me 'hey, you' if you like." He laughed and Pearl dissolved into giggles. "And if you do think of anything, you can tell me. Okay, little girl? But there's no need to worry about it in the meantime."

She nodded happily, her eyes shining.

He bent down to kiss her lips. Gentle ones to begin with, then deepening into long sensual explorations. Pearl felt herself melting in his arms. A small sound rose in her throat, and she slipped her arms around his neck as his lips continued to torment her. She could feel his body tensing, his breathing quickening and, under her, she could feel him hardening. His hand moved to cover her breast and a wave of sensual pleasure washed over her. She relaxed against him, opening, available, ready, but he broke away and, lifting her off his knee, stood up.

"Don't look like that," he said seeing the confusion and concern on her face. He bent and kissed her. "It's still quite early; I thought we might go out and get some exercise in the fresh air. Would you like to go down to the river?" He knew this part of town and that there was a grassed area with paths and playgrounds along the edge of the river in easy walking distance.

She nodded vigorously.

"Right then, let's do that. We can go for a run when we get there. Do you need a jacket?"

She shook her head and went to the front door.

"Ready?" he asked, joining her.

She nodded and he let them out and locked the door behind them.

Chapter 12

Marcus

"Come on," Marcus said, encircling her waist with his arm as they reached the street and headed towards the park. Pearl reached her arm around his waist and they walked in step without trying, their hips moving in unison.

"Oh, this is magical," Pearl whispered when they reached the river and she stopped to gaze awestruck at the glassy water glowing pink and yellow as it reflected the evening sky and setting sun.

"It is," Marcus replied, standing behind her and holding her in his arms. "Do you feel like a run, then? If we follow this path, it breaks off a little way up and that other one," he pointed across the grassed area to where she could see another path, "comes back around so it makes a good circular track. It's not far. About three kilometres, I think."

Pearl slipped from his arms. "You can't catch me," she cried gaily taking off at a brisk run.

"Hey, slow down." Jogging behind her, slowly enough so

as not to catch up, he watched her, admiring her delightfully plump bottom bouncing as she ran.

She'd surprised him when she'd said she didn't know what to call him; he knew what he wanted her to call him — Daddy, but it was probably too soon to spring that on her unless he got an inkling she was thinking the same thing. He was still worried she might run away if he pushed her too soon. The more time he spent with her, the more he saw of the Little girl inside. Whether she was consciously aware of her need to be a Little girl sometimes, he didn't know; he didn't even know if she was aware that some big girls were Little girls as well.

He'd deliberately brought her to the park to give her another opportunity to let her Little girl out. He'd told the truth about feeling the need for a run, but he had also brought her here because they would pass a playground and if his suspicions were right, he expected Pearl would want to stop and play, and he would stand at the bottom of the slide and catch her and push her on the swing.

Pearl had slowed from her first burst of speed, and he had no trouble drawing alongside.

"How are you doing?" he asked.

"Whew!" she giggled breathlessly, skipping sideways so she was facing him. "It's hard work. My legs are getting tired."

"Well, that's probably because you took off so fast instead of pacing yourself. And because you've only got short legs. We can rest if you see a place you want to stop," he said easily. He was used to running and could easily run twice the distance they were going.

"I'm okay," she said determinedly. "I can do it."

Marcus loved that about her: her perseverance. She didn't give up when things got tough, despite being such a little thing in such a big world. And when she got knocked down, she bounced right up. How many people would have been able to go back to Mon Addi after what Marcie had done to her? Probably not many, but she didn't suffer from false pride. She knew what she wanted and was prepared to make the required effort. It made him even angrier that Marcie had tried to bring her down for her own selfish ends.

Pearl reminded him of a tenacious puppy, smart and strong while still being ingenuous and unspoiled. It tugged at his heartstrings and roused his protective instincts. He wanted to be by her side, encouraging her, helping her if he could, keeping an eye on her, and taking care of her.

As they ran comfortably together, he wondered what was going through her mind. Was she attracted by his wealth? She hadn't had much experience with men; was she just enjoying the attention? Was she going to learn about being with a man from him and then go in search of someone else? Or, and his heartbeat quickened, would she truly surrender to him and be his Little girl?

As if to give hope to his last question, she stopped and cried out, "Ooh, goody! There's a playground. Can I have a swing? Please? Oh, please? I love swings. And slides."

Marcus laughed, feeling a rush of relief. He wasn't wrong about her. Surely not.

"Of course. Let me push you."

"Whee," she cried with glee as she climbed onto the swing and he pushed her high. "Higher," she demanded. "Higher."

"Had enough," he asked twenty minutes later, after she'd swung and slid and climbed numerous times on everything the playground had to offer, and evening was beginning to close in on them. He was way too big to fit on most of the playground equipment, but had been perfectly content to watch from below as she played happily. "It's getting too dark to see what you're doing. And I'm about ready to eat."

Pearl laughed, jumped down next to him and patted his belly before collapsing onto the sand and making a sand angel.

"Can we have pizza for dinner? I love pizza and I haven't had it for ages."

"Not since last weekend, anyway," Marcus said with a laugh, holding out his hand to help her up and then brushing the sand off.

"Can we anyway?" Pearl pleaded, clasping her hands together under her chin and adopting the most pleading expression she could. "Please? Please?"

"Of course," he agreed with a grin and kissed her nose. "Let's get going then before it gets dark."

"I'm going to race you," Pearl cried gaily, dashing off, but Marcus was quicker and caught her before she'd got far.

"No. No racing. Not in the dark. It's too dangerous. You might fall or bang into something or get run over by a bicycle."

"All right," she said innocently, but the minute he let her go, off she ran. Again, he caught her and took hold of her hand.

"Hey, naughty girl. I said no running around in the dark. Hold my hand and walk with me. Do you hear? I'm serious."

"But I want to run," she said. "I won't fall over." She tried to wriggle free but he held her hand too tightly.

"And I don't want you to. Behave yourself, Pearl," he warned her. "We've had lots of fun in the park, but it's dark and I don't want you having an accident. If you don't behave, you will be having pizza for dinner and a spanking before bed. Do you understand? I'm not kidding."

It had become a battle of wills and Marcus was surprised. He'd not seen this aspect of her before. She wriggled her arm, trying to pull her hand free, but he held it tightly. "I said walk with me. Or are you trying to earn yourself a spanking?" He paused, but she didn't reply, just stared at the ground and kicked it with her shoe. "You're tired and hungry; aren't you, little girl?" he asked gently. "We'll be home soon, so behave yourself and you can have pizza and a bath and hop into bed with the new pussy cat cover without getting your bottom spanked first. Okay?"

Pearl didn't answer and the light was so gloomy, Marcus couldn't see her face. Again he wondered what she was thinking. Had he frightened her with his threat to spank her? He felt her relax and loosened his grip on her hand.

"Come on, then, sweetheart." He let go of her hand to put his arm around her shoulders but she took off into the dark.

"Damn! Pearl? Pearl?" Marcus called, following in the direction he'd seen her shadowy figure disappearing. Peering into the steadily enveloping darkness devoid of artificial lights, Marcus pulled out his phone and switched on the torch. Scouring the way ahead, all he could see was a garden surrounded by an ankle-high picket fence. It surrounded a clump of bushes, ranging from waist to chest-high, quite big enough to hide one small, naughty runaway.

"Pearl," he called as he neared the bushes. "Pearl!" His reply was a muffled giggle followed by a scuffling and then the thudding of feet as she jumped the fence on the other side of the bushes and headed towards the road.

"Damn!" he growled, hurrying after her. He had no choice but to try and outrun her. She had taken a turn in the park that led to a different road than the one they'd come in on, and there was every possibility she may not easily, or at least quickly, find her way to the flat. While it's true that most young women move safely around the streets, for an unlucky few it is a tragically different story, and Marcus couldn't bear to think of Pearl winding up in that second group. It would break his heart if anything happened to her. He had to find her, and get her home safely and then…!

He caught sight of her as the lights from the street illuminated the edge of the park; she had reached the pavement and was about to cross the road. He sprinted the last bit catching up to her at the precise moment a group of four youths came around the corner and blocked her path.

"Whoa! Hey, little lady," one of them said as the others milled around her, looking her up and down and making lewd remarks.

"See that, lads? She couldn't get to us fast enough."

"Hahaha. Don't sweat it, baby. We're yours for the taking."

"Show us your tits."

Marcus stepped into the light. "Fuck off." His voice was a deep, menacing growl.

The younger men shrugged and held their hands up in mock surrender.

Pearl seemed entirely unaware of potentially having been in danger and was bent over, giggling and puffing. Marcus was also puffing and the rapid beating of his heart, which had only a small amount to do with his recent exertion, was making it almost impossible for him to speak. He pulled her into his arms and clutched her to him, watching warily as the youths sauntered past staring rudely at them, making comments too low to be heard and laughing loudly.

Pearl giggled and snuggled into his chest.

"You nearly didn't catch me," she teased him.

"Why did you do that?" he asked calmly, not allowing his concern to cause him to lash out at her in anger.

"What?"

"Run away from me like that after I specifically asked you not to?"

She shrugged, made a feeble attempt to loosen his hold and avoided his eyes. "Fun?"

"Look at me, Pearl." He paused until she did. "All I asked was that you walked with me, holding my hand. It's dark and there could be strange people about. To be honest, I'm confused about why you would behave like that. You've been so sensible and good up until now. What got into you?"

Pearl kicked at the ground with her foot, her signature move whenever she was feeling discomfited. She shrugged again. "Are you angry with me?"

"I'm trying not to be. I don't want to be angry with you, but you frightened me. What if I hadn't seen which way you went and hadn't been right behind you? What if you'd run into someone like you nearly did there and they'd hurt you? Could you even find your way home from here?"

Pearl frowned, confused about why he'd asked her that until she suddenly realised that the streets were not familiar and she had no idea where she was.

"I thought I was going the way we came," she said in a very small voice.

"Well, you were wrong. And although you are a smart, capable woman and can mostly take care of yourself, there's no need to take unnecessary risks. You scared me." He wrapped his arms around her and kissed her forehead. "You're so precious. I couldn't bear it if anything happened to you, especially while you're with me. Please don't ever do that again. Promise?"

"I won't. I promise," Pearl said contritely.

Marcus kissed her on the mouth, long and hard. "All right," he said gruffly, taking her hand. "Let's go home and have pizza. And then we'll have another chat about this."

They crossed the road and headed toward the flat.

"Erm," Pearl mumbled as they got closer.

"Yes, my precious but naughty girl, what is it?"

"Well, remember how you said you'd spank me if I ran away?"

"Yes, I said that."

"You didn't mean it. Did you." She said it as a statement not a question.

"I most certainly did mean it. I fully intend to put you over my knee and spank your bare bottom before you go to bed. You can get into your bunny onesie after your shower. That is your spanking pjs."

"I don't want you to spank me."

"Don't you?" Marcus pulled a fake sad face, then a serious one. "Well, you could have fooled me. I warned you explicitly that if you ran away, I would spank you, and you ran away. That seems to me to be a little girl asking to have her bottom spanked."

"Not really," she argued, "because I didn't think you'd actually do it."

"Well, you are going to find out that I will actually do it, and you won't make that mistake in future. So, what sort of pizza would you like? I may as well order it and it should be delivered about the time we get home."

Chapter 13

Pearl

Walking home, holding hands, Pearl and Marcus might have been any relaxed couple on a date, except for the turmoil in Pearl's mind. They'd be home soon, pizza would be delivered and they'd have dinner together. Then, Marcus had said, she would have to put on her bunny onesie with the flap at the back so he could spank her. Part of her didn't believe he was serious, but the other part remembered all the times since she'd met him that he'd talked about spanking her.

What would she do if he wasn't just teasing? Well, he couldn't make her. Would he spank her hard? Would it hurt?

"Erm," she said, wanting to say something but unsure what and embarrassed to broach the subject.

"What is it, little girl?"

"Nothing." She turned away, and he squeezed her hand so she'd look at him. He smiled encouragingly and her heart flip-flopped. He was so lovely. She smiled bashfully. He dropped her hand, put his arm around her shoulders and pulled her to him, bending to kiss the top of her head.

"My little girl, aren't you, baby?" he murmured.

"Yes," she whispered with a soft giggle as she snuggled against him and wrapped her arms around his waist as they entered her apartment building.

"The pizza should be here in about five minutes. Why don't you run along and wash up and I'll make a cup of tea while I wait for it," Marcus suggested as they let themselves into her flat. "Would you like one?"

"Yes, please," Pearl replied heading for the bathroom.

A short time later, they were seated at the table with their hot steaming pizza and cups of tea. Marcus hadn't mentioned spanking again, and Pearl was starting to believe it had been a warning but not something he planned to follow through on. She would have to be careful, though, in case she pushed him too far. She shivered, not with cold and not with fright, but wondering what that would be like, what he would be like if she pushed him too far.

"So, I've got some news," Marcus said between mouthfuls, breaking into her thoughts.

"Oh? What? Good news? Not bad news." Pearl made a sad face.

Marcus patted her hand. "No, not bad news. I hope not anyway. I guess time will tell. No, apparently my brother is coming home."

Pearl's hand stopped mid-air, her mouth agape. "Oh, I didn't know you had a brother."

Marcus paused, picked up a small piece of tomato that had fallen off his pizza onto his plate and put it in his mouth. "Well, he's been gone awhile. Didn't seem any point in suddenly blurting it out. Not that I was hiding it from you. I would have told you eventually."

"Where's he been?"

"Overseas. Drifting around. Taking drugs. And money from Mother."

Pearl frowned. "You don't like him?"

"It's not that I dislike him. We were close as kids. He's two years older than me, and we were pretty much brothers-in-arms from the time I was about two. We'd both joined the family business and were working together when he suddenly quit his job, took off overseas and went completely off the rails, drinking, taking drugs, not working. That sort of thing. It's been a terrible worry for Mother. I think she tried to wipe him from her mind, figuring one day he'd be found dead somewhere or disappear forever. But," he paused and opened his arms, palms up, "he's decided to come home apparently, and bring a sackful of money with him."

"How long has he been gone?"

"Hmm, three or four years, maybe. Must be nearly four, I guess. I was sent after him a couple of times, but he was adamant he was staying where he was. He was a mess last time I went. I honestly didn't think I'd ever see him again." He gritted his teeth, hardening his cheek, but that was the only indication of how painful it had been. "So, I don't dislike him, but I am pretty angry and I did lose a lot of respect for him."

"That's sad. I love my family so much. I couldn't imagine being on bad terms with them, even though I don't see my brother much either."

"You're lucky." Marcus pressed his lips together and sighed. "Yeah, we've never done family particularly well."

"So, when is your brother – what's his name? – coming home?"

"Ray. Not straight away. He's going into rehab for a while and then, when he's ready to leave, he's going to work in London for about a month or so. Mother is flying out tomorrow to see him and make arrangements. But she's already planning a welcome home party for when he does arrive, so I guess you can meet him for yourself then. If you'd like to come, that is?" he added hastily, realising he was taking her acceptance for granted.

"You mean meet your family?" Pearl sounded overawed by the thought.

"Yes. Why not? I mean, it's basically only Mother and Ray, and it's not for ages, so you have plenty of time to think about it. And I'd understand if you didn't want to. They can be trying, as can their friends, some of whom I'm sure you will have met in Mon Addi. I believe most of them shop there and they're always dripping with new jewels."

"Oh! I probably shouldn't come then," Pearl said, shaking her head. "I don't have any jewels except my diamond studs, and they're tiny."

Marcus shook his head, too, in reply, but his was in frustration, not refusal. "You don't need jewels. You will be the loveliest woman there – inside and out – I can promise you that, and all their fancy jewels don't make them any better than they are which, in some cases, is not that great."

"What's wrong with them? Most of our clients are lovely."

Marcus snorted. "They may be polite to the servants – it's considered crass not to be – while they stock up their treasure chests with ostentatious trinkets to flaunt their wealth, but most of Mother's friends rarely give a thought to anyone but themselves. Of course, it's not true of everybody that will be at her extravaganza, but Mother does seem to attract a surfeit of the shallow kind for some reason. Anyway, I shan't press you for an answer. Think about it. I'd like you to come. I want you to meet my family at some point. Or rather I want them to meet you." He smiled and squeezed her hand.

"But not yet. I think a party with lots of other people there would be a good time."

"I want to go. I want to meet your family. And I haven't seen your house either. I imagine it's enormous. Not like the farm." *Ping!* "Oh, I've got a message." Pearl looked over to where she'd left her phone. "Should I see who it's from?"

"Yes, go on." She jumped up, collected her phone and re-joined Marcus before checking the message.

"It's from Tony! It says: *Hey Pearl. Pierre and I are going OS on Monday and wondered if you want to catch up for lunch on Sunday before we go.* "Oh goody," she said wriggling with pleasure, then her face fell and she pouted. "But they're going overseas! I wonder how long for." She chewed her bottom lip for a moment in thought, then looked up at Marcus. "Can we have lunch with them? Can we? Please? Oh…" she paused, blushing as she realised what she'd said. "I mean, would you, could you…?"

Marcus chuckled and tousled her hair. "You are utterly delightful. Do you know that? I was fully planning on spending tomorrow with you and would love to meet your friends, especially your BFF. Tell him yes, and see if one o'clock is good for them. We can meet in the mall."

Pearl fired off her reply, and wriggled and bounced once the arrangements were finalised. "Oh, I'm so excited you're going to meet Tony and Pierre. You'll like them. I know you will."

"I'm sure I shall, and I'll be able to find out all the mischief you got up to as a teenager, won't I?"

"What mischief?"

"Aha, that's what I plan to find out," Marcus replied, tapping the side of his nose. "I bet you have some skeletons you haven't told me about yet." He winked at her to show he was teasing as he finished off the last piece of pizza. "Have you had enough to eat? Shall we clean up?"

Pearl leaned in her chair, rubbed her tummy and puffed up her cheeks. "Yes. I'm so full. I think I'm going to burst."

Standing up, Marcus pulled her to her feet and into his arms and kissed her firmly on the lips. "Don't do that! I much prefer you in one piece. There's not much to do here. I'll tidy up, while you have your shower, get into your spanking pj's, and wait for me on your bed."

"Oh!" The colour drained from Pearl's face as the import of his words sunk in.

Seeing her hesitation, Marcus tilted his head to the side and raised his eyebrows. "Yes, little girl?"

Blushing, Pearl stared hard at her toe, which was poking the ground, and shook her head. "Nothing," she managed to mumble. *Do I really have to? You're not serious about spanking me, are you?* was what she said in her head, but there was no way she could get those words out. She sighed. She still didn't fully believe he would spank her, deciding instead that he was teasing her so she would behave in the future.

"Very well, then. Off you go. And make it quick. I don't want you to make me come and get you."

Pearl collected the bunny onesie from her wardrobe and took it into the bathroom. It was absolutely the cutest thing she'd ever seen, and she would be so excited to be wearing it if Marcus hadn't called it her spanking pj's. She decided that, even if he was only teasing her about the spanking, she'd best not do anything else to make him think spanking her might be a good idea after all. Stripping off, she jumped into the shower, soaped herself all over, rinsed herself clean, brushed her teeth, then turned the shower off, dried herself and slipped into the full-length onesie. She stood in front of the mirror, pulled the hood with its long floppy ears over her hair and twitched her nose while she made tutting noises. Giggling, she strained her neck to see over her shoulder and tried to watch her fluffy tail as she wiggled her bottom. Then she did a bunny hop into a patch of water.

"Ugh." She wiped her foot on the bathmat, which didn't do much to dry her soggy paw. The mood broken, she collected her things and went to wait for Marcus. She could hear him in the living room on his phone, but couldn't make out what he was saying. She fidgeted as she sat on her bed, hugging her teddy bear and wriggling her damp foot. She wondered if she should get a book and be reading when he came in. Would he disturb her if she was reading? Maybe. Perhaps she should get right into bed and pretend to be asleep. He could hardly spank her if she was asleep, could he? And he wouldn't be so unkind as to wake her up. Surely not. She leaned up to pull the bedclothes from under her when she heard him coming. Quickly, she sat down as though she was about to get caught doing something she ought not be doing.

Her eyes opened wide as he came in and sat on the edge of the bed. "Come and stand here next to me," he said, pointing to the floor next to his knee.

Pearl held her teddy in front of her face so only her saucer-sized eyes were visible.

"Are you mblmblmbl?" she said in a tiny voice, her words disappearing into the bear.

Marcus kept a straight face, but she saw the corner of his mouth twitch.

"What was that?" he asked.

She hid her whole face behind her bear. "Are you going to spank me now?" she repeated, audibly this time, but only just.

"Yes, little girl. That's exactly what I'm going to do. So, up you get. Come and stand here, please."

Without letting go of her teddy bear, Pearl dragged

herself reluctantly off the bed and stood where he'd told her to.

"I don't want you to spank me," she said in a whisper.

"I don't suppose you do. And I don't want to do it either. But you were very naughty, weren't you? You were warned at least three times, and you went ahead and did exactly what I'd told you not to do, even though I said I would spank you if you did. I can't not do it after I said I would, can I?"

"Yes, you could," Pearl said, wriggling and peeking hopefully at him from around the bear.

Marcus swallowed a laugh and poked her gently in the tummy. "Nah." He shook his head. "That is not going to happen. I'm going to spank your bare bottom, like I said I would, and then you're going to get into bed and I'll read you a story if you like."

Pearl fidgeted and danced on the spot. "Couldn't I just have the story?"

"Nope. Spanking first. Then story. Come on. I think you're deliberately stalling. Let's get this over with, shall we? Turn around, please.'

Pearl's feet ran on the spot as though they were trying to carry her away and her breath came out in a muffled wail, but she turned as he said and squeezed her knees together.

"That's a good girl." Marcus ran his hand over her hip and then over her bottom, which contracted at his touch as though anticipating a smack. He undid the two buttons at the top of the flap and let it drop down leaving her perfectly framed milky globes exposed to his eyes and his hand.

Slipping his hand in, he cupped one cheek and squeezed it. Pearl shuddered. "Oh my, what a perfect little bottom," he said, cupping and squeezing the other cheek. "It was made to be spanked. And it has never ever been spanked before?"

"No," Pearl wailed as it became increasingly certain he

was going to be as good as his word and absolutely meant to spank her.

"What a waste," he muttered, giving it another squeeze. "Turn around then."

Pearl obeyed wondering why she didn't run away or jump into bed or simply refuse to be spanked. But she seemed unable to resist him.

"Are you seriously going to spank my bottom?" she asked one last time, clutching her teddy against her belly with one hand and bending over to wrap herself around it, while her other hand covered her exposed bottom.

"I am, naughty girl. I am."

"Will it hurt?" Pearl asked, finally accepting he was deadly serious about punishing her.

"It's a spanking. Because you were a very naughty and disobedient girl. Don't you think spankings are supposed to hurt, at least a little bit?" he said sternly as her nervous toe prodded the ground almost hard enough to make a hole in the floor.

"I don't want you to hurt my bottom," Pearl said sadly, her eyes filling with tears.

"Sweet baby girl," Marcus said, pulling her onto his knee. She buried her face on his chest and he stroked her hair. "I will never ever really hurt you. I promise. Never. Do you believe me?"

She nodded. He kissed her hair, then lifted her face up.

"It's just a little spanking on your naughty bottom to remind you to be more careful in future. Okay?"

She nodded but didn't move.

"Good. Then let's get it done, shall we?"

Pearl reluctantly dragged herself off his knee and stood next to him, her bear covering her face.

"So, a not-too hard spanking this time, and will you be a

good girl in the future so I never have to give you a harder spanking?"

She didn't lift her head, but peeked one eye around from behind her bear and looked up at him from under her fringe, nodding hard.

"Good. Come on, then. Give me your teddy." He tried to take the bear from her arms, but she clutched it tightly and wouldn't let go. "All right. You can keep hold of it if it makes you feel better. Lay yourself across my lap." He tugged her hand gently and guided her over his knee so her exposed bottom was perched high and ready.

Pearl had not been in this position before and it felt strange and precarious. Her toes barely reached the carpet on one side and, as her hands were full of bear, she couldn't hold onto anything for balance. She wriggled.

"If you're too uncomfortable holding the bear, you can give it to me and either put your hands on the floor or hold my leg for support. Would you feel more secure like that?"

Pearl nodded and didn't resist when he reached down and took her bear. "He's waiting for you up here to give you a cuddle when it's over."

Pearl nodded, her throat too full and tight for her to be able to speak. She clutched the leg of his trousers as she felt him arrange her onesie. When she'd lain over his lap, the onesie had ridden up so some of her lower back was exposed by the flap in her pj's but the area between her bottom and thighs was covered. Marcus pulled it down until he had unfettered access to her plump white bottom. Then Pearl felt him lay his left arm across her as he raised his right hand.

"Here's your spanking then, naughty girl," he said as his hand came down and smacked her right cheek. She blinked hard with surprise but didn't move. "This is for running away when I told you not to," he said as he rubbed her other cheek and then raised his hand and smacked that one.

"Oh." This time Pearl gasped at the sensation of his hand cracking against her flesh even though he wasn't spanking her hard.

"Keep still," he ordered as his hand rose and fell, her bottom coloured a rosy pink, and every nerve in her body focused on the plump flesh currently suffering under his hand.

Chapter 14

Marcus

Marcus was captivated by the round cherubic bottom framed by the flap of Pearl's bunny onesie and his heart felt fit to burst. She was completely bewitching, and he couldn't deny he was utterly smitten. He was in heaven. She was absolutely everything he'd wanted, and he couldn't believe his luck in finding her. He'd felt it the first time he'd seen her at Mon Addi. She might have been an adult doing an adult's job, but there was a childlike innocence she couldn't hide. He didn't think she had even been consciously aware of it, and doubted other people noticed.

But he had been searching for a long time, and he'd spotted it straight away, and this latest confirmation that he'd not been mistaken filled his heart with joy. She was submitting to his spanking exactly as he would expect a Little girl to submit to her Daddy. His heart and cock were both bursting, and he had to wriggle to try and ease the discomfort in his groin.

He brought his hand down again on her bottom, revelling in how it flattened under his palm and then jiggled as he raised his hand. He wasn't spanking her hard. He had no intention of making it too painful. He didn't want to hurt her. She was too precious.

"How are you doing, naughty girl?" he asked, pausing his hand.

"Okay," she whispered.

"Do you deserve this spanking?"

"Yes," she whispered and he heard the breath catch in her throat.

"Good girl. Your punishment is nearly over. Are you ready for the last few?"

She nodded, and he felt her brace herself.

He raised his hand, and a line from his favourite childhood book, "*Where The Wild Things Are*", flashed through his mind: "*We'll eat you up, we love you so.*" That was exactly how he felt about this completely captivating girl. He was thoroughly enjoying every minute of having her over his knee and spanking her slowly but not too harshly, pausing sometimes to take in the visual beauty of her blushing cheeks and to squeeze their firm softness.

"All right," he said, when he'd decided the session was over. "Come here, darling." He helped her off his knee and stood her with her freshly spanked bottom facing him. Before he fastened the buttons on her flap, he rubbed her punished bottom. "Not too sore?" She shook her head. Her flap refastened, he sat her on his knee and cuddled her into him, and she hid her face against his broad chest. "What a good girl you were," he said kissing and stroking her hair. "You didn't wriggle or make a fuss. It didn't hurt too much, did it?" She shook her head. "Can you look at me, Pearl?" She tilted her head just enough so one eye could see him. He chuckled and squeezed her tight. "Would you like to hop into bed then, and I'll read you a story?" She nodded, sliding off his lap, picking up her teddy bear and slipping into bed keeping her face hidden.

"What story would you like?" Marcus asked flipping through the books in her bookcase.

"*Winnie-the-Pooh*", please. When Eeyore has a birthday. I love that story. It's so sad even though Eeyore loves his presents."

Marcus laughed. "Oh, yeah. I read those stories as a kid. I enjoyed them then, but I haven't read them for ages."

He found the book and the story and sat on the bed next to her.

Pearl had the covers pulled up to her eyes. "Aren't you getting into bed too?"

"No, precious. Not tonight."

She pulled the covers down so he could see she was pouting.

He tapped her sticking out bottom lip and stuck out his own making a sad face. "It's not that I don't want to sleep with you," he explained. "I really want to. But I want to make love to you so much I don't know if I could spend the night in bed with you and resist the temptation. And when I do make love to you for the first time, I will be claiming you as mine forever. I want us both to be absolutely sure that is what we want. Do you understand, sweetheart?"

Pearl let out a huge sigh and shook her head, sticking her bottom lip further out. Marcus laughed, bent down and gently sucked it into his mouth, then turned the suck into a long slow, deep kiss. He scooped her into his arms, his heart melting. He never wanted to let her go. He hoped she understood that. He felt deeply that they were both on the threshold of knowing without doubt that this, her being his Little girl and him being her Daddy, was what they both wanted for the rest of their lives. But until then, he had vowed to be patient.

He laid her gently down and snuggled her bear up to her.

"Settle down and go to sleep, precious angel," he said, picking up the book again. "I'll let myself out when you're asleep and I'll see you tomorrow and we'll have lunch with your friends. Okay?"

"Okay," she agreed reluctantly.

"And can you do one other thing for me please, baby?" he asked.

She nodded.

"Can you stay in your pj's till I get here in the morning?"

Her eyes popped open wide in alarm. He grinned and stroked her gently. "Don't look so worried. No spanking. I promise. I want to help you get dressed. That's all. Would you like that?"

Pearl blushed and nodded.

"Right then, let's read a story, shall we?"

Pearl nodded and rolled onto her side. Marcus saw her hand automatically go to her face and for a moment he thought she was going to slip her thumb into her mouth, but then she didn't, just held it against her lips. He grunted quietly to himself. He doubted she would need much encouragement. He felt like it was something she unconsciously wanted to do but had probably trained herself not to because she thought it was wrong. He would happily change her mind about that. He stroked her hair, almost unable to believe his luck in finding her, and her apparently feeling the same about him as he did about her. Then he settled down to read her to sleep.

WALKING down the mall with her the following day, Marcus could not have felt prouder. He'd dressed her in the grey skirt and black tights he'd bought for her and a black T-shirt with a Minnie Mouse on the front, which she'd already, had in her wardrobe. With sparkly pink runners and grey cardigan completing her outfit, she looked utterly beguiling. And she'd been so compliant when he'd dressed her, standing quietly and holding up arms and legs when he'd asked as he took off her onesie, helped her with her underwear and then put on her tights, skirt and T-shirt.

"Oooh, there they are! Tony! Tony!" she exclaimed, letting go of his hand and running to meet the man who had stood up and was holding his arms open.

"Hey, sis," he greeted her.

"Mmm," she said hugging him tight and rocking them both. "Hi, Pierre," she added when she'd finished hugging Tony and hugged him too. "This is Marcus."

Marcus shook Tony's hand, immediately liking his big, open blue eyes, the smattering of freckles across his nose and the shaggy, red, brown, gold hair hanging over his ears.

"Hi, Tony," he said. "It's a pleasure to meet Pearl's partner in crime."

Tony grinned at Pearl and they both dissolved into giggles.

"Nice to meet you, Pierre," Marcus said, shaking Tony's partner's hand. Pierre was taller than Tony, with black hair, a brown complexion and friendly brown eyes. His handshake had a man-to-man feel about it that Tony's hadn't.

The greetings and introductions over, they made their way to a cafe and found a table. Marcus put his arm around Pearl's shoulder and helped her with her order, while Pierre and Tony discussed what they would have.

"So, what do you mean you're going OS?" Pearl

demanded of Tony after their choices had been made and they were waiting for their food.

"You're not going to believe this," Tony began and both he and Pierre laughed. "Not that it's funny. It's just that you think it's something that only happens in stories. Pierre, apparently, had a distant relative whom he'd never met and had no idea even existed until she died and left him some money."

"What? No? You're not serious!"

Tony and Pierre nodded. "Honest. Cross our hearts, and bless hers. She was in her nineties, so she had a good long life but no children or close family. She split her savings between all the relatives she knew of, which included Pierre's mum and dad and Pierre himself. It wasn't exactly a fortune, but it is enough for us to go backpacking in a few places, so that's what we're doing. We're starting in Paris – Pierre has some family there he wants to catch up with – then through Europe, the train from Berlin to Beijing via Russia, then across to South America and a few places there, then home. We're planning to be away about two months, but it's not set in stone, so we can stay longer if we want. Or come back earlier, which doesn't seem likely."

"Oh my," Pearl said. "That's amazing."

"It sounds fantastic," Marcus agreed, joining in the conversation as he filled everyone's glasses with water from a bottle the waiter had left on the table. "Have you been over-seas before?"

"I haven't, but Pierre has. What about you?"

They were still sharing travel adventures, Pearl leaning against Marcus who kept his arm around her, when their meals arrived.

In the lull in conversation while their plates were placed in front of them, Marcus took a napkin and tucked it into Pearl's T-shirt, picked up a chip and fed it to her, and topped up her glass with water. His movements were slow and casual, so he didn't appear at all to be fussing, simply attending to her. His eye caught Pierre's and he saw an imperceptible nod, which seemed to register approval. A tiny crinkle of his eyes showed he'd seen and he kissed Pearl's hair.

"I told Pearl I would ask you about what naughty things she got up to as a teenager," Marcus said to Tony who grinned.

"I was a good girl," Pearl protested.

"We weren't exactly the wild kids of the town, were we, sis?" Tony said. "But there was the time we wagged school on sports carnival day. Remember? We always hated sports carnivals," he explained to Marcus. "Sitting outside in pens pretending you cared whether the blues, reds, golds or greens won. I guess we weren't very competitive. And neither of us could run fast."

"Sports carnivals are horrid and silly," Pearl said adamantly.

"So you wagged?" Marcus gently prompted Tony.

"Yeah. We went swimming at the river and then to my place. No one was home, but the nosy neighbour saw us sneaking in and called the cops and then my dad. The cops arrived with their lights flashing and Dad was not far behind. He thought some major crime had been committed, and I think it was only the relief of finding out it was nothing more serious than Pearl and me skipping the sports carnival that made him forget to be mad at me."

Pearl and Tony both laughed at the memory.

"They called us Bonny and Clyde for a while after, hey, Tony?"

Tony nodded. "They did. Of course, the school was notified and Pearl and I had to appear before the headmaster the next day for a telling off, but even that was better than the sports carnival." He made a face, and Pearl laughed again.

"The worst thing that ever happened, I think," Tony continued, "was the time Pearl walked into a patch of double gees with bare feet. I was behind her and she suddenly stopped and screamed. Her feet were full of them and she couldn't move. I found some bark I could make a bridge out of. It was only a couple of feet, and I managed to walk across it to get to her, and help her balance while she got them out of one foot, then the other and then to safety."

Pearl shuddered. "Oh, that was awful. I hate those horrid things. They look kind of cute, like tiny foxes, but they hurt so much! I was lucky you were there! You were like my big brother, eh Tony, always looking out for me?"

"Uh-huh. Especially after John joined the army. Now we're all grown up, eh? And I've got someone to look after me." He snuggled against Pierre who tucked a few wayward strands of shaggy auburn hair behind Tony's ear. "And I reckon you have too."

"Wha…?" Pearl's nose wrinkled as she turned to Marcus.

"Yup. I guess it's my job to pull you out of prickle patches now, eh?" he said with a smile. "Although I wouldn't say that brotherly is exactly how I feel about you. Damn, there's my phone, and I can tell from the ringtone it's my mother. I'd better take it. Excuse me, please." He stood up as he answered the phone and politely moved out of earshot.

"He's gorgeous!" Tony whispered conspiratorially. Pearl blushed, but Marcus was off the phone before she had time to answer. He sat down, picked up a napkin and wiped a crumb from Pearl's mouth before kissing her.

"I'm sorry, baby, but I have to go," he said softly, then turned to the others. "Please excuse me. I'm afraid duty calls. My mother is flying overseas later, and she seems to be having some sort of crisis. Would you guys be able to see Pearl safely home for me, or should I take her now?"

"I don't want to go yet," Pearl said with a disappointed pout. "We've barely had a chance to catch up. I can go home by myself."

"If she'd like to stay longer, Tony and I will make sure she gets home safely and that she lets you know once she's there," Pierre answered with a nod to Marcus, ignoring Pearl.

Marcus met his gaze directly and knew he could trust the other man with his precious girl.

"Thanks, mate. I appreciate it. Pearl, you behave yourself and do whatever Pierre says. I'm taking Mother to the airport at midnight, so I won't come and wake you as you have work in the morning, but I'll see you tomorrow." He kissed the top of her head.

"I wish you could stay."

"Me too, baby. Me too."

He kissed her gently on the lips and left after shaking hands with Tony and Pierre, wishing them safe travels, and saying he hoped to catch up with them after their trip.

Chapter 15

Pearl

Pearl's eyes followed Marcus until he disappeared out of the cafe door and she couldn't see him any longer.

"He's a keeper," Tony said seriously, nodding his head.

Pearl giggled and dropped her eyes. "He is amazing, isn't he? I can't believe he's interested in me. He could have any woman he wanted."

"I'd say he's got exactly the woman he wants," Pierre observed. "You two seem perfect together. Like me and Tony, eh, ginger boy?"

Tony nestled his head under Pierre's chin and grinned at Pearl. "Yep. I reckon my little sis has found herself a Daddy."

"What? I don't know what you're talking about! That's silly," Pearl exclaimed, blushing and squirming. Maybe to herself she'd secretly felt like Marcus was a kind of Daddy and she was maybe a little girl, but how did Tony know that?

"Do you call him Daddy?" Tony went on, ignoring her discomfort.

"No," Pearl said, drawing the 'o' out to give it emphasis, but feeling a jolt of recognition at the suggestion.

"What do you call him, then?" Tony demanded. "I didn't hear you call him anything, not even Marcus."

With no room under the table for Pearl's foot to poke the ground, her finger drew circles on the table instead. She shrugged. "Everything sounds strange. I mean 'darling' or something like that. I call him Marcus when I call him anything, but... Why are we talking about this? Tell me everything about your trip. I'm so jealous."

"Okay," Pierre said kindly, letting her off the hook. "Tony, stop pestering the poor girl, or else."

"All right," Tony said reluctantly. "But if that guy's not your Daddy, I need glasses because I can't see straight. Check out the way you dress. I bet he picks your clothes, hey? And he was feeding you and wiping your mouth. Do you get bedtime stories too? And spankings?"

Pearl's eyes darted around as her cheeks burned brighter. "I... I..." she stammered.

"Don't be embarrassed," Tony said comfortingly. "It's not a bad thing. It's a lovely thing if you've found each other. Like us."

"Yes, and you might find out more about spankings than you want, naughty boy," Pierre scolded him, "if you don't leave the poor child alone."

"Yes, sir," Tony said quickly and meekly with a secret wink at Pearl, and the conversation reverted to talk of travel and jobs, but it had left Pearl with much to think about.

ON HER OWN for the evening after Tony and Pierre had seen her safely home, she'd searched Daddy on the internet and discovered lots of grown up girls who liked being Little girls whenever they could and who had a man they called Daddy to take care of them. She instantly recognised herself and wondered if Tony was right in thinking Marcus regarded himself as her Daddy. If he did, did he want her to call him Daddy? To herself, that was exactly what she had started calling him, but she had no idea how she would ever be brave enough to say it out loud.

The more she thought about Marcus and the more she read about D/lg relationships, the more convinced she was that that was what Marcus wanted with her, and the more convinced she was that that was what she wanted with him. Her heart fluttered as she remembered the girly clothes he had bought for her, how he tucked her in and read her stories, how he fed her and wiped crumbs from her mouth, how he helped her shower and dress, and all the other ways he looked after her. She loved all of it, even when he spanked her, and especially when he licked her pussy and made her orgasm. She definitely wanted as much of that as she could get, and she wanted all the rest as well.

Ping! Her phone alerted her to a message at seven o'clock the next morning. *Good morning, little girl. Are you getting ready for work?* Pearl felt a thrill shiver through her as she saw the 'little girl'. She had always liked that he called her that, but it had suddenly taken on an additional meaning. And it wrapped itself around her like the big, strong arms of a Daddy on whose lap she was snuggling. She couldn't imagine being brave enough to call him Daddy without him first telling her to, but she could at least try and let him know it was what she wanted.

I'm still in bed, she replied. *Teddy doesn't want to get up today.* She added a blushing smiley emoji.

Lol. Aw, I don't blame him if he's snuggled up with you. But you'd better tell him you can't be late for work. It's time to hop up and take your pj's off and put your big girl clothes on.

Yes, she paused, but it was no good; she couldn't bring herself to add Daddy. *I will.*

Good girl. Have a wonderful day. I'll come over after work. I want to see you in your pyjamas and ready for bed.

I want to see you too xxx. And she signed off with a bunny emoji, hugging herself with excitement as she imagined finding the courage tonight to call him Daddy.

She was deeply disappointed then when he dropped into Mon Addi that morning to tell her he had to go away on another business trip.

"Again!" she blurted out before she could stop herself, but she was busy with clients and, in her new role as trainee manager, she had to maintain her professional persona so they couldn't speak openly and he couldn't kiss her goodbye.

"I'm so sorry, baby," he'd whispered so no one else could hear as she'd seen him to the door after he'd imparted his unwelcome news. "This is not going to keep happening. I promise. But Mother is away and I can't get out of it. I'll call you tonight. I still want to see you in your teddy pj's," he said with a wink. "Behave yourself while I'm gone. I'll miss you."

"I'll miss you too," Pearl said truthfully, feeling tears pricking her eyes.

"I'll bring you a present. Text me if you think of anything you want," he said as he squeezed her hand and left.

All day, she kept thinking of him and calling him Daddy until it didn't seem strange at all, and she was confident she'd have no trouble saying it to him in person. That night, dressed in her pink, teddy bear pyjamas she waited eagerly for his call. When it came, however, and she heard him, her heart began beating so loudly and she felt so confused about wanting to call him Daddy and discovering she didn't have the nerve, it was hard to get any words out.

"What's up, baby girl?" he asked.

"Nothing," she lied.

"I don't believe you. Next time I see you, I shall insist you tell me or I might get a bit cross," he warned her, but he said it like he was teasing and she blushed and giggled and squeezed her thighs together. Then it was easier to talk so long as she didn't think about wanting to call him Daddy.

He rang the next night but didn't ask her about it, instead he'd found a book he wanted to read to her, so he started that while she curled up in bed and listened to his lovely, deep voice. He'd read to her both Wednesday and Thursday nights as well and at last it was Friday and he would be here in person. Pearl was longing to see him and call him Daddy, but hadn't plucked up the courage to do it or even talk to him about it. Wandering around the shops at lunchtime, she saw a T-shirt with 'Daddy's Little Girl' written on the front and bought it quickly before she chickened out.

When she was changing out of her work clothes at home, though, she took it out of its bag, scrunched it into a ball and hid it in a drawer. She settled instead on the pink skirt with the white heart, the white blouse with the red hearts and the pink, sparkly runners. She pulled her hair up in bunches on either side of her head and fastened them with ties each of which had a plastic red heart attached.

She poured a glass of milk, got her teddy bear and sat on the couch to watch the "*Shaun the Sheep*" movie for the millionth time while she waited for Marcus, but couldn't stop wriggling and checking the time and wishing he would hurry. At last she heard his knock, leapt up and flew to the door, flinging it open.

Without even waiting to close the door behind him, he scooped her up and spun her around. She squealed and laughed until he set her down so he could shut the door. Then he led her to the couch, sat down and pulled her onto his knee.

"Did you miss me, precious girl?" he murmured, nuzzling her neck. "I missed you."

"I missed you heaps and heaps and heaps and heaps," she replied, giggling and squirming as he tickled her neck with his lips.

He raised his face and kissed her and she melted into him, her body moulding against his, her mouth soft and pliant as his lips and tongue revelled in her sweetness. She wanted him to keep on kissing her forever, but he stopped.

"I think we have something we need to talk about, don't we, little girl?"

"What?" popped out of her mouth before she realised she was going to say it.

"Well, that's the question," he went on seriously. "I got the distinct impression during the week that you were keeping something from me, and we need to sort that out. I don't want you keeping secrets from me, Pearl." His voice had deepened and Pearl closed her eyes, her mind scrambling for something to say.

"So, baby. Tell me what's been bothering you, and don't lie or you might find yourself in your spanking bunny pj's."

Pearl buried her face against his chest and resisted as hard as she could as he tried to get her to sit up. Silently she was begging and begging him to guess what she wanted without her having to say it.

"All right, precious. If you can't talk at the moment, we'll wait till later, shall we? See how you feel then?"

Her face peeked up at him, and she nodded. He smiled gently, and she relaxed, relieved he wasn't cross with her.

"I think we should have dinner, though, before it gets too late," he said, changing the subject. Pearl scrambled off his knee and jumped up and down.

"Can we have burgers? Can we? Please? Please, Da…" She stopped abruptly, realising 'Please, Daddy' had almost slipped out in her excitement. She saw from Marcus's expression that he had noticed that she'd stopped herself.

"Please what?" he asked quietly. "Or, please, who?"

"Oh!" Pearl gasped, running for the bedroom, diving onto the bed and hiding her head under a pillow.

"Hey, little one," Marcus said as he followed her in and sat on the bed beside her. "Come here." He pulled her to him and plonked her on his knee despite her squirming and hiding her face. "I have a secret. Do you want to hear it?"

Pearl nodded but didn't lift her face.

"I can't tell you unless you lift your head. I have to whisper it in your ear because it's a very secret secret."

Pearl raised her head just enough so she could see him. "What is it?"

"Let me whisper in your ear," he said again. Pearl raised her ear to him. "Are you sure you want me to tell you?" he asked, teasing her.

"Yes," she nodded, adding slowly and seriously. "I love secrets, and I won't tell anyone else in the whole wide world."

"Do you promise not to tell?"

"I promise."

"Okay then." Marcus put his lips to her ear and whispered softly. "I want you to call me Daddy. Could you do that, do you think? For me?"

Pearl shuddered at his words, a shiver rippling through her as her heart beat so fast from happiness she could scarcely breathe or talk.

She pressed her face flat against his chest and then almost imperceptibly nodded her head.

Marcus kissed the top of her head and laughed. "Are you going to hide from me all night? Or shall Daddy and his Little girl go and get some burgers for dinner?"

Still unable to look at him, Pearl nodded and allowed him to slip her off his knee.

"Yes, Daddy?" he prompted her. "I'll close my eyes so I can't see you."

"Yes, Daddy," she whispered to the floor with a little giggle.

"That's my baby girl," he cried, picking her up and whirling her around as he kissed her, then putting her down.

"Come on," he said gaily, and taking her hand, he led her from the flat.

Chapter 16

Marcus

Daddy or not, Marcus could easily have whooped and jumped for joy like a kid himself. He had been almost one hundred percent certain that he wasn't mistaken in thinking Pearl had a Little inside who would love to have a Daddy, but having it confirmed was a huge relief. He was confident they wanted the same thing and he couldn't wait to care for her, spoil her, and give her full rein to explore her inner Little. He felt himself immediately harden as he also realised that there was no longer anything in the way of him fully claiming her as his own. His one experience of introducing her to love-making had left him hungering to not only repeat that but to introduce her to all the other big girl delights that awaited her. Tonight would be the night.

He didn't press her about anything else while they ate. He bought her the kid's meal she asked for, fussed over her, wiped her face, listened to her chat about the week, laughed at her funny stories, and by the time dinner was over, she had relaxed. She was still a bit tentative, but he loved that about her, finding it ineffably heart-melting. He so badly wanted to wrap her in his arms, but resisted the temptation until they were at the flat.

"Well, little girl," he said once they were inside. "I think it's almost time for bed, don't you? Would you like Daddy to run you a bubble bath first?"

Pearl's eyes opened wide at the easy way he had called himself Daddy. She hid her face so he couldn't see her happy expression, and nodded.

"Can you say 'Yes, Daddy'?" he prompted her gently. "Like a good girl."

"Yes, Daddy," she said softly. It was still hard, but not quite as hard this time.

"Good girl," he praised her, gently tugging one of her bunches. She bent forward slightly, tucked both her hands between her knees and grinned up at him. "Cheeky girl," he said with a laugh and pulled her other bunch. "Do you want to take those out or leave them in while you have your bath?"

Pearl's hands went to her head and covered her tiny pigtails. "Leave them in," she said firmly.

"All right. You can leave them in. I'm going to start the bath and fetch your pyjamas. Would you like to keep watching your movie while you're waiting? I'll turn it on for you before I start the bath."

"Yes, please, Daddy," she managed to add all by herself as she ran to the couch and plonked herself on it, pulling her knees up, hugging her teddy bear to her and putting her hand to her face as though to suck her thumb, but only gently brushing the bear's paw back and forth across her nose.

Marcus turned on the taps, added some bubbles, put a towel on the chair next to the bath, then joined her on the couch while they waited for the bath to fill.

"Shall Daddy undress you, baby?" he asked when the water had been running for a while. She nodded, but made no move other than clutching her bear tighter. Marcus chuckled. "You'll have to put the bear down for a minute." He took the bear and she reluctantly let go. "He can keep watching the movie, while you get ready for your bath. Stand up here in front of me."

Pearl slid on her bottom off the couch and onto the floor. Marcus leaned down and tickled her. She giggled and rolled over, gasping for breath. He joined her on the floor and tickled her again. She laughed and tried to wriggle away but he held her down with both hands.

"Do you want Daddy to stop tickling you?"

"Yes. Please!" she gasped breathlessly between giggles and wriggles.

"Yes, please, who?" Marcus asked, raising one hand as though to tickle her again.

"Yes, please, Daddy!" Pearl said loudly. "Please don't tickle me anymore."

"All right," Marcus said, after pretending to consider whether he would or not. "I'll stop but only if you are a good girl and let Daddy undress you. Will you?"

"Yes, Daddy." This time it was more confident, and Pearl smiled coyly at him as she used the new moniker.

"Come on, then," Marcus said, standing up and pulling her up beside him. "Let's get you undressed in the bathroom."

He held her hand as they went to the bath, letting go so he could turn the taps off after first swishing the water to check it was a good temperature. Then he knelt down so he could untie the shoelaces on her shoes, and pull her shoes and socks off. He tucked the socks into the shoes and set them neatly under the chair in the bathroom. Standing up, he took hold of her blouse. "Arms up." Pearl lifted her arms above her head so he could pull her top off. Next he undid the zip on her skirt and picked it up after it had fallen to the floor and she'd stepped out of it. He folded both garments and placed them on the chair.

He reached behind and unhooked her bra and, as it slipped over her shoulders, her breasts tumbled out and he had to fight to stop himself from cupping his hands around their plump, pink-tipped beauty. "Right, pants off and then you can hop in." He kept his voice calm so as not to break the mood as he slid her panties down over her legs. "Foot up," he said. "Now the other one." And then she was completely naked. He quietly sucked in his breath as he covertly admired her loveliness. Kneeling by the bath once she was in, he soaped her as she played with the bubbles, and they blew them at each other. She giggled when one got caught on his hair and sat there for a second like a tiny round hat. He ran the soap over her breasts but allowed her, this time, to wash between her legs herself.

"Would you like to come out and play grown-up games with me?" he asked once she was clean. He was impatient to have her on the bed so he could explore all her succulent treasures with his hands, his mouth and his cock, the last of which was so rock hard it was beginning to ache. Release was becoming uppermost in his mind.

He picked up a towel and held it out for her, encouraging her to step out of the bath. "Come, baby."

He pulled the plug as she stood up and climbed out. Then he wrapped the towel around her, picked her up and carried her to the bed. Stretched out next to her, he leaned over and gently kissed her, letting the kiss linger and feeling her relax under him.

"Did you enjoy your bath?" he asked when the kiss ended. She nodded. Her eyes, dark with expectation, held his and he could see her breasts under the towel rising and falling with shudders as her breathing became erratic. "Can I unwrap you?" he asked. She nodded. His own throat was tight making speech difficult so he didn't press her for a verbal answer. He could see she was tense, but hoped it was nervous excitement brought on by unfamiliarity not fear or reluctance. "First I want to know that you are absolutely okay with anything we do. Remember, if you want me to stop at any time say barlese. I will stop straight away and will never be cross with you. Okay?"

"Yes," Pearl said, frowning. "But I don't understand why I wouldn't be okay. What are you going to do?"

"Nothing that will hurt or harm you, precious girl. I promise. To start with, all I want to do is unwrap your towel so I can see your beautiful body. Will you let me?"

She nodded shyly and didn't move as he peeled away both sides of the towel. He gazed at her body in lustful admiration for a few seconds then into her eyes.

"I want to make love to you so much, my darling. Do you want me to do that too?"

She nodded harder, bouncing her head up and down to show how much she wanted it.

"Good," he growled thickly, unable to hide the relief in his voice. "And remember you can say barlese at any time if something hurts or doesn't feel good or you get scared or anything."

She nodded, reaching her hand up to touch his face and then slipping it behind his head and gently pulling so he would bend down and kiss her. The ground rules laid down, her willingness and own desire matching his, the dam burst and his passion spilled out in a flood engulfing them both.

Snatching her to him, he crushed her mouth, all but devouring it with his lips and tongue. Inexperienced as she was, he could feel her surrendering herself to voluptuous abandonment, her body pressed against him, her mouth locked in a passionate duel with his. Pushing her down, he raised his head then lowered it to catch a delicate pink bud gently between his teeth before he closed his whole mouth over the plump flesh of her breast. Her hands clutched at his hair as she gasped for breath, every new sensation sending hot chills through her.

Leaving that breast, he moved his attention to the other one, savouring its slightly soapy flavour as he licked her nipple and then teased her by flicking it with his tongue.

"Do you want this, baby?" he murmured.

"Yes. Yes, please," she cried, desperate to gift him her other cherry, something she knew without any doubt she no longer wanted. She pushed him up. "Let me take off your shirt," she begged breathlessly, her fingers already pulling at his buttons. As she pushed his shirt open, she sucked in her breath at the sight of his naked chest, sculpted to perfection and decorated with a patch of black curly hair that she immediately ran her hands through as she looked up at him in adoration. His face was taut with desire as he slipped his shirt off so she could explore the curves of his arms and chest and the hard flatness of his belly.

"Shall I get rid of these too?" he asked, undoing his trousers.

Her eyes wide, she nodded, watching him as he stood up, pulled a small packet from his pocket and then took off his trousers and boxer shorts. Fully naked, he took his bursting erection in his hand, searching her face for a reaction as he slipped on a condom. He was comfortable with his body, but unsure how she would feel confronted with the reality of what was about to happen. For what seemed forever, she stared, her mouth open, then she raised her eyes to his and smiled an invitation.

Lying next to her, he kissed her tenderly as his hand roamed across her breasts and belly and then stroked her thighs before sliding up and over her mound. Unlike most women he'd been with, she had a small cluster of blonde curls, which he found, like everything about her, utterly enchanting. He gently squeezed and rubbed her plump folds, alternately kissing her and lifting his head to watch the expressions flitting across her face.

"Okay?" he asked, gently probing her with one finger.

She slowly blinked and let out a long trembling sigh.

While his fingers gently dipped into her hot, slippery wetness, sliding a little further in each time, he kissed her mouth, then moved down her body, kissing every inch of the path between her lips. He wanted to make sure her first time was as delicious and blissful as it could possibly be, and was using every ounce of self-control he had to get her completely ready before he took possession.

Sliding his mouth down, he parted her thighs, noting no resistance as she arched her hips up to him. *Excellent.* She was greedy for the pleasure he could give her. Pushing his hands under her bottom, he held her up against his mouth as his tongue lapped at her little hard nub, pacing himself to match her increasing agitation. He could hear her breathing becoming louder and quicker as her hands fluttered against the bed, clutching the bedspread. Then a deepening moan on each breath as her body went rigid told him she was close, and he pushed her harder until she cried out as her hips thrust up and her head rocked from side to side. He quickly moved his mouth to her belly, kissing up towards her mouth as he moved over her and she threw her arms around his neck.

"Open your legs a bit wider, my darling," he whispered, feeling her immediately part her thighs and draw her knees higher. He slid his finger in and out of her, then two fingers as he prepared her for the final invasion. He used his hand to line himself up perfectly, then pushed forward. "Relax, baby.

Relax as much as you can. This might hurt," he whispered, feeling resistance. "But it will be over quickly." He gave one short, sharp thrust, felt her give, heard her cry, and at last was right inside. His heart swelled; he was home.

He paused for a moment to look tenderly at her. "You okay, baby?"

She nodded, her wide eyes shining in the light like two round full moons.

Not taking his eyes off her, he slid out and then gently in. Her eyes folded shut with the pressure inside her and then opened. He moved in and out again and this time as her eyes opened a happy smile played about her mouth and he knew she was his.

Slowly at first, he introduced her to the pleasure another body could bring hers. She moved under him, her breathing quickening and she began moaning with every new thrust. He'd waited so long and she was so intoxicating as she matched his rhythm, he felt his control slipping and all too soon he tipped over the point of no return. "I'm going to take you now," he growled as he plundered her velvet treasure, riding her harder and faster until he cried out, shaking as his body climaxed and pumped out its seed into the waiting sheath.

Chapter 17

Pearl

The weeks until Ray was due flew by, and for Pearl they were the happiest of her life: she had her dream job, a beautiful apartment to live in, and she was hopelessly in love with the gorgeous Marcus Holding who seemed to feel the same about her. He hadn't declared his love in so many words as yet, but she didn't think she could feel more loved if he shouted it from the rooftops.

Even though he had his own key, they were not yet officially living together, and much of his time – way too much according to Pearl – was consumed with work and out-of-town business trips, but whenever he could get away he was with her. He took her to different parks to run and play on the playgrounds. They went rowing on the river, swimming, roller-skating, to the movies and anywhere else they could think to have fun. Whenever he could get away for the weekend, he drove her home to spend it with her parents, and Pearl was amazed anew each time at how easily he fit in and how comfortable everyone was together. He'd become good friends with her father, and together they spent hours wandering about the farm, discussing the inefficiencies of old-style farming in the light of modern problems such as hotter temperatures, decreasing water supplies and depleted soils. In the evening, though, he and Pearl walked in the moonlight, listening to the music of nature and kissing under a billion stars.

In the city, he loved to take her shopping and buy her presents, but she was uncomfortable about him spending too much money on her. He'd offered to buy her jewellery from Mon Addi but she'd begged him not to and he'd reluctantly agreed. "For the time being", he'd said, tapping the side of his nose mysteriously.

But knowing how much she loved *"Shaun the Sheep"*, he'd surprised her with Shaun, Shirley and Timmy stuffies, a T-shirt, hoodie, and cup, all with pictures, and even a *"Shaun the Sheep"* backpack. He loved to buy her clothes: miniskirts and short, girly dresses, and shoes with spots, sparkles, and pictures. She had a new onesie in her wardrobe, too, but the bunny one remained the only one with feet and a flap.

She hadn't worn it often. The second time was after she had stayed up late one evening watching a movie and had overslept the next morning. The most disappointing part, Marcus had told her, making her want to cry with shame was that she'd told him she was already in bed when he'd texted her to say 'goodnight' and that had been a lie. He'd also scolded her for being irresponsible, resulting in her being late for work. Marcie couldn't punish her for that, so he'd included it in her spanking for lying to him and being disobedient.

She'd stood next to him as he scolded her and tears of misery had rolled down her face. She hated hearing him say that she had disappointed him. Somehow, she thought, it would have been easier if he'd been cross with her instead.

"I'm sorry, Daddy," she'd told him. "I won't ever do anything like that ever again. I promise."

He'd pursed his lips as he shook his head sadly. "I hope not, baby. You're such a good girl. I can hardly believe you lied to me."

"I was very bad," she'd cried. "I have never told you a lie before, honestly, Daddy."

"So, you think you deserve this spanking?"

Pearl had clutched her teddy to her face and nodded miserably as a single tear slid down her face. "Yes, Daddy."

"Give me your bottom then, naughty girl, so I can let the flap down and bare it for its spanking."

Once the flap was released, Pearl had put her teddy bear on the bed and lain across Marcus's knee.

"Will you be a good girl for Daddy and not wriggle around too much?"

"Yes, Daddy."

It hadn't been easy, though, as Marcus had spanked her harder than the first time. Still nowhere near as hard as he could, but enough to make her squirm and yelp, and he'd held her firmly in place as he'd spanked her bottom until it was a dark rosy pink.

It had been especially lovely when it was over, though. Sitting on Marcus's knee as he'd kissed and cuddled her, she'd told him how sorry she was and how she promised to be better in the future, and he'd promised her it was all over and forgotten, and then he'd made love to her so tenderly she'd felt their very souls had merged. For the first time, she'd orgasmed while he was thrusting inside her; sweet sensations and luxurious heat had radiated from where their bodies were melded together, and her insides had felt like they'd dissolved into a blissful, warm pool, leaving her so completely languid and peaceful, she'd fallen asleep in his arms certain she was the happiest person who had ever lived.

Their relationship had developed in other ways too. Pearl often thought of the day in Mon Addi when she'd first met him, and how she'd known immediately that if he asked, she would obey. What she hadn't realised then was how much she would love doing it and how close it would bring them.

She was his little girl, his pet, and she surrendered to him without question. She did anything he wanted, like when he'd decided that she was always to sit on the floor by his feet when they watched television. She'd hugged his leg and he'd stroked her hair and the nape of her neck so tenderly, she thought her heart would burst. And when they were ready for bed, he picked her up and carried her in and made love to her fiercely and passionately until she was drenched, spent and deeper in love than ever.

Tidying up her apartment and making dinner as she waited for him, she was thinking about sex. It was a few days since she'd seen him, and she was desperate for his loving. She ruefully shook her head, remembering how innocent and naive she'd been when they met. She couldn't believe he could have been attracted to such a mousy country bumpkin, but she thanked her lucky stars every day that he had.

Her natural shyness hadn't translated into sexual reticence though. Her body had responded to his as though it had been waiting all its life for this man, springing to life under his touch. She had no other lover to compare him with and was glad that he was the only man she'd ever made love with. She wanted to die in his arms, an old woman, and for that to still be true.

As he'd explored her body and found it's secret hot spots, she'd become impatient to do the same with him. At first she'd hesitated to touch him intimately, but then when she'd been running her hand over his belly and he'd gently taken it and put it on his cock, her inhibitions had given way to curiosity. It was like a new toy she never tired of. She would watch fascinated as it came to life in her hands. She had learned how to torment and pleasure him by running her fingernails lightly along it, gently squeezing it and, after he'd shown her how to wet her hand, slipping it's length through her fingers. The first time he'd shown her how to grip it firmly as he slid it back and forth until she felt it bulge and then pulsate as he came, she had watched in fascination as it spurted its sticky fluid.

And then she had become hungry to taste it, all of it and, as always, he had been the patient teacher and she his willing pupil. The tip of her tongue slid out and licked her lips as she remembered how they'd been watching television, her sitting by his feet, him playing with her hair, and how as she'd swiveled around to say something, her hand had slipped into his lap and she'd felt how hard he was. Their eyes had met, hers wide, his narrowed with desire, and she'd seen the tension in his body mirrored in the hardness of his cheeks. Swinging fully round, not taking her eyes from his, she knelt and unzipped him as he caressed her hair. He was rock hard and ready for her, and she took him, at first hesitantly, then greedily into her mouth. He was big and it was hard at first not to gag, but his cries as he emptied himself into her mouth and she hungrily swallowed every drop were the most ecstatic she'd heard, and his eyes as he gazed at her afterwards overflowing with love. She'd understood without him having to explain, and happily and willingly knelt before him as she worshipped his manhood.

As the weather had grown warmer, he had gently instigated something else new. Before she sat by his feet in front of the television or to chat, or knelt to take him in her mouth, he would take her into the bedroom and slowly remove each garment, touching and kissing her and telling her over and over how beautiful she was, then lead her to the couch where she would sit naked at his feet. There had been times they hadn't made it to the couch, times when his kisses had become hard and demanding and he'd pressed her shoulders so she would kneel then and there as he hurriedly opened his bursting trousers.

The one thing he still hadn't done, though, was introduce her to his mother. When she'd accused him of being ashamed of her, he'd threatened her with a spanking if she talked such nonsense. "I am not ashamed of you, beautiful girl. I couldn't be prouder to be seen with you. But my family isn't like yours. I want you all to myself for a bit longer, that's all. Be patient. You can meet them at Ray's welcome home party. I'm just worried that when you do meet my mother, you might decide you want nothing further to do with me." He'd grinned to take some of the seriousness out of his words, and she'd giggled at such a ridiculous notion as her not wanting him.

She heard his key in the door and rushed to greet him as he came in carrying roses.

"Oh, Daddy," she cried merrily as he handed them to her and bounced her pigtails. "They're beautiful. Hmm, and they smell divine. Quick. I'll put them in water. And, look, I've made us some dinner and laid the table and everything. There's salad and fruit and delicious sandwiches. Nothing hot. And I didn't use any sharp knives." It wasn't that she couldn't use sharp knives, she had many times in the past, but he had forbidden her to unless he was supervising so she wouldn't hurt herself, and she'd discovered that obeying him gave her a special thrill.

He pulled her into his arms, chuckling with delight, and kissed her until she was breathless.

"What a good girl, you are," he said at last, letting her go and gently touching the end of her nose with his finger. "And cute as a button." She blushed with happiness as she carried the plates to the table.

As they ate, she chatted about her work and the diploma course in gemmology she was doing online.

"I'm already starting to be able to tell the difference between the quality of the stones we have in the shop. Some really aren't that great. I don't think Marcie has a good eye for stones, but I'd never tell her that of course!"

Marcus grinned. "Probably better at this stage not to, but tell me if she ever gives you a hard time in any way, and I'll sort her out."

"I will, Daddy. And I won't say anything about the jewellery she's bought; I'd have to be absolutely certain, and I'm not. But it's such fun, and I'm starting to see the gems quite differently the more I know about them."

"You're such a clever girl, aren't you?" Marcus praised her. "Daddy is so proud of you. Shall we clean up then? I shan't be staying tonight. Mother is insisting I have breakfast with her in the morning. I guess it's about Ray. The party is supposed to be next week even though he's not even here yet."

Pearl pouted. "But I want you to stay, Daddy. I haven't seen you all week!"

"I know, precious. So let's get cleaned up in here as quickly as we can. I'm ready for some big girl games." He winked at her and she felt her breasts tingling in anticipation and her thighs squeezed together in response to the immediate ache.

Chapter 18

Marcus

The only blot on an otherwise perfect evening had been his having to leave Pearl, but his mother was adamant he have breakfast with her in the morning. She'd refused to give him a time, and he guessed it was her way of ensuring he had to come home for the night. Damn her! Saturday morning, for crying out loud. But try as he may, he had not been able to dissuade her and he'd eventually decided to give in, make it short and get back to Pearl as quickly as he could.

It was time for him to have that conversation with his mother again, though – the one about it being time she left him alone or he would leave altogether. He was tired of her trying to control him. She could, and would, threaten to cut him off from the family, the business and the money, but maybe it would be a blessing if she did. She didn't realise, and wouldn't accept even if it did cross her mind, that he was ready to leave Holding Corporation and the billionaire lifestyle and make a different life for himself.

Linda had organised for breakfast to be served on the patio, and was waiting for him as he crossed the lawn from his apartment.

"Good morning, dear," she said as he came up the steps, stopping at the buffet table to pour himself a coffee. "Have something to eat?"

"No, thanks. Coffee will do," he replied, sitting down at the table with her. "I honestly have no idea why you insist on having your cook prepare so much. Who's going to eat it?"

"Don't be vulgar. Max is not a cook; he's a chef. And I invited you to breakfast. It would be rude of me to not have any available. If you want to be disagreeable and not eat it, you can't blame me for that."

"Where's yours then? You only have a coffee."

"I never eat breakfast, and I have no idea why you are making such a fuss unless you are determined to start an argument."

"Nope. I definitely don't want to argue. Forget breakfast. What was so important that I had to join you this morning? It was very inconvenient."

Linda's only indication that she had reacted to his complaint was a slight narrowing of her eyes. She sipped her coffee, and made him wait for her answer.

"I'd expected Ray before this but, as I've told you, rehab took longer than we'd hoped. Nonetheless, I have no intention of cancelling next Saturday's party, so he can't delay any longer. Bob says he appears to be clean and has worked hard, so I've told Len he's coming and to organise a job for him at head office, and we'll just have to hope Ray doesn't let us down this time."

"When's he coming?"

"Tomorrow evening. You will pick him up from the airport."

"Is that absolutely necessary? Couldn't you go, or send a car?"

"Yes, it is necessary. He's been away a long time, and considering how he spent most of that time he might be unsure of his reception. I don't want him feeling he's being fobbed off with a car. He is to be properly met so he feels welcome and that his family is glad he's home. I can't meet him, so you will have to."

"Why can't you?"

"That's irrelevant." Linda dismissed his question. "I'm asking you to go."

"What time is his plane?"

"I'll text you the flight details and you can check tomorrow in case there's a change."

Marcus rolled his eyes. "I guess I don't have a choice then as it seems you have it all planned in your usual inimitable way."

"You don't seem particularly eager to see your brother. I hope you are not going to be difficult and unpleasant. While it's wonderful he's finally coming home, it's not easy for any of us. But, it's easier for you than it is for Ray and me, so I have no idea why you're acting so hard done by."

Marcus felt the deep irritation his mother managed to engender in him rising up through his chest, and he sighed to release as much tension as he could before he answered.

"Don't you? Do you seriously not understand why I am tired of being at your beck and call? My time is never my own. Matter of fact, I'm overjoyed Ray is coming. It means you won't need me so much. Perhaps I can finally start taking control of my life."

Linda's shoulders rose and her hand clenched into a fist at Marcus's words. She looked away, out across the garden, staring at nothing until her shoulders relaxed and her hand slowly unfolded, and when she spoke her voice showed no indications of her reaction.

"You know that's not true, dear," she said mildly. "You and I are the only ones who truly know the business now. Ray has been gone too long. Besides, you're the only person I trust. Ray let us down once; who's to say he's not going to this time? He's going to have to earn our trust, and that will take time. I need you there to keep a close eye on him until we can be certain he's not going to relapse, or change his mind in five minutes about being here and want to go gallivanting off somewhere else."

Marcus gritted his teeth and didn't reply. Linda was right. Until they saw Ray in person, they couldn't be certain that he had recovered and was serious about starting work again. Maybe he had grown tired of living in poverty and squalor and missed the luxury of the family mansion; saying he wanted to get clean and join the business might simply be a ruse so he'd be allowed home.

"And on that matter," Linda went on, "have you done anything about organising yourself a wife? Time is running out; I want an announcement next Saturday night."

"I told you I wasn't going to."

"Yes. Yes." Linda waved her hand as though shooing a fly. "You did, but I told you you *were* going to. I had a meeting with Len and some people from finance while you were away, and if we don't get some additional capital soon, it will mean a major restructure that will substantially reduce the size of the company. I have worked too hard – since your father left us in that dreadful mess – to build it up to where it is today to stand by and see it cut into pieces."

"Isn't Ray offering to invest his money in the business?"

"That's what he said. But even if he sinks everything he says he has in, it might not be enough. Besides, we've agreed we can't entrust him with the future of the company at the moment. He simply doesn't have the knowledge, and we have to be sure he's reliable before we take any risks. And, of course, until we actually see that money and it's handed over to the business, it's only his promise." She reached across and put her hand on his arm. "We need to be sure. Holding Corporation, and I need you more than ever." She paused and observed him through lowered lashes.

"Anyway, what are your options? Get a job somewhere else and earn peanuts? Get a mortgage and buy a house in the suburbs? You won't get a penny from me. I mean that. How long would it take before you were begging to come home? This is the only life you've known. You've had it easy because I've spent my life working to make it easy for you. You've led a very sheltered life and I don't think you fully understand what leaving would entail. Don't forget what happened to Ray."

Marcus looked down at his mother's perfectly manicured hand, the fingers covered in gold and diamond rings, flaunted symbols of his family's immense wealth. In some ways his mother was right: he had had an easy life, not that he hadn't worked and worked hard, but he'd had every luxury money could buy. He hadn't had to fight for a job; an executive position was always waiting for him as soon as he was ready to fill it. He was only nominally answerable to the board; as a Holding, his position in the company would never be under threat. Could he make it on the outside without family protection?

Linda took her hand away, leaned both elbows on the table, clasped her hands together and rested her chin on them. "You know what you must do, Marcus, and I promise it will be the last thing I ask of you."

He knew what she meant, but he waited for her to say it. He glanced up, then back down at the table.

"You haven't made a decision so I've made it for you. I've

spoken to Tina Fielding and she has agreed to marry you. You will announce your engagement next Saturday at Ray's party and marry quickly afterwards. Our lawyers are drawing up contracts to cover the financial side of the union, which includes Tina making a large portion of her money available to the business. You will have absolute control of that, and it will be sufficient to solve the company's immediate financial problems. Then you will assume the position of CEO, and together – I'll continue as a consultant – we will clear the debris and get the business performing better than ever. Tina has also agreed to have at least two children as soon as possible, and then as many as are needed to produce a son if the first two are girls. And, lastly, the marriage will be permanent; divorce is too messy and expensive."

Marcus's face darkened, but his thunderous expression didn't faze her.

"There's no need to pull that face," she admonished him without rancour. "As I said, this is the last thing I will ask of you. Once done, the business and family will be in safe hands and provided for into the future. What you do apart from that, as long as it doesn't threaten the business or the family, is entirely your own affair. Tina is not a fool. She's aware you won't be marrying her for love and she might have to... turn a blind eye at times, shall we say?"

Marcus shook his head, but before he could say anything, Linda continued.

"One last thing, Marcus. If you refuse to do as I've asked, I *will* cut you off without a cent. You will leave here with nothing but the clothes you are wearing, and your name will be taken out of the will. And if I were you, I wouldn't consider testing me to see if I mean it. I am absolutely serious. I will not see everything I've worked for destroyed by selfish and irresponsible sons. Are you hearing me, Marcus?"

Marcus stared through slitted eyes at her. "I hear you, Mother," he growled.

"Go ahead. Sulk all you want, if it makes you feel better, but Tina needs an engagement ring. I would prefer you go with her and help her choose, but if you refuse, I will give her a company card and she can buy one herself. The announcement of your engagement will be at Ray's party, and I have nothing further to say on the matter."

Marcus stood up. "In that case, I'm off," he replied tersely, and all but ran down the steps and across the lawn. He dashed inside, packed an overnight bag, picked up his car keys and headed for Pearl's apartment, his mind whirling as adrenaline pumped through his body. He needed time to think, not about whether or not he would do as his mother had ordered him to – that was never going to happen – but about what he should do to ensure the best outcome for himself, Pearl and Holding Corporation. Like his mother, he'd invested too much of himself in the family business to walk away and let it fall to pieces, but he wasn't going to marry Tina and he didn't want to be the company's CEO. He had to come up with another solution that he could convince his mother was equally as good, or preferably better, and he had to do it quickly.

He had a few ideas, but he wasn't going to waste this weekend thinking about them. Until Ray's plane arrived, he was going to think only about Pearl. But there was at least one thing he was more determined about than ever, and that was that Pearl would accompany him to Ray's party, he would introduce her to his mother and his brother, and they would be left in no doubt that he planned to make his future with her. Knowing how excited Pearl was about the party, he couldn't wait to tell her that Ray was on his way and she would be introduced to his family next Saturday as planned.

Chapter 19

Pearl

Pearl greeted news of Ray's impending arrival and confirmation of her introduction to Marcus's family the following week with mixed emotions. She couldn't entirely suppress her apprehension about what they would think of her and about whether she would fit in with Mrs Holding's wealthy friends, but she also wanted to know everything about Marcus, and he was so lovely she couldn't believe his mother was the dragon he portrayed her to be. Plus, she was also deeply curious to meet his brother. It was hard for her to picture another man bearing a strong resemblance to him in either looks or mannerisms.

As well as trepidation and curiosity, though, she was beside herself with excitement to dress up like a princess and attend a lavish party, the likes of which she'd only seen on television and in movies. Marcus had offered to buy her a dress, but she was adamant she would rent one for the night as she couldn't see herself wearing a designer gown often enough to warrant the expense. He had agreed, adding he had something special for her, though, that he would insist she wore with her rented dress. She'd pleaded with him to tell her what it was but he'd just laughed and told her to wait and see, then kissed her quickly to prevent any further pleadings.

"I think we might be quite busy this week," Marcie said on Monday morning. "Linda has confirmed her party for Ray is definitely going ahead next Saturday and I've issued invitations to our VIP clients to come and view our latest collection. I am acquainted with most of the people who attend Linda's parties, many are my friends too. I know what they like and they are used to dealing with me, so I will be serving them. You can attend to anyone else who comes in."

"Yes, Miss Jones." Pearl said, stowing the vacuum cleaner under the desk.

"Linda throws the best parties," Marcie continued, leaning her elbows on the counter with her chin in her hands as she watched Pearl begin wiping down the display cabinets. "It's a shame you'll miss it."

"But I'm going," Pearl said, surprised by Marcie's assumption she wouldn't be. She didn't discuss her relationship with Marcus at all with her boss, but Marcie had seen them together enough for it to be no secret.

"Oh? Well, that *is* brave of you I must say. I thought you would definitely want to stay well away, unless..." Marcie said cruelly, her eyes squinting to slits.

Pearl realised Marcie was baiting her and pretended not to hear as she unlocked the front doors. She had no idea what Marcie was talking about and didn't care. She was well aware that Marcie deeply resented having been caught out lying to get rid of her and even more so because Marcus had chosen Pearl over her. But no matter how angry and bitter she was, she was unable to do anything about it if she wanted to keep her job and not risk anyone else finding out she'd falsely accused Pearl of stealing. Not wealthy herself, she relied on the willingness of the Holdings and other wealthy people to include her. Her position was tenuous, she understood that, and she didn't want to lose favour. She hadn't yet found the rich husband she was seeking.

The bell on the front door tinkled.

Pearl glanced up from the display case she was rearranging to see Marcie smile ingratiatingly and nod at the two women who had entered. She was about to continue with her display as it appeared Marcie knew the women when Marcie caught her eye and gestured for her to attend to them.

"Good morning. Can I be of any assistance?" she asked after closing the cabinet and approaching the women. She was used to dealing with wealthy clients, and these two women certainly fit that description. Her increasingly experienced eye for jewels told her that the considerable number of rings and other jewellery the women were wearing were all high quality and worth a small fortune. She liked this type of customer because they could afford the absolute best, so she could show off the shop's most expensive treasures and potentially make big sales. This boosted the shop's profits and allowed her to buy new stock, which was her favourite part of being a manager. At this stage in her training, while she was allowed to make suggestions, the final say remained with Marcie. So far, she'd accepted most of Pearl's suggestions, and the jewels Pearl had brought into the shop had mostly sold well.

After a cool nod at Marcie, they turned to Pearl.

"We'd like to see what you have in the way of engagement rings."

Up close, Pearl could see the women were not, as she'd first thought, of the same age, but were likely mother and daughter, although the older woman had almost certainly spent a pretty penny on trying to deny her years.

"Certainly, Madam. Were you thinking a diamond ring? A solitaire or cluster? Do you have a preference for cut?"

"Show us the largest diamond you have," the older woman demanded imperiously.

"Of course," Pearl replied politely, realising ostentation was probably the most important criterion for this client, but she had one ring that had both size and quality. The most expensive ring in the shop, it had only arrived the previous week. Pearl hadn't been entirely confident when she'd ordered it, despite its quality. It was more expensive than the shop usually carried and larger and bolder than the other engagement rings. Pearl had thought Marcie might veto the purchase, but she'd encouraged Pearl to go ahead; perhaps, Pearl worried, because she believed the ring wouldn't sell, and she was hoping Pearl was making a very expensive error of judgement.

Pearl took the ring from the display case and encouraged the young woman to try it on. While the customer moved her hand about so the enormous stone showered them with sparkles like tiny coloured rain drops, Pearl pointed out the diamond's quality, cut and other attributes that made it such a valuable stone.

"There aren't many women who could wear this ring with style and grace," Pearl said, "but I can see you are one of those who can. Without the right flair, such a ring would be out of place, but it might have been specially made for your lovely hand."

The woman, holding up her soft, white, slender hand with its perfectly manicured fingernails to admire the ring, glowed with pleasure at Pearl's words. She felt their sincerity, and Pearl was speaking from her heart. This woman could indeed wear an ostentatious ring. Such a ring would look ridiculous on her much smaller hand, but its beauty would be displayed to full effect if this client decided to buy it.

"What do you think, Mama?" she asked her companion who was eyeing it covetously.

"They can afford it," was her only comment as she drew herself up and folded her hands under her bosom.

"Marcie?" the young woman said loudly, flashing her hand in Marcie's direction. Marcie, who'd been watching from a distance came over. "Do you think Linda would approve of this one? She asked me to choose something suitable for the announcement on Saturday night. I think you might have excelled yourself this time, Marcie. I love it. It makes quite the statement, doesn't it?"

"It does, and it looks fabulous on your hand, Tina. I'm sure Linda will think it is perfect. Are you having to choose it on your own, then?" Marcie replied, prepared to take the credit and not reveal it was Pearl who had selected the ring for the shop.

"Yes." The woman called Tina laughed, a controlled titter honed with years of practice. "But Linda gave me her card to pay for it, and at least this way I can be certain of getting one I like."

"It is a beautiful diamond," Marcie said, not wanting to praise Pearl's work but well aware of the ring's six-figure price tag. "I think Linda will approve."

Tina winked at Marcie. "Good enough for her favourite son, then?"

"Never mind him. Is it good enough for you?" her mother interjected.

Marcie's mouth creased, but her lips stayed shut and her eyelids lowered.

"I'll take it," Tina announced, tossing her shoulder-length black hair and opening her ostrich skin Hermès Birkin bag to take out a Chanel wallet. She flipped it open and handed Pearl a card. "Put it on this."

"Will you be there?" she asked Marcie while Pearl conducted the business side of the deal with hands she was fighting to control. "Linda usually allows you to drop in, doesn't she?"

"Yes, Linda has invited me," Marcie's eyes squinted further closed and her lips tightened, but her voice was low and even. "I wouldn't miss it." Her eyes opened sufficiently to glance triumphantly at Pearl. "I'm quite excited to see Ray again, too, the naughty boy. I wonder how Marcus will enjoy having his brother home."

"I love it when those boys get all manly and competitive," Tina went on with an exaggerated shimmy. "They were forever locking horns when they were young men, and now it's been so long since they were together, things could get most interesting, don't you think? Especially as I heard Len is stepping down as CEO of Holding Corporation, and both boys are apparently vying for the position. Did you hear?"

Marcie shook her head, and was about to speak when Tina declared loudly. "Well, my money is on my man anyway, even if his brother thinks he can slip in and walk away with the prize. I reckon he's going to be disappointed for sure—in more ways than one. Being CEO is not the only thing he's always wanted and isn't going to get." She grinned and winked, and the grin broke into the carefully orchestrated titter.

Pearl's heart was beating furiously and she felt faint, but managed to retain her polite and unemotional persona until the sale was finalised and the women had left.

"Excuse me," she said immediately to Marcie and rushed to the bathroom, the only private place in the shop.

She was trying to make sense of the conversation she'd just heard between her customer and her boss. That woman had bought an engagement ring and all but said that she was to be engaged to one of the Holding men, their mother's favourite. Of course she couldn't mean Marcus, but she'd also said the other brother needn't think he could 'slip in' and take the top job. Ray was the only one that seemed to be doing any 'slipping in', so she must have been talking about Marcus, but that couldn't be!

She washed her hands and face to try and calm herself and regain her composure. She wanted to present Marcie with a completely calm exterior whatever was going on inside. It was to no avail, however; Marcie was waiting to pounce.

"You seemed surprised, Pearl," she said silkily. "Hasn't Marcus told you about the purpose of the party?"

"To welcome Ray home, you mean?"

"Oh, that." Marcie scoffed dismissively. "That's not the real reason. Hasn't he told you then? Naughty boy. How mean of him. I was surprised you were going, but I guess that explains it. No, dear," her eyes glinted sharp enough to cut a diamond. "I have it on good authority that Linda has ordered Marcus to announce his engagement to Tina. Or else! Oh dear, are you shocked, sweetie?" Marcie feigned concern. "But you can't have imagined Marcus would ever marry *you*. Even *I* don't qualify through lack of fortune."

Pearl pulled herself up to her full height. She wasn't as tall as Marcie but she felt bigger. There was no way she was going to allow this horrible woman to bully her.

"I have work to do, Miss Jones, as do you," she said and walked away.

Chapter 20

Marcus

"Hey, bro." Marcus, meanwhile, had said earlier that morning looking up from his lounge by the pool as his brother appeared in the doorway. "There's coffee in the pot. And a feast to feed an army which hasn't arrived as yet." He gestured to a table holding heating dishes filled with bacon, eggs, tomatoes, mushrooms and sausages, toast in a toast rack, butter and jam, and a percolator of hot coffee. "It's been there for a while, though, but might still be edible, or I can organise some fresh."

Dressed only in boxer shorts, Ray stretched in the doorway. The preceding few years of self-abuse had left him pale and thin; nonetheless, he was in far better shape than when the brothers had last seen each other. Ray had been such a stoned, dirty, sick mess when last they'd met, Marcus had doubted he would ever see his brother alive again. Yet here he was, looking not unlike a ghost but not actually being one. He wasn't letting it show, but Marcus was deeply relieved.

Despite it all, he loved his brother, and he was glad the worry seemed to be finally over.

"Nah. Thanks, but it's so late anyway, I'll wait for lunch I think," Ray said, pouring a cup of coffee and making himself comfortable on a lounge next to Marcus. He closed his eyes and breathed a deep, satisfied sigh.

"I used to think I might never come back, but I have and I'm glad. It's where I want to be," he said. "And, apparently everything has survived without me."

Marcus grinned. "Yep. Not much has changed."

"You're still in the flat on your own, then? I thought you'd be married by now." It was an observation, not a criticism, and Marcus was not offended.

"I've been too busy filling the role of son and heir," he said calmly but pointedly.

"*Touché*! Ah, so I guess that's changed, then, with the return of the prodigal son and true heir?" Ray's voice was even, but both men were acutely aware that this was a foray into potentially dangerous territory.

Marcus took a mouthful of his coffee, drawing out swallowing it while he paused. Then he shrugged, stared out at the garden and spoke.

"*Que sera, sera*, I reckon."

Ray was also staring straight ahead, like a dog that knows that looking into its rival's eyes will be taken as a challenge and it had best be prepared to defend itself.

"So, you all ready for the big party?" Ray changed the subject.

Marcus laughed mirthlessly. "I'll happily eat a slab of roasted fattened calf in your honour, bro, but the rest I could do without."

"I'm quite looking forward to reacquainting myself with some of the fairer sex, sex being the operative word here," Ray replied, leering suggestively. "Never mind my pale, flabby, scrawny appearance, I've always found there's no aphrodisiac like a fat bank account. I reckon I'll be fighting the money-grubbers off with a stick, and I'm guessing most of the ladies gracing us with their presence will fit into that category."

"Doesn't it turn your stomach?"

"Nah, not really. And, remember, some of the pretty little money-grubbers have fat bank accounts of their own. I'm ready to settle down and can't say I'm averse to beautiful, flexible *and rich*."

Marcus laughed. "You're right, bro. Some things don't change. And you will gladden Mother's heart with words like that."

"Words like what?" Wearing a long, black, lace robe over a black silk nightie, and black, heeled, feathered bedroom slippers, Linda joined them on the patio, running her fingers gently down Ray's face before pouring herself a coffee and taking a seat in a comfortable chair by the table.

"Ray was just saying he's looking forward to the bevvy of well-heeled beauties who'll be buzzing around the party following the scent of money. He might even marry one if you get lucky."

Linda's eyes, meeting Marcus's, flashed with anger before she composed herself. Ray was oblivious to what had passed between the other two.

"You could do worse," she said calmly, betraying no emotion.

"Yeah, I don't suppose Tina Whatsername is still about? I always had the hots for her, but she apparently couldn't see past my little brother who stupidly kept turning her down. I guess she's married to some ancient gazillionaire, but if not, I wouldn't mind another crack at her."

Marcus shrugged disinterestedly. Linda stiffened.

"Mother?" Ray persisted.

Linda's face briefly revealed her annoyance, before quickly resuming its practised impassiveness. She smiled at Ray like a doctor delivering bad news. "Tina will be here, and no she's not married yet, but I don't think you'll have much luck there. I suggest you focus your attention elsewhere. What about Wilma Pleasance?"

"Willow," Marcus corrected. "Filthy rich blonde with a big arse," he said to Ray who arched an eyebrow at him. "Mother's description. Not mine," he added, shrugging and holding his hands out palms up.

"Can't say I can place her immediately, but she sounds delightful. I have no particular aversion to a big arse to keep me warm in my marriage bed. So long as the bank account is at least as big."

"I'm glad one of you appears to have some sense," Linda said to Marcus with a dramatic sigh. "Maybe you can knock some sense into your brother, Ray."

Ray laughed. "I tried pretty hard when we were kids to no avail." His amusement gave way to a more serious expression. "I don't think you should be too hard on Marky," he said. "He's not the one that's been missing in action. I am." His features tightened further and his empty fist clenched. Then he relaxed and sighed. "But I'm here now, hardly the worse for wear surprisingly, and ready to get stuck into making large bags of money. When do I start?"

"I figured you might as well hit the ground running, so I've asked Marcus to take you into the office today and show you around, point out the changes, introduce you to new people, start catching you up on the various divisions and how they're doing. It will be good to get your input. Some changes need to be made, and those decisions have to be made soon. I'd like to discuss them as a family, so the sooner you familiarise yourself with the current state of play the better. Marcus is at your disposal for the rest of the week. I might even get you to take a short trip to the mine and logistics head office. But I don't want you to overdo it, Ray, if you're not up to it. You've cost me too much already. I don't want any backsliding."

Marcus drifted off. The tension that had sprung up between Ray and Linda was palpable, but not his business. He was thinking about Pearl. It was going to be hard to find time to see her this week, and he didn't like the thought of that at all. His mother had been right when she said some changes needed to be made, but he was thinking of personal changes not business ones. His thirty-third birthday had been and gone and he was effectively still living with his mother. Maybe it wasn't quite as bad as that; he had his own luxury flat, own garage, and could come and go as he pleased, but nonetheless... It hadn't worried him to date. If he'd wanted to spend the night with a lady and she hadn't had a private place, he could always afford a comfortable hotel. Occasionally, he'd taken a date to his flat without being disturbed, but there was always the chance his mother might intrude at an embarrassing moment, so he'd mostly avoided doing that.

"And what about you, Mother?" Ray was saying. "Do you have a date for Saturday? I was half-expecting to find a man about the place. I can't think you haven't had a truckload of suitors. You got yourself a toyboy yet?"

"Don't be disgusting," Linda replied calmly.

"I can't see anyone referring to Alan Price as either a 'toy' or a 'boy'," Marcus remarked casually.

Ray swung around to face Linda. "Alan Price! Mr Moneybags! That old lech? My god, he was trying to get into your pants when we were kids and dad was still around." A tic pulsed in his cheek.

"Really, Ray. You're not in the gutter now," Linda chided him without changing the tone of her voice. "We don't need that kind of language here. Yes, I see Alan. He's been divorced for... it must be getting on for seven or eight years. He came around at the time, but I wasn't interested. Then," she waved her hand dismissively to emphasise the matter's lack of importance, "we got... close a couple of years ago. I'm not getting any younger and you boys are grown up. I don't deny I would like a man around to take care of me. But don't worry," she added standing up and placing her half-empty cup on the table, "the business and you take precedence. I'm going to get dressed. I've got a list a mile long of things to do for the party. Marcus, mind your brother. And apart from that quick hello last night, I haven't had a chance to welcome you home properly yet, Ray, so I'll see you both at dinner. *Both* of you. It will be our first meal all together in so long." The last was directed at Marcus in a tone that told him she did not expect to be disobeyed.

"Okay. Okay! I'll be there."

"Good." And she swept inside.

"What was that about?" Ray asked.

"Mother being Mother." Marcus dismissed the question. He wasn't ready to tell Ray about Pearl quite yet. Besides, they'd all be meeting her in a few days. It could wait. He changed the subject. "So, Brother, Mother tells me you have come home with a sizeable war chest. She was rather vague about how you came by it, other than to stress it was legal. No contraband, eh?"

Ray laughed. "Gawd, no. When I was hooked, any contraband that came anywhere near me didn't leave no matter how much money I was offered. To be honest, I couldn't be happier that's in the past. I hope to God I never fall off that wagon."

"So what then?"

"Good fortune, mostly. There's a lot to be said for hard work, don't get me wrong, but anyone who thinks hard work is the road to wealth is mistaken. There's plenty out there who have broken their backs all their lives with nothing to show for it at the end, and plenty (though fewer) of others who've barely done a stick of work all their miserable lives and money just falls into their laps. I'm one of those." He grinned. "So, I met this girl who'd had an idea for a survival pack and started a small business. We hung together for a while. I have no idea how she put up with me, or how she got any work done while I was passed out on her couch, most likely dribbling. Not an attractive sight. Anyway, the business started to take off. Opening lucky dips is the current zeitgeist, apparently. Who would have ever guessed?" He spread his arms in wonderment. "Anyway, she had a website and was doing pretty well. I think her turnover was edging up towards the magic million mark, but she needed a boost of capital and couldn't get anyone interested. I was flat broke, needless to say, but I'm nothing if not silver-tongued. I schmoozed around for a while and managed to borrow a couple of hundred grand, interest-free and on a repay whenever arrangement. No doubt the guy thought he'd never see it again but couldn't bring himself to refuse me anyway." Ray chuckled, seemingly pleased with himself, before continuing with his story.

"Suzie gave me an IOU for the money and ten percent of the business after going with me to oversee the transaction and make sure the dosh went straight into her bank account." He snorted self-deprecatingly. "She was smart enough to know you never trust a junkie. Anyway, the extra money was all she needed to get the company to go crazy. When its sales reached thirty million two years later, she looked me up. We weren't together anymore but, bless her honest heart, she found me, repaid the original loan and told me she'd sold the business to Amazon for an obscenely large stash of cash and gave me the ten percent she'd promised. So, while I was off my face on couches and in bars, I made a fortune without having to lift a finger. Like I said, money drops into my lap. I repaid the original loan with interest, much to the lender's surprise, and hid the rest in an obscure bank account. I'd been hanging around too many scumbags to risk anyone finding out about my good fortune, so I decided it was best to hightail it out of there as quickly as possible."

While Ray was telling his story, Marcus sat up and rested his arms on his knees, his eyes on the ground. As Ray's story came to an end, he looked up without raising his head. "You're right, bro. More arse than class, eh?" he observed with a grin.

Ray nodded. "Fair cop. To date. I'm going to see if I can manage to switch that around though. And the honest truth is that even getting all that lolly and being a sitting duck if any hard boys heard about it didn't change anything straight away. Then I got up one morning, or should I say afternoon, and saw a revolting, decrepit man in the mirror who looked like he was at death's door. I mean, I must have seen him many times before that, although I mostly avoided mirrors for that exact reason, but that day, I saw him. I mean, I really saw him. It seemed to flick some kind of switch in my brain, and I thought what the hell am I doing? I called Mother on the spot, she flew over and saw me into rehab, organised for the job when I got out, and booked my ticket home. I've a lot to be grateful to the old girl for. She could have told me to bugger off after all the trouble I'd given her, but she was right there the minute I called."

"Yep, that's Mother. Eager to help if you want to return to the fold bringing your pot of gold with you. Not so accommodating if you want to leave."

"What's that mean?" Ray asked quickly. "You want out?"

Marcus shook his head and sighed. "Nah, shooting the

breeze. That's all. So, how are you feeling? Want to head into the office?"

"Yep. Give me half an hour or so to spruce up and I'll be good to go. I'm looking forward to it, although not the curious stares and whispering so much, but I don't suppose that will go on for too long." He stood up, clapped Marcus on the shoulder, and went inside.

Marcus had dressed before coming to breakfast so was ready to leave. He pulled out his phone and checked the time. It was already after midday so Pearl might be at lunch. He called her.

"Hey, precious," he said when she answered. "I'm not going to make it over today, damn it. Mother is insisting I take Ray to the office this afternoon and then be here this evening for a family dinner."

"Oh, okay," Pearl answered. Her voice sounded flat.

"What's up, baby?"

"Nothing."

"Pearl." He'd spanked her for lying before and would do so again. Open and honest communication was one of the few things he demanded without exception. He was well aware that secrets and misinformation can kill a relationship, and he wasn't about to allow that to happen if he could prevent it. "Tell me."

"Just something that happened at work," Pearl said quickly. "I'll tell you about it when I see you. It's not important."

"Marcie's not giving you trouble, is she? Do you want me to call her and tell her to watch herself?"

"No," Pearl said firmly. "It's not Marcie. Like I said, it's not important. When will I see you?"

"As soon as I can, baby. I promise. I might be going out of town this week with Ray. Mother is kind of insisting but

I'll see you before Saturday so we can get you a dress. I want to go with you."

"Can I go and have a look first and then you can help me decide?"

Marcus pictured her sweet upturned face as she asked his permission. God, she was lovely. He wished she was with him in person so he could kiss the tip of her nose and her sweet lips.

"Wait and see how I'm going, can you? Would you mind, baby? I want to go with you, but if I'm too tied up, then of course you'll have to go on your own. I'll talk to you tonight after dinner when I have a better idea of what the next few days look like. All right, baby?"

"All right, Daddy," she said. His heart melted.

"Okay, little girl. I have to go, so take care of yourself and be good."

"I will."

Marcus hated leaving it like that. This arrangement, him living at his mother's, was no longer tenable. He would introduce Pearl to the family on Saturday night and tell his mother he was moving out of his flat and in with Pearl. He couldn't wait to see the expression on Pearl's face when he told her as well.

Impatient, but satisfied he had a plan in place, he went to find Ray.

Chapter 21

Pearl

At home alone in the evenings that week, Pearl sat on the couch hugging her teddy and missing her Daddy terribly. He was out of town with Ray until Thursday afternoon. He called every day and texted whenever he could, but she longed to see him in person. She couldn't get that customer, Tina, out of her mind and didn't want to talk to him about it over the phone. She wanted to snuggle on his lap in her favourite pink teddy bear pyjamas and feel safe, but she had to wait until Thursday. She was trying to be patient, but as she huddled further into the couch, pressed her hand, thumb first, to her mouth and brushed her teddy bear's paw back and forth under her nose, she felt very small and alone.

Her own problems vanished in an instant, however, on Thursday morning when she got a phone call from the small country hospital servicing the area, which included Darling Flats. She didn't take personal phone calls at work, but the hospital receptionist had called Mon Addi's landline when

Pearl had failed to answer her own mobile phone. Pearl's parents had been in an accident but were in no danger, she told Pearl. They could go home but would need someone with them for the first few days.

"What happened?" Pearl asked, her face ashen with shock.

"I haven't got all the details," the woman replied, "but I gather they were shifting something heavy and it appears your father injured his back, and let go of his end and the object dropped fracturing one of your mother's wrists and spraining the other. The doctors have prescribed bed rest for your dad for three or four days, only getting up to wash and go to the toilet, and your mother has one arm in a cast, and the other is in a sling and she's not allowed to use it for a few days so she's not able to take care of your dad and needs someone to help her as well. So I was wondering, is there a family member they could call in, or a friend or neighbour?"

"I'll come," Pearl said without hesitating. "I can take care of them. I don't have a car, but I can catch the bus. Should I come to the hospital or go straight home?"

"The bus to Darling Flats stops almost right outside the hospital, so why not jump off here and I'll organise transport home for you and your parents from here. How does that sound?"

"Perfect. Thank you so much. Can you please tell them I'll be there mid-afternoon?"

Sitting on the bus a short time later after handing over to Marcie and organising a few days leave, Pearl texted Marcus to tell him what had happened and to say she wouldn't be able to go to the party on Saturday night after all.

Okay, baby. Do you need anything? I'm in a meeting. I'll call tonight

No. I'm fine xxx

Once off the bus, all thoughts about her own life evaporated. As relieved as she was to find her mum and dad in relatively good, if somewhat subdued, spirits, and the prognosis for their recovery excellent as long as they rested for the next few days and then took things easy until they were fully healed, it was unnerving seeing them both so weak and virtually helpless.

"We're so sorry to burden you like this," her mum said, but Pearl waved away their apologies.

"I want to help you, Mum," she said, giving Mary a hug. "You've done so much for me all my life, it's the least I can do."

"I've spoken to Nancy," Mary went on, referring to her sister. "She couldn't come this weekend, but is going to come on Tuesday and stay for a week. Longer if need be, but I'm sure your dad and I will be right as rain by then."

"Okay," Pearl nodded. "I'll tell Marcie I'll be at work on Wednesday, but I won't leave until Auntie arrives."

She filled Marcus in on the day's events when he called her at bedtime.

"I wish I was there with you," he said echoing her own desire, but she didn't want to worry him and everything was manageable and her parents were both resting comfortably, so she put on a brave face.

"I know. Me too, but I can manage. There's not that much needs doing around the farm apart from keeping an eye on the watering and feeding the animals. Stuff like that. And answering the phone and cooking for my folks and doing the housework. That's about it."

"You're such a good girl, aren't you, baby. I'm so proud of you. I'd come but Mother has booked me in to help with preparations for this damn party Saturday night. Even so, if you get into any difficulty you are to call me immediately and I'll come straight away. Okay? Promise?"

"Yes. I promise."

"Who are you promising, baby? Can you tell me, or is someone listening?"

"No, I'm in my room at the moment. Mum and Dad are in bed. I promise you, Daddy." Pearl giggled as she felt the familiar rush of panty-melting heat between her thighs that happened whenever she called him Daddy.

"Ah, that's my precious Little girl," he said, and Pearl could hear how his own voice had thickened and knew that he was feeling as amorous as she. She sighed. That would have to wait.

"I'm sorry I'm going to miss the party, though," she said. "I was so looking forward to meeting your brother and mother." That was true, but she was also still curious about what Tina had meant when she bought the ring, and she hadn't been able to find the words or courage to ask him straight out.

"Is there no way you can be here?" he asked. "I could fetch you."

"No. I can't leave in case anything happens. I would never forgive myself. It's a shame but I won't miss anything too important, will I?" She was fishing.

"Nah, just the usual crowd of sycophants and snobs, showing off to people with less money and sucking up to people with more."

Pearl laughed. "It won't be that bad, will it, Daddy? Won't there be lots of pretty ladies in beautiful dresses wearing all kinds of heavenly jewels. I've never been to a party like that in all my life."

Marcus sighed ruefully. "And I've been to too many."

"Is it just a party for Ray? Marcie said maybe there's something else as well." Still fishing.

"There is nothing else, trust me, baby. Nothing at all. What did Marcie say? I feel like something is on your mind. Out with it."

"It's nothing," Pearl said quickly. She trusted Marcus absolutely and if he said nothing was going on, it meant either nothing was going on or, at the very least, nothing he knew about. Tina must have been talking about Ray, and Marcie was just being mean. "Really. I was just curious about what I'll be missing." As many times as she said she didn't mind not going to the party given the circumstances, she couldn't keep the wistfulness from her voice. "Uh oh, Mum's calling me. I have to go."

"Okay, baby. I'll call you tomorrow night. Take care, precious girl."

"I will. You too, Daddy."

But instead of calling on Friday night, he texted to say he was going to be busy until late and she was to be in bed early and get a good night's sleep.

"What is it, Pearl?" her mother asked on Saturday morning noticing Pearl's lack of usual bounce. "You seem so flat. Are you all right? We're not working you too hard, are we? I can do more if you want me to. Honestly. Or are you sad you are going to miss the party. It's tonight, isn't it?"

Pearl jumped up from the table where they were sitting having a cup of tea, Mary drinking hers through a straw as her unbroken wrist was still too painful to lift anything, and ran around to her mother and hugged her gently so as not to jar her injuries.

"No, Mum. I'm fine. Honestly. I don't need or want you to do anything. I can manage. All I want is for you to get well and, as for the party, I'm sure I would have been a fish out of water anyway. It's a bit of a relief I have an excuse not to go."

She wasn't actually lying; both those things were true, and she wanted to ease any guilt her mother was feeling about her and Pearl's father being the reason their daughter was missing out on wearing a designer ball gown and attending a magnificently splendid party with the man she loved.

"If you say so, darling, but you do look quite peaky. Maybe you should take it easier today. We can have sandwiches or something so you don't have so much cooking and washing up."

"It's fine, Mum," Pearl said, getting up and clearing away the breakfast dishes. "*I'm* fine. Honestly. I'm going to do the floors today. I like having something to do to keep busy."

And that's exactly what she was doing mid-afternoon as the sun was heading toward the horizon, mopping the kitchen floor with her sleeves rolled up, when she glanced out of the window and saw a car arriving. Her brow wrinkled in puzzlement. It appeared to be a limousine, but what was a limousine doing in her drive? She stood her mop in the bucket and went outside to meet it as it stopped near the house. The doors opened and three people, two women and the male driver, none of whom Pearl had ever seen before, got out and walked towards her. The man held out a phone and gestured for her to hold it up to her ear.

"Hello?" she said into it, a puzzled frown wrinkling her brow.

"Hi, baby," she heard Marcus's voice say at the other end. "This is Dave, who's a driver; Lisa, who's a nurse; and Georgia, who's a stylist. Georgia has a gown for you and is going to help you dress. Lisa is going to stay at the farm with your parents tonight. Dave is going to bring you and Georgia to the party, and then I'll return you to the farm sometime tomorrow. Lisa has friends who live not far away that she's going to stay with for a couple of days, so she doesn't mind at all hanging about until we get there and then her friends will collect her from there. How does that sound?"

"What? No." Pearl could barely take it in. "But Mum, Dad…"

"They don't want you to miss the party, do they?"

"I guess not," Pearl admitted. Her mother had already said as much.

"Let me talk to them," Marcus insisted. Pearl had no option but to comply, and to leave the room at Marcus's behest while he did so.

"Right," he told her when her father called her in and handed her the phone. "It's all settled. You are to do whatever Georgia tells you, and I will be waiting for you when you arrive. Lisa will stay with your parents till tomorrow, and she'll call me if there's anything you need to know. I have to get going, Mother's calling, but I'll see you tonight dressed up like a princess, baby girl. I can't wait. I've missed you so much, and I don't think I could stand this damn shindig without you by my side. We don't have to stay long, then we can go to your place and spend the night together."

It was two hours before the limousine set off on the return trip to the Holding mansion, and what a two hours it was. Before anything else happened, Georgia insisted Pearl try on the gown so she could see if any alterations were necessary and get started on them. She'd brought two big bags and a stool with her. As she opened one of the bags and took out the dress Marcus had organised, Pearl gasped. Figure-hugging but not revealing, it had everything she loved: champagne sequins and beads glittering like jewels in a pattern of vines trailing over white meshed lace. It sparkled and shimmered as Georgia held it up to the light and then helped her try it on in front of her bedroom mirror. She'd also brought a pair of low-heeled white shoes, which slipped on and fit perfectly.

"Oh my," she murmured, turning this way and that to see herself from every angle. "I feel like a princess. Did you choose this dress?"

"You look like a princess, sweetie," Georgia said kindly.

"And you are certainly beautiful enough to be one. And, no, the dress had nothing to do with me. Marcus chose it. He just asked me to bring it to you and help you get ready. It's a wee bit long. Hop up on the stool and I'll quickly pin it up, then you can take it off and settle Lisa in while I sew it. Apart from the length it fits perfectly, but you're such a tiny little thing… we don't want you tripping over it, do we?"

So, while Georgia sewed the hem, Pearl found Lisa, who'd been introduced to Jack and Mary and was chatting with them, and showed her around the house and explained what needed doing and where she could find things. Then she showered, by which time Georgia had finished sewing and was ready to help her get dressed, and do her makeup and hair. Since meeting Marcus, she'd let her hair grow because she liked wearing it in pigtails or a ponytail, and it was nearly down to her shoulders. With her skilled hands, Georgia pinned it up into a low messy bun with wisps of hair escaping each side. Satisfied at last, she surveyed her work.

"Okay, check it out in the mirror, and see what you think."

Standing in front of her reflection, Pearl could scarcely believe it was her. She felt like a little girl dressing up in adult clothes, but it was fun. She might be a princess, or model, or actress going to a party at the mansion of one of the wealthiest and most fashionable families in the city. It hardly seemed real.

"Thank you so much," she said to Georgia. "I can't believe it's me. I love my hair to bits. It's so pretty. I never would have thought to do it like that."

"Believe me, darling. It didn't take much effort on my part to make you stunning because you already are. And the hair was Marcus's idea. He specifically asked me to pin it up off your neck."

Pearl gently trailed her hand across her neck. "Does it

look funny without jewellery? I don't have any. Only these tiny diamond studs I always wear. All the other women will be wearing beautiful jewellery: necklaces and rings and tiaras and bracelets and dangling earrings."

"Don't worry, you don't need any jewellery. You are perfect without. There's no need to gild the lily. Now, let's get you to the party before you miss it all. Go and show your mum and dad how gorgeous you are while Dave and I pack the car. I reckon they'll be dying to see you all done up. Then we'll get going."

Chapter 22

Marcus

Marcus stood in front of the mirror, tweaking his shirtsleeves, collar, and tie. He would have much preferred casual clothes, but his mother had been adamant this would be an evening dress affair. He felt as though it was someone else staring back at him, as though it wasn't him at all. He half-expected the other man to hold out his hand and introduce himself as some big business tycoon, and Marcus would wonder how the stranger could be happy living the way he did.

He hadn't always been unhappy being a member of the Holding family. His childhood was idyllic; oblivious to the extent of his privilege compared to other children, he'd happily and innocently played with his brother and loved his mother. His father was so often not there, seemingly forever away on business, that he'd been almost a stranger when he did come home.

As time went by, it was better when he wasn't there as he and his wife had begun to fight. Although Marcus the child hadn't known him well, with hindsight he suspected his father might have longed for a different life far removed from the business world. Not his mother. She loved the thrust and parry, the lavish lifestyle and ostentatious displays of wealth. Life to her was a reality monopoly game: buying land, building businesses, and raking in dollars.

And Ray? Once they'd been so close, and Ray had been his best, possibly only true, friend. His mother discouraged friendships outside her vetted group and he'd found no other real friends inside. When he was young, it hardly mattered. He had Ray to adventure with, to share secrets with, and to share dreams with. Ray dreamed mostly of seeing the world, and spent hours researching different places around the globe and plotting journeys. Marcus wondered if Ray ever thought about the exciting journeys he'd planned as a boy, and how the reality of his time overseas had turned out so differently.

When Ray was thirteen and Marcus eleven, the carefree ambience of their childhood disappeared along with a substantial amount of money, which left the business floundering, and vultures circling. Like a suspense drama, the events unfolded quite slowly, over a couple of years, before reaching critical mass and rushing to the shocking and seemingly inevitable climax. Shortly after the discovery of his father's body in a car full of carbon monoxide when Marcus was thirteen came the discovery of precisely how much mess George had made of the business: debts were piled up, employees had been underpaid, businesses were running at a loss, and multiple writs had been lodged against companies in the Holding Corporation group for everything from poisoning towns to not paying government fees and taxes.

George's family were the Holdings who had started Holding Corporation, and they had been searching for money to expand when George met Linda, a beautiful socialite from another wealthy family. Linda had a substantial amount of her own money and an insatiable desire to make much, much more. It would have taken her a long time to amass a conglomerate as big as Holding Corporation if she'd started from scratch, so it had been a business deal for her when she married George; the only bad business deal she'd ever made she'd tell him when haranguing him about his lack of business acumen.

But on the odd occasion she slipped into castigating herself for it, she remembered Ray and Marcus. They were her silver lining. She'd tried to love George, and if he'd been successful, probably would have, but he was weak and incompetent when it came to being a business tycoon, and that she couldn't love. A hopeless businessman, whatever poetry might have lain fallow in his soul was of no interest or consequence to his wife or the world and went with him to his grave.

Linda played the part of grieving widow for about two days, then got to work. It would have been so easy at that point to just let the business go; she had no shortage of buyers, and despite the debts and bankrupt businesses, she would have been left with a small fortune to enjoy, but that was not what she wanted. She would not have her name associated with failure, and finally with full control of the business, she hungrily took on the challenge of turning it around. Intelligence, vision, lateral thinking, energy and perseverance were qualities she had in abundance, and she brought them all to bear with grim determination.

Their mother conscripted Marcus and Ray as soon as they were old enough, and any protestations were futile. The Holding name, her sons' name, would not be allowed to sink in shame; it would rise up in greater glory, and the sons were expected to do their part in ensuring that happened. Linda brooked no dissent. Private tutors worked with them ensuring they were accepted into the best universities in the country, and plush offices waited for them every holiday and welcomed them with doors bearing their names after their final graduations.

Ray joined the company full-time two years before Marcus finished his engineering degree, and they had been there together for five years when Ray suddenly quit and disappeared overseas. His mother was devastated. This was not part of her plan, and for the first time since George's death, she floundered. Hoping that an overseas holiday would bring Ray to his senses, she made sure he had sufficient money to enjoy himself. As it happened, though, it was also sufficient for him to party long enough to develop a drug habit and lose all desire to return to work.

With his father dead and his brother gone, Marcus was the only one who saw how close Ray's departure had come to breaking the previously apparently unbreakable Linda. She refused to overtly show any weakness, but Marcus saw her stumbles, heard her private, muffled sobs and saw the dark circles under her eyes before multiple applications of make-up covered them. In subtle ways, the child became the adult. His mother wouldn't allow open shows of affection or admissions of weakness, but Marcus was able to find small ways to show his support. He worked harder than ever. He spent hours discussing how different arms of the conglomerate were doing. He researched and implemented new strategies for additional potential profit. This is what made his mother truly happy, and it satisfied within him a need to protect and take care of her.

Gradually, though, Linda had been able to wrap a cocoon around the wound that was Ray and thus shield herself from the worst of the pain. Not that she forgot or abandoned her elder son; she sent him money whenever he asked and twice sent Marcus to try and bring him home, but gradually she was able to compartmentalise her life and heart and get on with it. She never told Marcus how much it meant to her that he had stood by her; without him she would have been on her own. But together they not only continued the resurrection of the business through the making of many hard decisions that saw long-term employees swept off the payroll as non-profitable businesses were sold or closed, but they completely revitalised and grew it. The ship had been turned around before Ray left, and under the continuing careful steerage of mother and son it had been powering ahead, until the recent worrying signs that it was headed for new rocks and its course, once again, needed recharting.

Marcus sighed. He'd voiced concern about two of the corporations major businesses, one in manufacturing and the other a newspaper publisher, warning his mother that both were vulnerable to the rapid changes evident everywhere. She'd listened and taken his concerns to the board, but two of the power brokers were too conservative and set in their ways to countenance the need for change. They'd grown up in one business environment and had failed to make the necessary adaptations when that disappeared. Believing Marcus to be wrong but not brave enough to openly defy Linda, they'd managed to hide their subterfuge long enough for they themselves to be proved wrong and for Holding Corporation to take quite a big hit. In a better economic time, it wouldn't have mattered quite so much, but the economy was weak and the family business needed an injection of capital if it was to jettison its unprofitable businesses and ride out this new storm intact.

Falling on their swords, the board had been forced to reorganise and bring in people with the skills and experience needed for modern times. Len, the chief executive officer, a long-time family friend, had been allowed to stay on after the others had gone on condition he resign within six months and make way for one of the Holding brothers. Linda had assumed that would be Marcus but hadn't yet spoken to him about it when, out of the blue, Ray had rung to say he wanted to get straight and come home, and also that he had a significant amount of money he was prepared to invest in the company. She knew that meant the board would choose Ray over Marcus who had none of his own money to offer, and had come up with the idea that Marcus should quickly get married to a woman with money to invest in the business.

For Marcus, though, Ray's sudden and unexpected reappearance seemed like a gift. The time they'd spent together since their reunion had convinced him that his older brother was genuinely eager to commit his life to the family business.

"I've been to all the places I wanted to go, done all the partying I ever want to do, laid all the women, taken all the drugs, and wasted all the time," he'd told Marcus over a beer. "I'm not saying I regret it; if I hadn't done it I might have always felt restless, but I'm over it. Well and truly. And I'm well aware I've let the family down, you and Mother. I took off leaving you to do the hard work while I spent the money. That's changed. I want a proper life. I want to repay the money I've taken, and do my share of the work wherever I can be most useful. I expect it will be a while before I'm fully up to speed, but I'm prepared to do whatever it takes."

"How would you feel about being CEO?" Marcus had asked.

Ray's beer had stopped half way to his mouth. "CEO?"

"Yep," and Marcus had sketched out recent events for him, omitting the part about Linda's choice being himself.

"Why me? You've done the hard yards and have a much better knowledge of where things are at the moment."

"Maybe," Marcus conceded. "But to be honest, Ray, I don't want it. And not a word to Mother about this yet. I'm going to tell her soon, but I don't want to keep working so many hours. There's other things I want to do. Other places I want to be, and I want more time to myself." *To be with Pearl.*

"I don't think the old girl is going to be too chuffed about that, is she?"

Marcus shrugged. "Probably not, but she's got no choice but to learn to live with it. And maybe she won't mind so much. I suspect she and Alan are going to be married in the not too distant future, and you're home with a bag of money and apparently not averse to marrying one of her daughter-in-law picks. And, let's face it, you want to be in the business and you have money you want to invest in it. I don't want to be there, have no money I want to invest, and am not available for an arranged marriage no matter how wealthy the bride or how big her arse."

Ray laughed. "Well, when you put it like that! And me marrying into money is not a definite yet; I'll have to see what's available. But I am ready to settle down. I'd like one woman to come home to at night, and I'd like kids." He grinned wryly. "I'd like to see if I can do a better job of family life than our parents managed."

Marcus nodded. "Poor Father. He probably always felt he was living the wrong life, not the one he wanted or would have chosen for himself. In the end, he could only see one way out. I'm not going to let that happen to me."

"Good for you, and good luck with Mother! Also," he ducked his head and looked at Marcus from under his eyebrows, "talking of marrying money, are you absolutely certain you have no interest in Tina? Seriously, would you mind if I had a crack at her? She was always so besotted with you she'd never look at me, and maybe that hasn't changed, but I reckon she and I are a far better match than she and you ever were."

Marcus laughed. "That's true. I could never understand why both of us could see it, but she never could." He solemnly placed his hand over his heart. "I have no objection whatsoever, brother. You have my blessing and I wish you every luck." He paused, took a mouthful of his beer and said as casually as possible. "I have a date for Saturday anyway, a girl I've been seeing for a while. Pearl. Mother hasn't met her yet and I doubt she is going to approve, but while it would obviously make life easier if she does, nothing she can say or do will change my mind."

This time, Ray's eyebrows shot up his forehead as his eyes opened wide. "Do tell, Brother, do tell," he said, nodding his head. "Pearl, eh? Sounds serious. I can't wait to meet her. Right, then, let's drink to Tina and Pearl."

Now it was Saturday night and Marcus was dressed and ready. He'd spent the last two days helping his mother organise. No matter how many times he'd told her he was not a party planner and they were rich enough to employ the best, Linda was adamant that the two of them would do the bulk of it. She wouldn't admit it, but he remained convinced this was all a ploy on her part to keep him close to home and away from Pearl. His personal life was never discussed; it was as though Linda believed that if she ignored it, it wasn't really happening. But it was, and tonight Linda was going to have to accept that Pearl was part of his life. He planned to speak to his Little girl first and, if she agreed, he would tell his mother that he was leaving the flat and moving in with Pearl. He couldn't wait. He was sick of spending his nights alone, going days on end without seeing her, having to find opportunities to spend time with her, and of having to pretend at home that she didn't exist. That was over. It ended tonight.

Taking out his phone, he sent her a message. *How far away are you, baby?*

Dave says 20 mins

Okay. Can't wait to see my precious little princess

Me too. I'm so happy, Daddy. And my dress is so pretty.

Marcus slipped his phone into his pocket and then slid his hand down his trousers to rearrange himself and ease the discomfort caused by his reaction to his conversation with Pearl. He groaned softly to himself as his hand closed over his partial erection. It had been days since he and Pearl had made love and he had such an ache it was tempting to quickly ease himself, but he resisted. If he didn't go out soon, someone was bound to come and fetch him. Guests would be arriving, and his mother would expect him to be there to greet them, plus he needed to be able to see Dave's car pull in so he would be right there to greet Pearl when she arrived.

With one last look in the mirror, a check of his pockets to see he had all he needed, he let himself out of his door, locked it behind him, and made his way across the grass to join the party in the big house.

Chapter 23

Pearl

I nside the limousine, Pearl could barely sit still. She'd called her mother who had reassured her everyone was doing splendidly; Lisa had set up a bed on the couch for Jack, and the three of them had opened a bottle of wine and were about to settle down to watch a movie. Pearl gathered from the conversation that Mary had taken quite a shine to Lisa and was enjoying having the company of a woman around her age, while her dad was lapping up the attention despite his frustration at being forced to rest. Mary insisted Pearl stop worrying about them, have a lovely time at the party and not hurry back in the morning.

"All good?" Georgia enquired when Pearl ended the call. "Sounded like it. Lisa is an excellent nurse. She genuinely likes people. I guess that helps if you're a nurse." She pulled a wry face and Pearl's excitement erupted into bubbly giggles.

"Are you coming to the party, too?"

"No," Georgia said, shaking her head. "It's been a long

day. Lots of fun," she added quickly with a smile, "but all I want to do is go home and put my feet up."

"Oh," Pearl's face dropped. "I won't know anyone there. Except Marcus of course. Oh, and I think my boss, Marcie Jones, is going, but I don't suppose she will want to talk to me."

"You'll be fine." Georgia patted her hand. "And Marcus will take good care of you."

"Yes. He will," Pearl agreed with an excited but slightly anxious sigh.

"Here we are, Miss," Dave said as they passed through a pair of magnificent iron gates.

"Oh my!" Pearl could scarcely believe her eyes as the brightly lit mansion came into view. Marcus had told her that his family was fabulously wealthy and she had been expecting a big house, but this! It was more like a palace than a house. Other guests were arriving, men in dinner suits or tuxedos, and ladies in fine gowns, high heels, and jewellery Pearl couldn't take her eyes off and was dying to see up close. Unconsciously, her hand went again to her own bare neck.

"Have a wonderful time, sweetie," Georgia said as Dave opened the door and offered Pearl his hand to help her out.

"Thank you, Georgia. Thank you so much," Pearl said warmly. She picked up the old but adequate purse her mother had lent her for the night, took Dave's hand and stepped out of the car carefully so as not to catch her dress. A moment of panic turned to joy as she saw Marcus threading his way through the other guests towards her.

"Ah, there you are, baby, the belle of the ball. Wow! You look absolutely gorgeous," he said, reaching her and draping an arm protectively around her shoulders and squeezing gently with his hand. "Thanks, Dave, for getting her here safe and sound." He shook the driver's hand, then opened the car door and bent down so he could see Georgia.

"Thanks so much, Georgia. You've done an amazing job as always."

"Thanks, Marcus," Georgia said with a laugh. "I enjoyed it. It was fun. And you've scrubbed up quite spectacularly yourself. Well, don't just stand there you two. Go and enjoy yourselves. I'm going home."

"You are the most beautiful woman here," Marcus whispered to Pearl after the others had gone and he'd removed all her lipstick with a thorough kissing. "In the country. In the world! Quick come with me before anyone sees us. I want you to myself for a moment. Can you walk on the grass in those heels?"

Pearl tried and found she could, as he took her hand and led her to his flat.

"Come in," he said as he pushed the door open. "Welcome to my cubbyhole."

Pearl laughed at his deprecatingly incongruous description of the spacious, luxurious apartment. "It's huge," she gasped gazing around at the large living area the front entrance led into. "I thought my flat was big, but I think it's tiny compared to this one. And you live here by yourself?"

"Yes," Marcus replied easily, following her eyes around the familiar room, which had been his home for the past few years. "But that's not what I want to talk to you about, baby. Oh, come here, my precious girl. You've no idea how much I've missed you."

He pulled her into his arms and crushed her mouth with his. The effect on him was instantaneous, and she could feel his hard erection pressing against her. As his tongue pushed between her lips and invaded her mouth, his hand closed over a breast.

"Damn!" he exclaimed, pulling away and running his hand over his hair in frustration. "That's a beautiful dress, but it makes it damn hard to get to you."

"Shall I take it off?" Pearl asked simply, driven as much by her desire to serve and please him as by her own erotic arousal.

"Ah, baby," he growled, nuzzling into her neck. "I would love you to, but if I get you naked, I will want to keep you that way at least until morning, and Mother will send Ray to round us up if we don't put in an appearance soon. No, we'd better wait, hard as that is. I've missed you so much." And he kissed her again, groaning with desire.

"I can kneel in this dress," she said when he freed her mouth. She gently squeezed the bulge in his pants. "Let me kiss you here. Please, Daddy? I can make you feel better."

Marcus ran his hand agitatedly across his hair. "We shouldn't, but, oh my God, how could any man resist such an offer?" He grinned at her, one finger tenderly stroking her face. "You're such a good girl, Pearl. Honestly, that isn't the reason I brought you in here. I have something for you and something I want to ask you. But as you insist, here, come with me."

Taking her hand, he led her into his bedroom. "I have a present for you, my darling. I've been waiting for the right time to give it to you. *Can* you kneel in the dress? Here, I'll give you a pillow."

He put a pillow on the floor, and Pearl pulled her dress up far enough to allow her to kneel comfortably without stretching it. She could feel some of the beads digging in, but it wasn't too bad, and there was nothing she wouldn't do for her Daddy. When she was ready, he opened a drawer by his bed and took out a small coloured bag, then squatted down next to her so his eyes were level with hers and gently touched her face.

"I love you, little girl," he said and her heart felt like it was about to burst at his first declaration of love.

"I love you too, Daddy," she replied without hesitating.

"I have a special gift for you," he went on. "If you wear it, it means you are mine, body and soul. You belong to me, forever. Is that what you want, baby? Say you do."

"I do, Daddy. I do. I want to be your Little girl and belong to you forever." Her heart was pounding, her eyes were wide and brimming with tears of love and happiness.

"Then wear this for me and be Daddy's precious jewel." Opening the bag he removed the diamond collar he'd bought from her the day they'd first met.

"Oh!" Pearl was afraid she might faint, her head was spinning and her mind reeling as it struggled to believe what was happening.

"The collar... but," she blurted out, her eyes flicking between his eyes and the gorgeous jewel.

He grinned at her surprise. "Yes, my darling. I bought it for you. Right from that very first moment, I knew I wanted to make you mine. That's why I asked you to show me your favourite thing, and you showed me this. It couldn't have been more perfect. And now I want to put it on you and claim you as my precious Little girl forever. Will you let me do that?"

She nodded, too ecstatic to speak as he leaned forward and fastened the beautiful thing around her neck.

"You're mine now, my darling. All mine," he said as he stood up, unzipped his trousers and released his throbbing erection.

Raising her hands, Pearl wrapped them lovingly around it as she opened her mouth and used her tongue to tease the sensitive tip the way he liked before sliding her tongue along its length as she wrapped one hand around the base and squeezed while her other hand gently cupped between his thighs. Overflowing with love, she wanted to give him as much joy as he had given her. She couldn't give him fancy jewels, but she could give him her heart and her life, and as much pleasure as he could take from her willing mouth. Opening wide, she guided him in as deep as he could thrust, and then as he pulled out she allowed her teeth to gently tease him before opening her mouth fully again as he pushed in. She could feel his urgency, partly desire and partly because he knew they couldn't linger, so she used her lips, her tongue, her teeth, and her hands to help drive him on relentlessly until he growled deep in his throat, paused and shuddered. She felt him pulsing in her mouth as it filled with his seed and she swallowed hungrily, ignoring the bitterness, prepared to do anything for the man she loved.

Sated for the moment, he helped her up and fixed his clothing. "You haven't even seen your collar, yet," he murmured against her neck as he showered her with tiny kisses. "Come and see." He led her to a mirror and as she saw her reflection, her fingers automatically reached up to touch the lovely creation.

"Oh, Daddy. It's even more beautiful than I remembered." She stared at the exquisite necklace, the diamonds sparkling against her pale skin, and pictured it in the display cabinet where she'd first admired it. Her eyes refocused on her image in the mirror, and a shadow crossed her face. Marcus saw, and immediately his face clouded with concern.

"What is it, baby? Don't you like it? Is it uncomfortable to wear?"

She shook her head, and turned away from the mirror, the lightness of her heart from moments ago replaced with a dark foreboding. "No. It's still the most beautiful jewel I've ever seen. It's just... just... It's just that it cost so much money. I'm not used to wearing expensive jewellery. I guess it feels a bit strange."

Marcus smiled at her. "Well, my precious little girl, don't you worry about the expense; I told you, my family is obscenely wealthy and working hard to become even more so. Stop worrying, and have a glass of champagne with me. There's something I want to ask you before we join the others, and I'm expecting a knock on the door at any moment."

Pearl followed him through to the living room where a bottle of Dom Perignon was chilling in an ice bucket. She watched as he expertly popped the cork and poured her a small glass of the exquisite bubbles. Unlike the sparkles in her glass, however, she was feeling suddenly flat. She forced herself to smile, but her parted lips hid an anxiety she could neither name nor identify the source from which it had sprung. Such a short time ago she'd been so excited about this evening, sure it was going to be the most magical ever, but now she couldn't suppress a feeling that something some-where, as yet unnamed and unknown, was wrong, dreadfully wrong. Unaware, Marcus was looking at her seriously as he raised his glass. "To us," he said.

"To us," she murmured, allowing him to clink her glass and then taking a small sip as he raised his own glass to his lips.

"Precious girl, there's something I want to talk to you about, to ask you. You can't have any doubts about how I feel about you…"

Pearl's hands grew damp, her heart beat fast and her chest tightened. What was coming next? What was he going to say to her so seriously with champagne and diamonds? And what was wrong with her? She had everything she could ever want. But what could Marcus be going to say that was so important? Did it involve Tina? She didn't believe he was going to announce his engagement to another woman tonight. Maybe he was going to propose to *her*. Of course she'd dreamt of his asking her to be his wife, almost from the first moment she'd met him. Why was that thought suddenly filling her with panic? It must be because the day had already been so crazy; she'd barely got used to Dave, Lisa and Georgia arriving so unexpectedly at the farm, transforming her into a high-society party girl, and whisking her off to Marcus's mother's mansion. She needed time to gather her thoughts. That was all.

Cutting him off mid-sentence, she pretended not to have realised what he was trying to do.

"Mmm, this champagne is yummy," she cried, faking gaiety, and drinking it in one gulp. She put her glass down, picked up her bag and went to the front door.

"Come on, Daddy," she called. "Can't we talk later? Please? We're missing the party. I want to see inside your mansion, and meet your family, and see all the ladies dresses and jewellery. And eat. I'm starving. I think I'm going to faint if I don't eat something right this minute." She leaned against the door, closed her eyes and draped one hand across them while clutching her belly with the other.

Marcus laughed. "All right. Let's get you some food, and we can talk while you eat. I don't want you fainting on me. Here, let me fix your hair and lipstick. You're looking delightfully dishevelled and wanton. Here give me your bag. I presume Georgia provided you with a repair kit."

Pearl stood still while he pinned a few stray strands of hair up and then posed her mouth for him while he applied her lipstick. Once he was satisfied, she took the hand he held out to her and they set off across the grass to the party. As they approached the house and she could hear the music and laughter, she was very conscious of the weight of diamonds around her neck and the weight of dread in her stomach as she prepared to be exposed as Marcus's secret girlfriend. A nasty foreboding told her it was not going to go well. She clutched Marcus's hand tightly and prayed she was wrong.

Chapter 24

Marcus

As he led Pearl toward his mother's house, Marcus was absentmindedly chewing his lip. He was frustrated, not sexually for the moment, his precious Pearl had seen to that, but as sexy and luscious as that had been, the rest had not gone to plan. He'd dreamed many times of fastening that diamond collar around her neck, and in his fantasies Pearl had always been naked. That she hadn't been tonight when he had finally placed it around her neck was a disappointment, but a small one and one he'd decided he could live with. Things aren't always perfect, after all, and he wanted to mark her as his and get things settled between them before he introduced her to his family.

It hadn't felt right to propose marriage tonight, although he would happily marry her tomorrow. He didn't want a rushed proposal before his mother's party. When he did propose to his precious Pearl, he intended making it the most romantic night she could imagine, so he'd decided tonight, in the meantime, to put the collar on her and ask her if she would be his Little girl, body and soul, forever instead. And that part had seemed to go exactly as he'd hoped. She'd promised to be his, and he'd seen the emotional tears welling in her eyes and had had to fight to control his own tears of joy.

And then, his darling Little had sealed her promise by giving him her mouth for his pleasure. And what a pleasure it was! She had practised following his gentle instructions, and knew exactly how to give him the most enjoyment and satisfaction, and how to take it slowly if they had plenty of time, and how to make it faster if, like tonight, they didn't. He felt a new stirring in his groin, and grunted inaudibly and wryly to himself. There was no denying the physical effect she had on him. He simply could not get enough of her, and if he thought he could get away with it without the possibility of having his door virtually broken down by demands to join the party, he'd whisk her straight to his apartment and take her to bed and stay there. Let the party go hang; it wasn't really necessary for him to be there. It was, after all, Ray's party, not his.

But he also wanted to bring Pearl out into the open, and introduce her to the part of his life he'd kept hidden. He had no doubt his mother would be difficult. He couldn't imagine the first time Pearl met her being at a private family meal where Pearl would be too exposed, too vulnerable, too much at Linda's mercy. At least tonight, with so many other people around and so much interest on Ray, he could introduce Pearl without her having to be the centre of attention all evening. He felt Pearl's hand grip his more tightly as they approached the steps leading up to the wide open, magnificent double wooden doors. Pausing for a moment, he turned to face her.

"You ready, baby?" he asked, searching her face and finding it unusually inscrutable as she silently nodded. He couldn't shake the uncomfortable feeling that something was going on that he wasn't privy to. He didn't like it. The sooner the introductions were made, a polite amount of time elapsed, and his duty done he would be getting her out of here and into his arms as quickly as possible. He dropped a small kiss on her lips. "Then let's find you something to eat, and introduce you to the family. Don't worry, they will be stunned that I have managed to find such a beautiful girl. And they will love you, too. Of course they will. How could they not?"

They both pretended not to notice that Marcus's voice was just that bit brighter than usual as they went in through the doors.

"Marcus! Where on earth have you been? I have been searching all over for you. Who is this person?"

They were barely inside before they were arrested by Linda's commanding voice. Marcus froze. This was it. Breathing deeply, he forced himself to relax, laid his arm possessively around Pearl's shoulders and faced his mother who, the minute she'd caught sight of her son, had crossed the room swiftly and effortlessly despite six-inch heels and a vivid red dress that could have been painted on.

Glaring imperiously, Linda's eyes travelled slowly down the length of Pearl, then up again stopping at the diamond collar. Her expression didn't alter as she swung her eyes from the jewel to Marcus, but Marcus felt the immediate drop in temperature. His mother was the only person he'd ever known who became colder and more impassive the angrier she was. He'd never seen her so much as raise her voice, but her icy displeasure could burn as effectively as the hottest rage.

"Mother," he began, keeping his voice calm and his arm around Pearl, "this is Pearl Sinclair. Pearl, my mother, Linda Holding."

Pearl offered her hand to shake, but Linda didn't even dignify it with a glance. Pearl withdrew her hand, clasping it to her other and squirming her fingers. Under her dress, her toe, trapped by its shoe, was trying to mimic the movements it so desperately wanted to make poking the ground.

"I'm disappointed, Marcus," Linda said calmly. "You should have told me you'd invited the lass from the shop. Anyway, I told you I needed to speak with you before people arrived. I *will* speak with you now." Her voice was too low for anyone but Marcus and Pearl to hear, and she kept her expression polite as she nodded and greeted people walking by without missing a beat.

"There's nothing for you to say to me that you can't say in front of Pearl."

"Oh, but there is."

"Well, I'm not leaving her here alone if that's what you think."

"I can't think why not. There's plenty of rich men," Linda replied coolly, raking her eyes up and down Pearl again with no attempt to conceal her contempt. Marcus's face froze with suppressed fury and he was about to take Pearl and leave when Linda stopped him with a hand on his arm. "Very well. Ray!" Linda called, having spotted her elder son in a nearby group. Ray, who appeared immediately, had been hidden from Pearl's view, so to her it was as though he had mysteriously materialised in obedience to her call. Somehow, Pearl thought, with this woman, it didn't seem entirely without the realms of possibility. She felt her skin crawling.

"Yes, Mother," Ray said as he joined them, then caught sight of Pearl. "Hello," he said, drawing it out and running is eyes appreciatively over her.

"Ray. This is Pearl Sinclair. Pearl, my prodigal brother,

Ray," Marcus introduced Ray who didn't hesitate to hold out his hand to Pearl.

"Delighted indeed, Pearl. And I see why Marcus has been keeping you hidden and all to himself!"

"Don't be vulgar, Ray," Linda said in the same tone she might use to offer a guest a piece of cheese. "I need Marcus for a moment. Look after this girl, please. Perhaps she'd like a glass of lemonade. And see she doesn't disappear or get robbed while we're gone."

Marcus's fists clenched in rage at his mother's cruelty towards Pearl. She was deliberately reducing her to nothing by refusing to use her name, treating her like a child by offering her lemonade, and even insinuating she might run off with the collar she'd rightly guessed he'd bought.

"Go on, brother," Ray replied amiably, ignoring his mother's scolding. "It will be a privilege to be seen with the loveliest woman at the party. And I can find out all your secrets." He winked at Marcus, who grimaced. "Come on, beautiful, I want to flaunt you and see if I can't make some of these other single lovelies jealous. They might see me in a whole new light if they see me with you."

Marcus saw Pearl smile shyly at Ray's good-natured flattery, and he felt a pang as he watched Ray tuck Pearl's arm around his own and lead her off. He trusted his brother to take good care of her, but her innocence and lack of artifice shone like her diamonds among the sophisticated set around her. She had so wanted to enjoy tonight, and he was furious with his mother for being so unpleasant and spoiling things.

"I will *not* have you being rude to Pearl, Mother!"

"I have no idea what you mean, dear," she replied, taking his arm and acknowledging everyone around them. "Come. We will speak in private."

"It had better be important," Marcus growled as Linda

led him out of the salon in which the guests were gathered, down a short hall and into an office. "And quick!"

Switching on the light and closing the door behind them, Linda poured two glasses of fifty-year-old Glenfiddich single malt Scotch whisky, handed one to him and bade him sit down.

"I think I'd rather stand," Marcus said grimly, but took the glass. "What do you want? You go first, then I have something to say, and as soon as I'm done, I'm fetching Pearl and we're leaving. So, get on with it. I don't like her being out there on her own when she doesn't know anyone."

"Well, she wouldn't know anyone would she?" Linda waved her arm airily. "She's obviously not from the world we inhabit. And there's no need to worry about her. Ray will keep her amused. He's had plenty of experience with girls like that." Her voice was calm and her body relaxed as she leaned against the desk and regarded him. Only a narrowing of her eyes, betrayed the emotions behind them.

Marcus strode over to her and slammed his glass down on the desk beside her. "You will not refer to Pearl as 'a girl like that'! I love her and I intend moving in with her immediately. Tonight. I also plan to make her my wife sooner rather than later if she'll have me."

"That would be a huge mistake, dear, and one I'm not willing to let you make. My marriage was a mistake, but at least it had its compensations. Marriage to that girl won't. I can see she is pretty enough, but girls like her are a dime a dozen. What else does she have? Money? Breeding? Class? Family?"

At the mention of family, Marcus was transported to Jack and Mary's kitchen with its comfortable and cosy ambience. It was a different meaning to 'family' than his mother was using, but one that he was beginning to think he might greatly prefer.

"Marcus, dear," for the first time, Linda's voice had softened. She put her hand on his arm. "I owe you a lot, I know that, although I don't often say it."

Marcus almost jumped in surprise. His mother had always been reluctant to give praise or show her emotions. He stiffened, immediately wary, sensing a trick.

"Don't make that face," Linda patted his arm. "We owe each other. I looked after you and Ray, the business, and our future after your father deserted us leaving the gigantic mess he'd created. And you looked after me when Ray ran off and left us in the lurch. We're a good team. We've accomplished a lot. We saved the business and built it up, bigger and stronger than it's ever been, and together we can do it again. But I want you as CEO. You can hand over to Ray later if that's what you decide to do. But for the foreseeable future, you are the best man for the job. You know the business inside and out. You might think I've pushed you too hard, but that's why. No one is better qualified to lead the company than you. You can't let us down."

Marcus was silent. He wanted to tell his mother she was wrong, but she wasn't. It would take Ray time to learn everything he needed to know, and the business would not survive another mistake. At its heart, it was solid, but it had a crack. It needed the right action to fix it. The wrong action could destroy it. He shrugged.

"Very well. I'm prepared to make a deal. If you can talk the board into appointing me despite me having no dowry, I will step in as CEO for as long as it takes to get the company back on track, and I will ensure Ray has all the training, help and support he needs to take over from me. As soon as he's ready, I'll step down and hand over to him."

Linda allowed herself a rare smile.

"In the meantime, though," Marcus continued. "I will

move in with Pearl and you will accept her as part of the family. That is my condition."

Linda's face recomposed itself into fake concern. "But, Marcus, that's not possible, is it? I've talked to the board, and they are adamant they will only appoint someone if they bring capital with them. I'm sorry, Marcus, it's time to repay everything the business has done for you and to do your duty. Once you are married, have a baby on the way and have settled into your new role at the company, you'll be quite happy. You'll see."

"Are you still on about this marriage nonsense?"

"Of course. It has to be done. There's no other way. I've spoken to Tina. I like her. She's a lot like I was at her age. She'll make you a good wife. She's always had a thing for you, Marcus, although sometimes you can be so difficult I begin to wonder why. She'll keep you satisfied in bed. She's prepared to have your children despite her figure, and she will give you access to the bulk of her money—with the usual pre-nup and caveats, of course." She made the same airy hand-waving gesture, which she'd used earlier to dismiss his concern about Pearl.

Marcus was staring at her in disbelief. He thought he had made it absolutely clear that he would not be going along with any arranged marriage nonsense to Tina or anyone else, but Linda was acting as though it was a done deal.

"I gave Tina my card to buy a ring." She grimaced as though with pain. "She made rather a big hole in it, but it *is* a magnificent ring. She bought it at Mon Addi obviously, so it would seem Marcie has developed new skills when it comes to choosing jewellery for the store."

"Pearl does the buying." Marcus mentally slapped his forehead. That's what had happened at work on Monday to upset Pearl! Something must have been said about the ring being for Tina and him.

Linda ignored his comment. "I've told everyone we're making an announcement tonight. I'm prepared to give that little girl a cheque to disappear, and you can be adult about this and get on with your proper life."

Marcus suddenly felt all the tension leave him. "No, Mother," he said calmly and firmly. "Not in a hundred million years. It's not going to happen. No matter what you say or do, I shan't be marrying Tina. I love Pearl, and she is the only woman I will be marrying."

A ripple ran through Linda as her lips tightened, but was gone almost immediately. "I was afraid you might have some silly romantic notion like that, so I have another proposition. Tina and I have had frank discussions about all options and although this isn't our preferred one, we are willing to compromise. Have another whisky while I explain."

"Make it quick!"

Chapter 25

Pearl

Through the growing throng of guests, Pearl was glancing in the direction from which she was expecting Marcus to reappear. He'd been gone for ages. What could his mother have wanted? Certainly not to tell him how happy she was to have met her! Pearl's hands rubbed each other for comfort as she remembered how blatantly her extended hand had been rebuffed by Linda.

She'd been so excited about coming to the party, but so far it was nothing like she'd imagined. She was glad Ray was with her; it would have been too ghastly if Linda had whisked Marcus off and she'd been left on her own. She could see a family resemblance between the brothers, she decided, although Ray looked more than the two years older that he was, and he was pale and thin while Marcus was strong and muscular. There was also an edge to Ray that Marcus didn't have, a hardness that reminded her of her quick introduction to Linda. She wondered if he had it in him to be as kind and caring of others as Marcus.

"Can I get you something?" he was asking her. "Food? Drink?"

"I am quite hungry," Pearl admitted. "I haven't eaten since lunch."

"Then food you shall have," replied Ray gallantly, taking her into the next room where a large dining table was over-flowing with every gourmet delicacy imaginable including, right in the middle, a roasted pig's head with a sad expression and an apple in its mouth.

Averting her eyes, she helped herself to a sandwich and a few pieces of assorted chopped fruit, and then moved away from the table and started edging out of the room. Ray, chatting about some of the more exotic things he'd eaten in different places, including dog, which put Pearl off the rest of her half-eaten sandwich, didn't seem to notice her discomfort at all.

"So, tell me about yourself, Pearl. How did you meet that handsome brother of mine?"

Pearl started to tell him about Mon Addi, but every few words they were interrupted by a man shaking Ray's hand or a woman hugging him and kissing his cheek. While, they clearly wanted to catch up and welcome him home, they were also obviously curious about the woman in the diamond collar who was with him.

After the third time he had introduced her with, "This is Pearl," without elaborating, Pearl started to feel he was deliberately not mentioning that she was Marcus's girlfriend. This was supposed to be the night her relationship with Marcus stopped being a secret but, although Marcus wanted to make it public, it seemed the rest of his family were not so keen. She looked around, willing Marcus to reappear, but there was no sign of him. She was starting to wish she hadn't come. The gown, the shoes and the diamonds weren't hers, and she felt like she was in dress-ups, pretending to be someone she wasn't. She didn't know any of these people, and unlike Marcus who had always been so friendly, none of them had shown any interest in her at all apart from a few winks and lewd leers from men old enough to be her father, or even her grandfather!

One of the staff, unable to locate Linda, approached Ray to request assistance on a catering matter.

"Excuse me, Pearl," Ray said. "I'd best go see to this. You'll be right on your own for a minute, won't you? Have something else to eat. And drink. Marcus should be re-joining the party soon and I won't be long."

Finding herself alone, Pearl wondered what to do. She couldn't just stand there like a bump on a log. Keeping her head up and telling herself that, as the girlfriend of Marcus Holding, she had more right to be there than most of the other guests, she wandered out onto the patio area where, under coloured lights, champagne was flowing freely for the party-goers flirting, smoking, chatting and laughing in the balmy evening air.

No one appeared to notice her as she found a place to sit in the shadows. One thing she observed as she watched the guests arrive and settle into the party groove was that they stuck closely to their established groups. As each man arrived, he would scour the room for his tribe and head over with a loud "Hello, Bob!" or Fred or Roger or whatever. And the women were doing it no less than the men, clustering in cliques, eyeing outsiders suspiciously. Pearl was very much an outsider and with no clique of her own, it seemed she had effectively vanished into the woodwork as far as the other guests were concerned.

From her hidden spot, she could see past the open doors through the next room and down the hall, so she would be able to spot Marcus as soon as he reappeared.

"So, when's the big announcement?" she heard a

woman's voice ask. It appeared one of the cliques was gathered on the other side of the large potted bush Pearl was sitting next to.

"Soon. When everyone is here." Pearl immediately recognised the important-sounding voice as belonging to Tina, the woman who'd bought the engagement ring. "Although I'll be glad when it's done; my hands are getting hot in these gloves. Linda insisted I wear them to hide the ring until the engagement is public."

"Didn't I see Marcus arrive with a blonde, though?"

"Her?" Pearl heard that practised titter. "She's the sales girl at Mon Addi. Marcus, bless him, was being his usual chivalrous self, escorting her in when she arrived as apparently she couldn't find a date, poor girl. Mon Addi's manager, Marcie Jones, was invited too. Linda always invites some shop staff or other plebs to her parties. She likes to do something nice for people that would otherwise never get the opportunity to attend a party like this."

"I heard Marcus has a secret lover. Maybe it's the sales girl." It was not offered as information; it was a saccharine-coated barb.

Tina's laugh in response was brittle and the tone of her voice as fakely sweet as her antagonist. "Oh, Jasmine, I hardly think bonking a sales girl classifies as a secret lover. But it doesn't matter anyway. Once we're married, I will have his name, and my children will be heirs to the Holding fortune. I've agreed to allow him to play around on the side, although don't be surprised if he no longer feels the need for variety once we're married. I have some tricks up my sleeve he doesn't know about yet. But who cares? Money and name is what matters, not outdated ideas about marital fidelity."

Another woman laughed. "God, yes. I can't think of anyone who is actually having sex with the person they're married to. Well, not if they can avoid it!"

"I've managed to not have sex for over a year," another woman confided. "If he wants to share Marcus's piece of arse, I couldn't care less. I refused to marry him until we had a water-tight pre-nup that was all in my favour. He won't ever divorce me. It will cost him too much. I've kept my side of the bargain and given him a son and heir; from here on in, he can keep that wrinkly old cock well away from me."

Another burst of laughter erupted over which Pearl heard someone say, "No shortage of hot pool attendants and gardeners," and they all laughed louder.

"Ah, there's Marcus," Tina said. Pearl swung her eyes quickly around and saw Marcus walking amongst the guests, his eyes scanning the crowd as he went. She could see he was searching for her, and was about to go to him when Tina broke away from the group. "Excuse me ladies while I speak with my intended and find out the plan." Seconds later, she came into view as she went through the doors.

Pearl watched as she approached Marcus. It was clear Marcus was not interested but Tina was not to be deterred. Pearl moved out of the shadows to go to his rescue only to bump into Linda.

"Ah, I'm glad I found you before my son did. You and I need to talk, dear. At least I need to talk and you need to listen. I can see you don't belong in this world and have no idea how it functions, so I'm going to tell you. It's what some people might think of as incestuous, I suppose. Marriages are much better when they're kept in the extended family, as I like to think of the people you see here tonight. Occasionally, some men with bigger cocks than brains wind up marrying young and beautiful fortune-hunters." She paused for effect. "Like you, dear!" She held her hands palm up and opened her eyes wide in feigned surprise as though the thought had only just occurred to her. "But those marriages don't make anyone happy. The men wind up embarrassed, and their gold-digging wives end up with no husband, no friends and, if their husbands were at least smart enough to get pre- nuptial financial agreements, no money either. It becomes a sad and ghastly mess, I'm afraid, and I'm not about to let that happen to my son. You're quite a pretty little thing, aren't you? And I've no doubt you're well practised in bed, so it's been agreed that if Marcus insists on continuing his affair with you after his marriage until he has lost interest, he may do so. None of his other sexual partners has lasted long; I see no reason why you should be different.

"It's a shame you came tonight, though. I can't imagine what Marcus was thinking. It was cruel of him to expose you to embarrassment and humiliation like this. Why don't you slip away while you have a modicum of pride left, you poor little thing? It's obvious to everyone that you are hopelessly out of your depth. I feel a bit responsible for Marcus's cruelty in letting you think you'd be welcome tonight, so I've organ- ised a driver to take you home. See?" She pointed to a man standing by a car looking up towards the house. "You can leave quietly down these steps. That way no one will notice and you won't need to feel ashamed. Off you go. It would be silly if you were here when Marcus announces his engage- ment to Tina. Oh, but before you go, perhaps you'd like to remove the necklace which I am guessing Marcus loaned you for the evening. It's too valuable for you to be wearing while you're traipsing about in dingy streets and bars."

As Pearl listened to Linda's cruel words, her heart started thumping in her ears and her body broke out in a cold sweat and began trembling so violently she was afraid she'd fall over. Over Linda's shoulder, she could see Marcus still scan- ning the room for her as he tried to escape Tina, but people were coming from all sides, clapping him on the back and making small talk. Her eyes refocused on Linda's tight, baby- bottom smooth face, glinting eyes and curled mouth and suddenly, with absolute clarity, she understood the dread she'd had in Marcus's apartment.

"Don't worry," she said quietly to the older woman. "I will leave, but it's not because you want me to; it's because I wouldn't waste my time here with you for another second if you paid me."

Linda's face hardened and the curl of her mouth became a snarl. "Interesting you should mention paying you. I have a large cheque here. It's yours if you agree to never see Marcus again. It's extremely generous I think you'll find." As she spoke, she pulled a cheque from down the front of her dress and held it out.

Without missing a beat and without looking at it, Pearl took it, tore it in half, then in half again and handed her the pieces. "You're a horrible, horrible person," she said managing to keep her voice low and controlled despite the rage and sorrow flooding through her. "Keep your money. I want none of it."

"Ah, Linda, darling, how are you? Oh, and goodness, is that little Pearl all tarted up in her refashioned prom dress? I didn't realise it was a fancy dress party, but you've come as… Cinderella, is it?" Marcie said loudly as she joined them, gloating triumphantly at Pearl, enjoying her obvious humiliation. The colour drained from Pearl's face and the hot tears burning her eyes threatened to overflow. As awful and as cruel as these people were, though, she was going to retain her dignity.

"Mrs Holding. Miss Jones. Good night," she managed to say clearly, before making her way down the stairs, praying with every step that she would reach the waiting car without tripping or crumpling in a heap.

"Where would you like to go, miss?" her driver asked as she fastened her seat belt and he started the car.

She gave the driver the address of her apartment. "Please

219

hurry," she said, needing to get away as quickly as possible. Her stomach was churning. Her heart was broken. What a horrible, horrible night. But it had made everything crystal clear, and she tried to feel grateful that that had happened now and not further down the track. Marcus would come after her as soon as he realised she'd left, but she didn't want to see him. Not tonight. She guessed Linda and Tina would prevent him finding out for as long as possible that she'd gone, so she would at least have a bit of a head start. As they were driving, she blocked him on her phone.

Arriving at her apartment, she asked the driver if he could call her a taxi and wait for it. Then assuring him she would only be a few minutes, rushed up, threw off her dress, shoes and diamond choker and changed into jeans, jumper and runners. Closing her eyes to all the Little clothes Marcus had bought for her, she grabbed her other clothes and threw them onto the bed. Her Little was tucked away and adult Pearl was in charge as she fetched her bag and stuffed her possessions into it: clothes she'd brought with her from the farm, books, and Rusty, Moppy and her teddy bear. Then running into each room, she grabbed essentials and shoved them in as well.

When she had everything she wanted, she wrote a note and left it on the bed with her dress and the choker, picked up her things and left. A pain so sharp it caused her to softly cry out and double up ripped through her as she took one last look around the apartment where she'd felt such happiness. Biting her violently trembling lip, she locked the door behind her and hurried downstairs to where a cab was waiting for her. Jumping in, she gave the driver the name of the hotel where she planned to spend the night.

Half an hour later, with everything taken care of and nothing to do until morning, Pearl collapsed onto the pillow in her hotel room and sobbed, her heart broken, her dreams shattered, and her life once more in tatters. This time, though, there would be no going back. This time she had learned her lesson. She was done with Marcus, done with his family, and done with Mon Addi and all its clients. She would make a new future for herself, but first she needed to cry.

Chapter 26

Marcus

Marcus scanned the room again. Still no sign of Ray or Pearl. Damn. Where was she?

"I'm sorry, Tina. Please excuse me." He tried once more to extricate himself, but this woman who, with every passing minute he was increasingly in danger of disliking, clung to him like a limpet.

"Aw, come on, Marcus. It's a party and we almost never get time to talk these days. Remember when we were kids, sneaking downstairs to pinch food off the table and then alcohol when we were not much older." She laughed, and Marcus was struck by how much her head resembled a grotesque skull when she peeled her lips back like that. He didn't recall her laughing like that.

"I do remember," he said grimly. He didn't want to feel badly about Tina. He just wanted her to leave him alone to find Pearl who, artless and unspoiled as she was, could not be less like this calculating woman in front of him. But he also remembered when Tina had been a carefree girl, and one summer in particular. A few of the families with children made it an annual event to take a summer holiday together at an expensive lakeside resort. The parents were too busy with their own drinking, flirting and philandering to be interested in the children who were old enough to go off on their own without anyone noticing or caring. That had been the best summer holiday of his life, and he and Tina, friends then, and the others had swum in and boated on the lake, walked in the moonlight and sat around in the dark telling ghost stories.

When the summer ended and they'd packed up to leave, he and Tina had kissed as they said goodbye, and he'd been impatient for the next summer holiday. But when he arrived at the lake and rushed over to her chalet, he found a different person to the one he'd taken his leave of less than a year before. She'd been away, boarding at a new school, and the older girls there had taught the younger ones how to pout and simper and wheedle. "You have to practise if you're going to catch a rich husband," they'd been told.

Finally, when Tina had stamped her foot, pouted and pinched him one too many times, he'd pulled her over his knee and smacked her bottom. She'd jumped up crying and run off, threatening to tell her parents. He knew she wouldn't. She'd be too embarrassed. Alone, he'd sat staring unseeingly out over the lake after she'd gone, thinking about what had occurred. It wasn't planned. Until it happened, he'd had no idea he was going to do it. But, he'd admitted to himself, putting his hand down his trousers, he'd liked it and wanted to do it more. And he did, although not with Tina. Some business of her father's called them away before she'd forgiven him, and that was the last summer holiday they spent together at the lake. The next time they met up, they were both adults and Marcus didn't find the woman she had become at all attractive. She, however, seemed to think his spanking her was tantamount to a proposal and she firmly believed they were destined to marry.

Ray, meanwhile, had been hopelessly in love with her all his life, but had said nothing because he figured she was Marcus's girl. Marcus could see it in his brother's eyes, but spared him the humiliation of letting on he knew. When Marcus stopped wanting to spend time with Tina, she used Ray to try and get close to him. Ray knew she was doing it, but hoped that one day she'd look at him, instead of always past him at Marcus, and realise how good they were together. What no one else but the two of them knew was that one night, after too much to drink and Marcus having again told her he didn't love her and would never love her, she'd taken Ray into her bed. He wasn't aware of the conversation she'd had with Marcus, and foolishly believed the day he had waited so long for had finally come at last. He joyfully made love to her all night, whispering endearments, planning their future together, declaring his eternal love and loyalty.

In the morning she was gone. Then a text arrived. *How could you? You know I love Marcus. You've made me betray him. I hate you. I never want to see you again.*

Within days he had quit his job, packed a small bag and left the country. Tonight, Marcus thought he could still see an echo of the girl she'd been, and wondered if that part of her could be reached, or if the brittle exterior she'd cultivated had hardened over the top and made it impossible for anything deeper to get out.

"Why don't you find Ray?" he asked suddenly, interrupting her. He hadn't been listening and had no idea what she was talking about.

"What?" She started as though he'd slapped her face. "What for?"

"If you want to marry into this family, Tina," he told her gently, "you're focusing on the wrong brother. I am in love with Pearl and I intend to marry her if she will have me. I've told Mother, and I've made it clear there is nothing she can do to stop me. I don't know if Ray is still in love with you, but I think he would consider marrying you to unite our families anyway and he'd do the right thing by you. He's already told me he is keen to find a wife and have a family. He's a good man; in some ways better than I am. And you and he are alike. He likes this lifestyle. He'd love to have kids and go holidaying with the rest of our old crew and their families up at the lake, as the adults this time." He half smiled and shook his head. "It's not for me though, Tina, and neither are you. It's time you accepted that once and for all. I'm going to find Pearl. I think she's with Ray, so when I find them, I'll tell Ray to come see you, shall I?"

He'd expected her to make a scene, but she was just staring at him, her shoulders sagging, her face crumpled into sad understanding. He bent forward and kissed her on the cheek, thinking he'd not seen her look so beautiful since they'd kissed goodbye half their lifetimes ago.

"Goodbye, Tina. Be happy. Don't let Mother humiliate you by announcing a fake engagement to me. Talk to Ray."

He resumed his search for Pearl. There was no sign of her, of Ray or of his mother. He started to get a very uneasy feeling which was heightened when he saw Marcie and asked if she'd seen Ray and Pearl.

"I saw Ray a while ago. I think he and some others were going to the summer house for a smoke. Pearl probably went with them," she told him with a self-satisfied smirk which he didn't understand.

He made his way through the guests, out the back door and across the garden to the summer house, but before he even reached it he realised he'd been sent on a wild goose chase. No lights were on, and it was as silent as a grave. Angrily clenching his fists, he returned to the house. He saw

Marcie out on the patio talking to Linda and went the other way. After searching the house and asking everyone he could find, he caught sight of Ray coming in through the front door. He sped to meet him.

"Where the hell have you been? Where's Pearl?" he demanded.

"Mother sent me to the shop for these." Ray held up a packet of cigarettes.

"She doesn't smoke!" Marcus almost shouted.

"I know." Ray shrugged. "I thought it was odd but she was adamant she wanted them and that I was to get them. She said not to worry about Pearl because you were with her."

"I haven't been able to find her," Marcus growled, realising he'd been duped and that his mother had outplayed him as she'd done so often in the past.

Barging onto the patio, he grabbed Linda by the shoulders and swung her around. "What have you done with Pearl?" he demanded, not caring who heard.

"Ah, there you are, dear," Linda said smoothly and quietly. "I was beginning to worry about you. There's no need to shout at me. Pearl was with us a minute ago, but she felt ill and wanted to go home. I couldn't find you, so I organised a driver for her. Poor little thing. I think she felt out of her depth. She said I was to tell you that she wanted to rest and that you shouldn't bother her tonight, so why don't you have another drink and let's make this a proper party. Perhaps you could have a dance with Tina."

"I don't believe you," Marcus snarled menacingly glaring at her with utter contempt. "What did you say to her? Never mind. I'll find out from her." He made to leave, but Linda stopped him.

"Marcus, don't. Don't disregard your family or the business. Don't make a foolish decision and let your emotions run away with you. If you leave me, you will be doing exactly the same thing your father did, and you know it. You won't do that to me, will you, my darling? You and I both know Ray is not ready to be in charge of the company. If you walk out on me, you will be destroying me as surely as your father tried to."

Marcus shook his head as he ran his hand roughly across it as if to rub away her words, his thoughts and his pain.

"I have to go, Mother. I have to make sure Pearl is all right. If she would really rather be alone, I'll come back for a while. Otherwise, I'll see you tomorrow before I drive Pearl home. We can talk about the business and what we're going to do then. Okay? But I'm not marrying Tina. That's final, and I have told her so."

Linda shrugged sadly, but Marcus knew she was trying to manipulate him, and he was quite prepared to stand his ground. She had Ray and Alan to look after her; Pearl had only him.

"I have to go." He bent to kiss her cheek, but she moved away so he kissed the air. His mouth tightened and he snorted as he left, striding quickly to his apartment without another word.

What a disaster the night had been, he thought grimly as he jumped in his car and headed to Pearl's apartment. He was furious with his mother; maybe she hadn't said anything in particular to make Pearl leave, but she hadn't been welcoming and friendly, and it certainly felt like she'd deliberately kept him away from her. At least he'd made it clear that his marrying Tina was not an option even if they hadn't finally resolved the issue of a new CEO for Holding Corporation. The only solution he could see to that problem was a three-way agreement between himself, Ray, and the board, under which Ray would invest his money and be nominally appointed CEO while allowing Marcus to actually be in charge until he, Ray, was in a position to take the reins himself. It seemed like the perfect solution, but it might not be easy to get everyone to agree. He had made himself unpopular with some of the board who'd objected to changes he'd implemented, but fortunately most of them had gone. His mother would be seriously vexed that he wouldn't officially be the CEO. It was a shame she couldn't see that the harder she tried to cling to him, the more she was pushing him away. She had a lot of power with the board and if she decided to veto his plan, it was unlikely he would be able to get the board to override her.

He grimaced to himself as his mind went over and over the problem but he couldn't see a solution other than the one he'd articulated to himself. No amount of wheedling on his mother's part was going to convince him that he had an obligation to marry Tina for her money. He loved Pearl and he wasn't going to lose her but, and his gut tightened at the thought, he didn't know if he would be able to live with himself if his plan was rejected, he walked away and the business crumbled through lack of expert leadership. He'd seen his mother suffer before; he didn't want to be the cause of additional suffering. His hand thumped the steering wheel. He was the only one who could protect her. Damn Alan! It should be his job, but he'd made it clear when he'd started dating Linda that after three ex-wives had fleeced him of all they could, his money was locked away and not to share. Linda hadn't minded. At the time, she had enough of her own and wasn't about to share it with anyone else either, including Alan should the need arise.

Marcus suspected Linda hadn't told Alan about Holding Corporations current crisis. He briefly wondered if he should, but decided against it. This was family business, and as yet Alan wasn't family. He hadn't proposed to Linda, and Marcus was unsure of his intentions. He would feel he was betraying his mother if he went behind her back; if she wanted Alan to know, she would tell him herself.

For the rest of tonight, though, all he wanted to think about was Pearl. He'd been missing her terribly and was desperate to wrap her in his arms and tell her he wanted to move into the flat and be there when she returned from the farm. He wouldn't think about his family. That could wait. Tonight he would lose himself in Pearl. But the moment he opened the front door he could sense something was wrong. Switching on a light, he hurried through to the bedroom. The bed was empty, her teddy bear, Rusty, and Moppy were gone, and in their place lay the dress, the diamond choker and a note. He picked it up and his heart sank as he read *Goodbye, Marcus. I've taken all I want. I'm catching a taxi to a hotel and will be on the 10 a.m. bus home tomorrow. I'll be at the bus station at 9:45 if you want to see me before I leave.*

As his eyes flicked over the note, he pulled his phone from his pocket and called her. It went straight to voicemail. He rang again, but it was pointless. She wasn't going to answer. He left a garbled message asking her where she was and to call him, but without any real hope that she would. What could he do? How could he find her? There was no point ringing Jack or Mary. He doubted they would know anything and, if he rang, he'd only worry them. He reread the note. She'd covered her tracks to prevent him finding her tonight, so he had no choice but to wait till morning and go to the bus station. Curling himself up on the bed, his arms achingly empty, he steeled himself for a long night.

By nine o'clock the following morning he was already waiting at the bus station in case she was early. He bought himself a coffee and paced to and fro in the waiting room, taking his phone out every few minutes in case she contacted him. He'd tried calling her, but she wasn't letting him get through. Alternating between anger and misery, he tried to understand why she was doing this to him. His mother must be involved somehow, but Pearl wouldn't, couldn't be punishing him for something his mother said or did, could she?

And then he saw her walking towards him. He frowned. She was different somehow, her back was that bit straighter, her head that bit higher. He rushed to her.

"Pearl! Baby! Where have you been? What's going on?"

Snatching her into his arms, he had time to see the pain flash across her face before her mouth set hard in grim determination.

"Where have you been? What are you doing?" he asked again, scanning her face for an explanation. "Why are you catching the bus home, baby? I have my car. I'm taking you."

Pearl wriggled from his grasp and faced him squarely.

"No, Marcus," she said firmly. "It's over. I'm leaving and going home. For good. I'll send Marcie my resignation effective immediately. You can do what you like with what's in the flat. I have my things here. Thank you for all you've done for me, but I can't stay."

Marcus stared at her, then raising his head, his eyes cast desperately about but saw nothing. His hand violently ruffled his hair. He looked down at her. He was once more struck by what a little thing she was in such a big world, and he was overwhelmed by her self-possession. He knew there was a frightened Little girl hiding inside, but adult Pearl was in charge.

"For God's sake, what happened? What did my mother do to you?"

"This isn't your mother's fault. Honestly." She reached out to put a hand on his arm. "I thought being a princess would be fun, like a game, and everyone else would be having fun. I thought I could get your mother to like me; that she would like me when she realised I love you and am not after your money."

"And she will. I promise, baby. Come and have breakfast with us. I can take you home later." Marcus was speaking quickly and urgently, desperate to change her mind.

She shook her head and wiped away a tiny tear that had escaped. "No. I realised something last night. As much as I love you, I don't want to live in your world. I don't feel part of it and never will, and I doubt I would ever truly be accepted."

"No, that's not true," Marcus blurted out, but even he didn't really believe his words. They'd been living in a fantasy for the last few months. There was a good reason he'd not introduced her to his mother before. It was almost as if he'd known this would inevitably follow. "I love you!" he cried, his voice breaking. "I want to live with you. I want to marry you. You can't throw it all away."

"Oh!" A tortured cry escaped her, her bottom lip and chin suddenly trembled violently and her facade of self-possession threatened to crumble. She shook her head and kicked the ground with her foot until she regained control and could face him. "No. It wouldn't work. I would always be an outsider coming between you and your family. We would probably wind up hating each other. And I couldn't bear that, Daddy."

Her reference to their special relationship cut through his heart like the sharp blade of a sword, and he was suddenly hopeful, but she shook her head.

"No. I've been the happiest I've ever been in my life with you. Don't you see," she pleaded, "if I leave now, I will always have our beautiful memories, but if I stay they'll eventually be destroyed. I don't want that. I want to keep them as my most precious possession forever. Safe. Where they can never be damaged. That's why I'm leaving, and why we're never seeing each other again."

"You can't mean it!" Marcus could see Pearl's mind was made up but he didn't want to accept it, couldn't accept it. He chewed his lip and looked wildly around as though he might find something to change her mind. Then his shoulders drooped. "All right," he conceded. "Catch the bus if you must, but I'll come and see you. I have a meeting with Mother this morning, but I'll come after. If not today, as soon as I can."

Pearl sadly shook her head. "No, Marcus. I don't want you to. Please don't. If you truly do care for me, love me even, you will stay away. I don't belong in your world. I never will. You will only make me unhappy if you insist, and it will only prolong the pain of our break-up if we see each other."

With no words left, Marcus took Pearl's hand and led her to a seat. Sitting himself down he pulled her onto his lap and wrapped her tightly in his arms.

"I love you, baby," he murmured against her neck.

"I love you too, Daddy," he heard her whisper. No! His heart cried. Could he really be going to lose her? Surely life couldn't be so cruel. But he couldn't force her to stay if it would make her miserable; he loved her too much for that.

Adrenalin coursed through his body as he saw the bus that would take her out of his life pull into the bus station and people begin boarding. He couldn't let this happen. His mind was scrambling trying to think of what he could do.

"At least let me drive you home?"

"No! I couldn't be in the car with you all that time and then say goodbye again. Let me go while I'm strong enough. Please," she begged him.

His throat too tight to speak, he released her so she could climb off his lap, helped load her bag into the bus's luggage compartment, and walked with her to the steps. He was desperate to kiss her soft lips one last time, but when she hugged him, she turned her face away and he could only kiss her gently on the top of her head. He stepped away as she climbed aboard the bus, found her seat and locked eyes with him through the window, hers as big as moons in a face as pale as moonlight.

His chest was hurting so much he wanted to double over in pain, but forced himself to stand tall. He saw her spread one palm on the window as the bus pulled out of the station onto the main road and then headed out of the city taking his Little girl out of his life.

Chapter 27

Pearl

Pearl parked her boss's car outside the jewellery shop in the main street of Darling Flats, collected her things and went in.

"Ah, there you are," the owner, Reg Downey, greeted her. "Successful trip?"

She nodded, her eyes shining. "It was, I think. I might have even got lucky this time. And thank you so much for lending me your car."

"You're welcome. Lucky, eh? Well done," he replied as she handed him his car keys. "Can I see what you got?"

"Of course. I'll unpack them and then show you," Pearl promised as she went through into the back room. Sitting herself down at a table, she opened the briefcase and removed a black velvet cloth, a jeweller's loupe, a tablet and three small bags. When all was laid out and ready, she opened the bags and displayed their contents in front of her.

When she'd turned up at her parents' farm in Darling Flats the day after her horrible night at the Holding's party with her luggage and without Marcus, her mother had been sensitive enough not to ask questions until she was ready to talk. Her dad, apart from a few additional silent hugs when his back allowed, pretended nothing had happened.

Glad to have something to take her mind off her broken heart, Pearl dressed in her big girl clothes, locked her Little girl away and threw herself into caring for the farm and her parents. She rang her Aunt Nancy and said there was no longer any need for her to come as she would be there to take care of Jack and Mary, and then she made ready for the start of the fruit picking, pulling out and cleaning the pickers' baskets and tidying the packing shed. The picking started the following week by which time both Jack and Mary were able to start doing a few things, and Pearl could keep herself busy with hard physical work from sunrise until well after sunset and collapse exhausted into bed as soon as dinner was done and the kitchen cleaned.

After the last lot of fruit had left for market and the thick fog of pain shrouding her had begun to thin, she realised her love of jewels and her desire to have them in her life burned as bright as ever. After discussing her desire with her parents and getting their encouragement to look for work outside the farm, her first thought was Reg Downey's shop, the Darling Flats Watchmaker & Jewellers. Reg had started his business as a young man and done well enough to raise his family on the proceeds. In recent times, however, profits had been steadily falling and Reg, on the threshold of retirement, was considering closing down. The demand for watches had plummeted, he rarely sold any jewellery, and what he made from repairs barely covered the costs of keeping his doors open.

He wasn't quite ready to admit defeat, though, so when Pearl approached him about work, after an hour of her enthusiasm, ideas and encouragement, he agreed to employ her starting off at one day a week. That became two days a week, and then he began taking those two days off, leaving her in charge. Quickly seeing how the business could be improved, she found the courage to make some suggestions, in particular clearing out old stock by heavily discounting it, and replacing it with up-to-date, fashionable items with a wider range of prices.

At first Reg had been reluctant to sell his old stock at a loss and buy in new stock which he feared might be throwing good money after bad, but then Pearl offered to bring jewellery in and sell it on consignment and he agreed to that. Without a lot of her own money to buy from the wholesalers, Pearl had to go slowly, but she had an excellent eye and understanding of what customers wanted.

She sourced new wholesalers with fashionable jewellery and instigated a small advertising campaign. As turnover rose and his confidence grew, Reg allowed her to gradually discount the old stock and get rid of it, and before long he'd given her access to the shop's money so she no longer had to use her own, and full responsibility for purchasing stock. Soon the shop had a whole new vibrant look and feel about it. Not only did locals start spending more in the shop, but tourists were also dropping in and, increasingly frequently, leaving with something they couldn't resist.

Within a few months, Reg had felt confident enough to install Pearl as manager while he went into semi-retirement coming in only to carry out repairs and cover for Pearl, as he'd done today, if she wanted a day off.

While running the jewellery shop satisfied some of her ambition, she was as keen as ever to have her own jewellery business, so in her spare time she had set about building one online. She registered the name, Pearl's Oyster, and created a website. Her evenings were spent online checking market sites and auctions, and gradually she developed her own modus operandi. She bought some jewellery online, but almost always from reputable sites. When she found something she was prepared to buy, she would offer a much lower price which was usually, but not always, rejected. If the item hadn't sold after a certain amount of time, she repeated her offer, and sometimes it was accepted. Her success rate was low, but so were the prices she paid, so she could almost always resell the items at a profit.

Her preference, though, was to be able to see the jewellery before she bought it, and she managed to borrow a car frequently enough to be able to travel to auctions, market days, car boot sales, and anywhere else people might have jewellery for sale. She also took the bus on occasional trips to the city to follow up on jewellery advertised on online market sites and to scour second-hand shops. Tony, home from his travels, enjoyed driving her around and then dropping her at the bus station. It took up all her free time, but slowly and steadily she was creating a good business buying and selling jewellery.

The jewellery on the table in front of her she'd bought from private sellers in the surrounding towns. Reg had quite a few repairs waiting to be done, so it had suited him to spend the day in the shop leaving her free to go in search of stock. After looking at a considerable number of jewellery pieces of all types, she'd bought an antique emerald bracelet, a diamond pendant and a small plastic bag of unsorted cheap, costume jewellery. She wasn't at all interested in glass stones and gold plating, but had spotted an interesting ring mixed in with the others that had made her heart beat a little faster. Something about it, even though she couldn't see it properly, told her it wasn't fake like the rest. She'd asked to see it out of the bag, but the seller had refused. "Take it all and look at it when it's yours or stop wasting my time," she'd said, so Pearl had gambled on her intuition and bought the lot.

Teasing herself by leaving that aside for the moment despite dying to inspect the ring, she picked up the emerald bracelet. She'd been in two minds about this one too, unconvinced it was everything the seller claimed. In the end, she'd decided it wasn't suitable for Pearl's Oyster, but she would buy it for the shop. It was eye-catching and she had bargained hard so it should make a fair profit, especially as antique and retro jewellery was currently extremely popular and among the shop's best sellers.

Examining the emeralds minutely through her 10x triple-lens loupe, she decided her first assessment had been quite accurate. It was worth what it would fetch in the shop but probably not of sufficient quality to warrant the professional appraisal and certification required for sale through Pearl's Oyster.

She picked up the second item, a diamond pendant, and held the loupe up to her eye. She'd seen the pendant offered on the internet and offered half the asking price. Her offer had been summarily dismissed, but the seller had later made a counter-offer when no one else had shown any interest. Pearl didn't waver on her initial offer, and eventually the seller relented and Pearl bought it for the price she wanted.

Her commitment to quality had already earned her online business five-star reviews and plenty of positive feedback. Her goal was, one day, to be trading in expensive items, but that was for the future; for the present, she was content to keep learning, test her eye and praise herself for her successes. This diamond pendant, for instance, unlike the bracelet, seemed promising and was worth getting appraised.

Those two out of the way, her heart beating faster, she picked up the plastic bag and tipped out the costume jewellery, rifling through for the ring she'd glimpsed. She picked it up and turned it around in her fingers, savouring the look and feel of it. In a minute she'd find out if she'd been right and if she had indeed found a hidden treasure.

Firstly, was it silver, white gold or could it even be platinum? She checked inside the band and saw a tiny *pt.* It *was* platinum, then, which meant the blue stone was most likely a natural sapphire. She inspected it through her loupe. No air bubbles, no lines, nothing to indicate it was man-made. She breathed onto it. Two seconds later, the fog started to disappear and was gone in a second. All signs it might be an authentic, natural sapphire. She slipped the ring on her finger and held her hand up to admire it. She would definitely get a professional appraisal, and if it was as good as she hoped, on top of the likely profit was the huge satisfaction she got from having spotted an unidentified treasure.

After quickly making some notes on her tablet and taking some photographs, she collected up the costume jewellery in a bag to give to the local charity shop and took the bracelet, pendant and ring out to show Reg.

"I thought this would be good for here," she said handing him the emerald bracelet. "It's an unusual design, the stones are good and the bracelet is sterling silver. I don't think it will last long. It's very pretty and we can put an attractive price on it. Someone will love it."

Reg looked at it and nodded. "I'll take your word for it. You have a much better eye and instinct for what will sell than I ever had. Did you get something for yourself as well?"

"I did. This pendant and this ring. I paid peanuts for it, but it says *pt,* so I reckon it's platinum. Hopefully it will be as good a quality stone as it appears to be. I've got a diamond ring and ruby earrings going in to be appraised next week, so I'll get these two done at the same time. If this ring is as good as I'm hoping, I should be able to sell it for about ten times what I paid for it, which, to be honest, wasn't much, so I still shan't be able to afford the Hope Diamond quite yet." She made a sad face, then perked up again. "But, every bit helps."

While she was talking, Reg had put his own loupe up to his eye and was carefully studying the pendant and ring.

"Like I said, I think you've got a natural eye and instinct. They could both be quality and are definitely worth a proper appraisal I reckon, Hope Diamond or not."

"Aw, thank you," Pearl said gratefully. She locked them in the safe, and helped tidy the shop before closing as a 'thank you' for the loan of the car.

"You need a lift home?" Reg asked when they'd finished and were preparing to leave.

"No. I'll be right. Dad's picking me up. He should be here any moment."

They went out and Reg locked the door behind them, then went off leaving her to wait for her lift. In less than five minutes, she saw her dad walking up the pavement towards her.

"Good timing, Dad," she said, smiling up at him.

He greeted her with a half-smile and a nod. "You ready to head home then? The ute's over there, next to that empty shop that someone's been doing whatever it is to."

"Oh, look, they've started painting a name out the front," said Pearl as they crossed the road. "It wasn't there when I left this morning. They must be getting serious, whoever they are. Do we know what it is, yet? It's been such a mystery."

"There's some brochures on the door. I picked one up. Here, you can look at it on the drive home, and tell me what it says."

Settled in the ute, Pearl opened the brochure Jack had handed her. "It says *Sustainable Farming Foundation*. I wonder what that means," she said, scrunching her nose.

"Hmph," Jack snorted. "Nothing, most likely. Sounds like

city activists coming to tell us how to run our farms. Waste of time. Chuck it in the bin."

"Hang on," Pearl said. "I want to read it. It says: The SFF is a private, non-affiliated organisation, committed to partnering with farmers in the Darling Flats region to ensure their long-term viability and productivity. To help counter dwindling water supplies, SFF will provide information on the latest technologies to maximise water collection and usage. Experts will also be available on request to consult, free of charge, with farmers on the individual issues facing each farm and provide advice and suggestions for improvements and change. SFF will also offer loans to aid farmers who wish to future-proof their farms and crop production." As she'd been reading, her voice had been getting more excited and she was fidgeting in her seat. "Wow, it sounds pretty interesting, doesn't it?"

"Hmph," Jack scoffed again. "Sounds downright fishy to me. Who's behind it, that's what I'd like to know."

"Well, it says here there's an introductory meeting at the Town Hall on Saturday night at seven o'clock. Why don't we go and check it out? They might be able to help you with our farm, mightn't they?"

"Oh, Pearl. You're such a dreamer. No one is magically going to appear to help us. I may not know what this crowd's angle is yet, but I've been around long enough to know they aren't doing it for love."

"Let's go anyway, Dad. With Mum. We hardly ever go out together. We could go to the Chinese restaurant first and then to the meeting. Come on. I'm curious to see what it's about. It can't do any harm, can it? What a shame John and Debbie are away. I bet John would want to go."

Reaching over, Jack ruffled his daughter's hair and smiled affectionately at her. "All right, Pearly girl. Let's go see. I can't see me getting any peace until I agree, anyway.

And, if it's anything interesting, we can tell John all about it later."

A FEW LOCAL farmers had stated categorically that they didn't want any 'city-slickers poking their unwanted noses into farmers' business' and would definitely not be going to the information night, but others were driven by curiosity and the promise of a night out with friends somewhere other than the pub. Consequently, the rows of wooden chairs lined up in front of the stage were filling quite quickly by the time Pearl, Jack and Mary arrived. Around the edges of the room, not wanting to appear too keen in case they found out later it was some type of scam, small groups were hanging back, voicing their scepticism to each other.

Despite their natural suspicion of outsiders, over thirty local families were represented when the time ticked over to seven o'clock and a man, in his late thirties or early forties, stood in front of them. He introduced himself as Len Buckingham and told them he'd begin with a short presentation on SFF, and then answer questions.

"It's been hard for a while, and many of you are struggling and considering leaving the land," he went on after briefly outlining the structure of the foundation and its mission statement. "Some families have already left. This is a real shame as Darling Flats has some of the most fertile land around these parts. Food security is going to be an increasingly serious issue in the future, and we can't afford to let important food production areas like this one fall apart. SFF believes new methods and new technologies can help restore productivity to farms such as yours, and that, by working together, we can not only make this district the thriving food bowl it used to be, but even increase its productivity."

"What's in it for you?" a sceptical voice called out.

"And what's it going to cost us?" another voice chimed in.

"Two excellent questions," Len replied. "Firstly, what's in it for me? Well, I've been hired by the Foundation so, yes, I'm paid and this is my job. But don't think that makes me less committed to SFF's mission or to this district. We all have to eat." He smiled. "That's the very reason SFF exists, and we have the opportunity here to be a test case for other districts. I can't deny that excites me because if we can show other places how to better manage their farms in changing conditions, we will not only aid in the production of food, but we will also be helping rehabilitate land that has been degraded by outdated farming practices.

"And, as to what it is going to cost you: all SFF services are free of charge. What we are offering is, initially, a consultation service. Any one of you can book a time to meet with one of our consultants and discuss what particular issues and difficulties you are having. SFF's articulated mission is to come up with a strategic plan for any farm that wants help, and then to partner them to bring that plan to fruition. We can provide a range of resources like information, professional help with planning, budgets, farming practises and so on…"

"And money?" the heckling sceptic called out then grinned around at the audience.

"Yes," Len said, staring directly at the man and forcing him to look away. "And money. Obviously, we won't be just giving money to anyone who asks." Jeers and boos greeted this announcement, but Len calmly waited until it had died down amid shushing from those interested in hearing what he had to say. "SFF is prepared to consider any request for financial help, and if we believe the money is going to be practicably used to help future-proof production on the farm and the district, it will make funds available to help."

"What's the catch?"

Len grimaced and nodded. "I guess you could call it a catch. For any funds to be approved, SFF must believe that whatever the money is being used for will help increase productivity in a sustainable way. Some of you might not agree with all the conditions, and of course that is completely your right. No one is going to be forced to do anything, but what we hope is that when some farms start showing benefits, others will come on board. We're also actively seeking farmers who want to partner with us by setting aside a small part of their land which we will then farm jointly using some of the new ideas, technologies and products available, and those will become showcases. While we are not suggesting doing anything that hasn't already been tried and succeeded in other places, they will be experimental in a way because some adaptations to local conditions will almost certainly be necessary."

Sitting between her parents, Pearl listened carefully. It sounded like a good thing, and the district certainly needed help. She was wondering what her father was thinking about it all, when the side door moving caught her eye. It opened just enough so the man behind could see into the hall. Frozen with shock, her tummy getting a sudden breath-taking case of the collywobbles, Pearl watched his eyes glance around the room until they met hers and locked onto them.

Even in the shadow, even behind a half-closed door, Pearl would recognise those beloved eyes anywhere. Marcus! Her body began to tremble and she clenched her hands into fists as her palms grew suddenly wet. She forced her eyes away from his and looked to the front. What was he doing here? It was months since she'd seen or heard from him, and nearly a year since she'd fled the city to come home.

He had come to visit her at the start, but she'd refused to invite him into the house, telling him each time that his life was not for her and she couldn't be happy in it. It had taken all her courage to not give in to him. Every time she saw him, she was reminded, painfully, how much she loved him and how much she wished it could have worked out for them, but then she would remember that awful night and how alien his world had been.

She had built a life for herself in Darling Flats, and when she wasn't missing Marcus and crying softly into her teddy bear, she was quietly content and proud of herself for being strong and independent. She missed him terribly, but her one meeting with his family had convinced her that they couldn't be together.

Now he was here. Looking in. But why? Len also glanced at the door and Pearl saw the two men nod to each other. Then the door closed and Marcus disappeared. Did he have something to do with SFF? It certainly seemed as though he and Len knew each other. What was going on? Pearl couldn't stop her heartbeat from quickening at the thought of Marcus being as close as the other side of the door.

"Okay, well that about wraps up all I want to say for the moment," Len was announcing to the crowd. He gestured to a trestle table against the wall. "Please help yourself to light refreshments—there's tea, coffee and cake. There's also plenty of brochures and information sheets on this table at the front, so help yourself to those as well. If you have any questions, I'm here to answer them for you. If I can," he added with a smile, stepping back as people began standing up and milling about. A few left, but most stayed for refreshments and to discuss amongst themselves what they'd heard or to talk with Len.

"I'm going outside for a minute," Pearl told her parents and, before they could reply, she hurried across the room to the door, opened it and went through.

Chapter 28

Marcus

Anyone walking past and seeing Marcus leaning casually against the wall of the building, would never have guessed that his heart was racing and the hands in his pockets were tightly clenched into fists. It had been a shock seeing Pearl in the hall. He hadn't expected her to come nor seen her arrive. It had been months, maybe even a year since she'd broken off their relationship and broken his heart. He couldn't remember exactly how long off the top of his head; it seemed both aeons ago and yesterday at the same time.

His eyes were fixed on the door through which she would come. Now she knew he was here, she would come; he knew she would. The second their eyes had met, he'd felt the connection as strong as ever. And then the door opened and she was there, looking around for him. He kept perfectly still. For this brief second, he allowed himself to imagine that when she saw him, she would squeal with delight, run to him and throw herself into his arms with a cry of "Daddy!" In reality, though, he expected she would be as she had the last time he'd seen her: cool, distant, not wanting him to touch her and definitely not wanting to call him Daddy. He sighed and steeled himself. If he had to be patient, so be it; he was prepared to wait for as long as it took and to do whatever it took to make her his again.

He stepped out of the shadows and into the light, his movement catching Pearl's attention. She turned to him and he felt that same punch in the gut as their eyes met. Maintaining his outwardly relaxed demeanour, he strolled towards her.

"Hey, Pearl." What he wouldn't give to know what she was thinking, what she was feeling.

"Marcus? What are you doing here?" She sounded surprised. Was there a hint of pleasure, too? His every sense was straining to its limit to pick up the slightest nuance in her voice, her expression, her movements. The last time he'd seen her, like every time since that awful day at the bus station after the disaster party, she just wanted him to go away. Was that what she was thinking this time too? Was that what she was going to say?

"Same as you. SFF's information night. What did you think of it?" His voice was misleadingly calm.

"Oh. Good. I think. I'm not sure I followed all of it, but it certainly sounded interesting. A lot of it was stuff you used to talk about with Dad, I think. But you weren't in there. How come you were out here?" Her nose scrunched up in confusion as he'd seen it do many times before, and he felt that stab in his belly again and had to forcibly restrain himself from reaching out and pulling her into his arms.

He smiled gently. "No, I'm reasonably *au fait* already with what Len was talking about, so I thought I'd enjoy the evening air. I'll go in a minute, though. Are Jack and Mary with you?"

Pearl nodded. "Are you going to come and say hello?"

"Sure. I'm so glad you all came. I had no idea if you would or not. I'm dying to see what Jack thought of the presentation. I would have called him anyway if he hadn't come tonight."

Marcus's mouth twitched as he watched Pearl's expression change from bemusement to confusion to realisation. She was as captivating as he'd remembered, but also now had an air of quiet maturity that he found as appealing in its own way as her Little.

"Is SFF something to do with you? I mean, are you something to do with SFF?"

"Yes. Guilty as charged." He held his hands out, palms up, and adopted a remorseful expression.

"Oh."

He sighed. "Duty calls. I'm going to go inside and give Len a hand, but will you wait and let me drive you home? We could chat on the way."

He felt her defences shoot up. "What about?"

He grinned ruefully and gently shook his head. "Nothing in particular, I promise. But we haven't caught up for ages. I'd love to hear what you've been up to. Please, have a cup of tea or something while I finish up and I'll give you a lift home. What do you say? Or is someone else waiting for you?"

"No. I came with my folks." It was emphatic, as was the shake of her head.

"How about it then? Let me drive you home? Please?" He tilted his head sideways and scrunched his lips pleadingly.

She didn't answer, but glancing down he could see her foot move as her toe strained inside her runners. It meant she was conflicted, which wasn't an outright 'no'. It had always been hard for her to say what she wanted, and perhaps that hadn't changed despite her outwardly self-possessed persona.

He put his arm softly around her shoulders and led her towards the door. She didn't melt into him as she might have once done, but nor did she pull away.

"Come on. I should go in. Let's see your folks, and I can tell them I'll give you a lift home."

Pearl didn't resist as Marcus led her inside, dropping his arm from her shoulders before he opened the door and they went in. If he was unsure about whether Pearl was pleased to see him, Jack and Mary left him in no doubt.

"Marcus!" Jack said, grabbing Marcus's outstretched hand in a firm grip and pumping it. "Good to see you, mate."

"It really is," Mary agreed, giving Marcus a warm hug as soon as she could push her way in. "How are you, dear? I had no idea you were in town. Did you, love?" she asked Pearl.

Pearl shook her head.

"Are you here for this information night, too?" Jack asked him. "It covered a lot of the stuff we talked about last year, eh?"

"Marcus is part of SFF," Pearl told her parents realising that hadn't occurred to them yet either.

Jack's eyebrows shot up. "Is that right? Well, well…"

Marcus shrugged and nodded, then held his hand up with its palm facing Jack to stop any congratulations. "You know, Jack, if any of this comes off, you deserve a lot of the credit. I listened to what you were saying about farming in this area and how it hasn't changed as the land and water resources have changed. It used to be so fertile and productive, and with food production essential, it's a real problem places like Darling Flats are drying up and farmers are walking off the land."

"So is this your foundation?" Jack asked.

Again, Marcus shrugged to deflect the conversation from

him. "After talking with you, I wanted to see if there was anywhere in the world that was working on these issues, particularly new ways of managing soil and innovative farming practices that use less water. And also, of course, better water catchment and management to make optimum use of what water there is. I've had a good look at work being done all over the globe as well as here and where current research is at, and I decided I wanted to make a contribution."

Marcus was becoming more animated and Jack increasingly more interested as they started going over the major points in the presentation.

"I reckon they might be settling in for the night," Mary said. "Shall we get a cuppa?"

"Marcus wants to drive me home," Pearl told her mother after they'd poured their tea, taken a piece of carrot cake each, sat down and were watching Jack and Marcus deep in discussion.

"Are you okay with that?" Mary asked with a small frown of concern. "You don't have to if you don't want to." Pearl shrugged and sighed, her feelings so jumbled she wasn't sure what she wanted. "Well, whatever you decide, Marcus is always welcome," Mary continued. "And he's welcome to a bed for the night, too, if he wants one. Do you want a cup of tea, love?" she asked Jack who was joining them after Marcus had excused himself to talk to another interested farmer.

"No thanks," Jack answered, clearly excited. "Gee, this stuff is interesting. I've invited Marcus out to the farm so we can carry on our conversation there. I want to hear more about his plans for partnered experimental lots. This could be what we need at our place, and maybe even the thing that turns this district around. I'm reserving judgement until we see some results," he added, trying to sound cautious, "but it's definitely worth a try. Nothing else is working, the place is going downhill, and so far there's no help coming from anywhere else. Too many families are in danger of losing everything, but with the foundation offering financial help as well, it might give them a chance to save their farms or at least make them worth something if they decide they want to sell anyway."

Mary fondly observed her husband's enthusiasm. She hadn't seen him this fired up for a long time. "Do you want to talk to Marcus any more tonight?"

"Nah, I'm pretty right I think. He's coming over in the morning, so we can head off if you like, love."

"What about you, Pearl?" Mary asked. "Are you coming with us or waiting for Marcus?"

Pearl felt herself blush. "I'll wait," she managed to mumble.

From the other side of the room, Marcus saw the Sinclairs getting ready to leave and pursed his lips as Pearl stood up with them, but then Mary gave her a quick hug and she and Jack walked off leaving Pearl behind. He grunted with satisfaction as something inside stirred after being dormant for too long. He couldn't afford to get his hopes up. If Pearl remained adamant she wanted nothing to do with him, he would accept that, at least for now. She looked across at him and he winked. She sat down in a chair to wait.

The hall was emptying as people got answers to their most pressing questions, made appointments for meetings over coming days, or finished chatting with other guests and left after deciding not to do anything for the moment but to wait and see.

Marcus took down the contact details of the farmer he was talking to and promised to give him a call during the week, and then handed out his card to a few other men who were getting ready to leave. At last, Len, Marcus and Pearl were the only ones left, and Marcus brought his colleague over to meet her.

"Len, this is Pearl. Her dad, Jack Sinclair, has a property not far out of town along Forest Road. I met Pearl while she was working in the city and I've been to Jack's farm a few times. Actually, it was Jack who gave me the idea for all this and I think he's keen to get involved."

"Hi, Pearl," Len greeted her. "I hope you enjoyed the presentation. Marcus has often mentioned your dad. I don't know about you two, but I'm ready to get out of here, so I think I'll make a start on tidying up."

Pearl pitched in, cleaning away the refreshment things and washing up while the two men stacked the chairs and tables, and collected up their posters and brochures and carried them out to the car. When it was all done, they switched off the lights and locked the doors.

Len sighed loudly and clapped Marcus on his upper arm. "I think that went well in the end. Probably better than I expected. Of course, it's early days, but I think we can safely say we're not going to be run out of town just yet, and I reckon I've got at least a couple of good leads. Could be a few farmers around here willing to try something new if they think it might help. Well, I'm off then. Catch you guys later."

"Okay, mate," Marcus said with a nod. "You did a great job tonight, Len. Thanks. You're excellent at explaining things so they're easy to understand. I reckon that's why we got such a good reception. I'll see you in the office on Monday, eh?"

Their leave taken, Marcus led Pearl to a four-wheel drive.

"Thanks for waiting," he said opening her door and resisting an almost overwhelming urge to touch her. He didn't want to frighten her away, so he had to tread carefully. It was killing him, though, when all he wanted to do was scoop her into his arms and hold her there forever.

"New car. Yours?" Pearl asked as she climbed in.

"Yep. Ray's got the Jag, but this is much more practical out of town," he said without emotion as they pulled out of the car park and headed for the Sinclair's farm. "So, you've seen something of what I'm doing these days, but what about you? Still in the jewellery business? Or a full-time farmer these days?"

"I still help around the farm sometimes, but John and Debbie came to live here a couple of months ago. John's out of the army and they decided they want to raise their kids in the country, so John's working with Dad now. They're away visiting Debbie's folks for a week or so, that's why they're not here tonight, but I guess you'll get to meet them if you're around for a while."

"That's good news for Jack. I'm sure he appreciates the extra help, and I guess both he and Mary enjoy having their family closer," Marcus replied. "So, what about you?"

"I manage the jewellery shop in town and have an online jewellery business, and I'm still studying for my gemmology diploma." Shyly, but with pride, she told him about her work.

"Do you buy all the stock you sell online off the internet, too?" he asked. She shook her head.

"No. I get some pieces from other places. I travel around to local markets and swap meets, and deceased estate auctions are always a good place to find things. Most people who go to auctions can't value jewellery, so they have no idea what it's worth. They buy because they like it or they are hoping to snag something valuable. I only buy if I'm as sure as I can be that I can make a profit."

Marcus grinned proudly to himself listening to her. He admired her so much for following her passion, putting in the effort to become knowledgeable and then having confidence in herself to take risks.

"And it's going well?" he asked.

She smiled. "Yes. It's building slowly, but I'm happy enough. And I just gambled on a bag of junk jewellery because I thought I saw a valuable ring in it." She told him the story of the ring and then grinned mischievously. "I checked out the ring at the shop and it's definitely real and definitely worth way more than I paid for it."

"Well, good for you, Pearl," he said with a chuckle when she'd finished.

"What about Holding Corporation?" she asked. "You became CEO, didn't you?"

"Not really," he said. "I was only keeping the seat warm for Ray. I never wanted to be CEO, that was Mother's idea, but I had to take it on until Ray was up to speed. We talked it over and agreed he would let the company use his money for its restructure, in return for which he would be appointed CEO, but in name only for six months during which I would have final say on everything and he would be my shadow. We managed to rustle up enough support on the board to make it happen, and at the end of the six months he was doing great and I left him to it. He can call me if he gets stuck with anything, but he's actually very good at his job, and he loves it."

"Do you work there at all then?"

"Nope. As soon as Ray could fly by himself, I quit. I kept my office for a while so I was nearby if he needed anything, but spent my time researching, planning and setting up the foundation. Once that was off the ground, I packed my cardboard box and left for good. Holding Corporation will sink or swim without me now," he added with a wry smile.

"Wow. How did your mother take that?"

"She cut me off without a cent, as she'd threatened to do, until I came to my senses. Her words. So, you see before you a man who is financially independent." He grinned again.

"Oh. Are you living in the same apartment? At your mother's?"

"Nope. I moved into your apartment the day you left. I'd planned to move in with you that weekend anyway if you wanted me to, but I didn't get a chance to ask." He kept his eyes focused out the windscreen and his voice casual. This was dangerous territory. He didn't want her to think he was accusing her of anything or trying to make her feel bad.

"Oh." Pearl was also looking straight ahead. "What did your mother say about that?"

"Not much. She did try and make me change my mind but I moved anyway, so there was nothing she could do about it. And Ray moved straight into my old apartment, so that was that. He and Tina live there. They were married three months ago, and they're expecting a baby, I gather."

"Wow, that was quick. I guess. Tina? I thought she was planning to marry you?"

He pursed his lips. "That rumour was floating about for a while, but it had nothing to do with me. When I told her she was absolutely wasting her time and even if it meant Mother cutting me off without a cent, which of course she did anyway, there was no way I would marry her, she finally accepted it was a lost cause. Meanwhile, Ray was there, arms open, to pick up the pieces and offer her an alternative. They started seeing each other, and once she'd taken off her rose-coloured glasses with my name on them, she decided Ray would do instead. He's been in love with her forever, so he's been as happy as a kid in a candy store, and she's thoroughly enjoying being spoiled rotten by her husband and grand-mother-to-be."

"Your mum?"

"Yep. Mother is tickled pink, although you might be forgiven for not being able to tell. She's never been one for big displays of affection. So, that's all sorted. She's got Ray,

Tina and the baby, and I'm officially out on my own and out on my ear. I think Mother believes I will eventually come to my senses." He looked at her, his eyes dark, his cheeks taut and his voice low. "But I truly feel that that is exactly what I have done at last. Finally come to my senses and made a break for it."

"Oh," Pearl said, momentarily taken aback by his intensity. "So, are you still living in the other flat?" she asked.

"Not for much longer. I've taken a lease on a place here, on the other side of town, on Steep Gully Road. I've kept the apartment to use if I want to go to the city for anything, but I was fed up living there, and assuming SFF goes well, I'm going to be working around this district, at least for the foreseeable future, so it doesn't make sense for me not to live here too. And it's where I want to live. I want to listen to cicadas not traffic, and I want to see a billion stars at night. I've brought some of my stuff already, and the rest is coming next week."

"Oh."

Marcus looked across at her, trying to determine how she'd taken this last piece of news, but she was inscrutable, and it was too late to probe further because they'd arrived at her house.

Chapter 29

Pearl

"Would you like to come in?" Pearl asked as she opened her door to get out. She tried to sound sincere, but was hoping he would decline. It was late, and the lights were out, so Jack and Mary were likely in bed, and she was tired herself and needed time alone to think.

Marcus grinned, and she blushed in the moonlight aware he'd seen through her pretence. "No. I think I'll head off, if that's okay," he replied gallantly, going along with her charade. "Will you be around tomorrow? I'll be over, so perhaps we can catch up then. I'd really like to."

"Okay." Pearl dropped her eyes, then looked up, her body quivering. She'd almost forgotten how kind he was. Her heart contracted as she said, "Goodnight", and he smiled at her so tenderly. Dear Marcus. So gentle. So kind. So handsome. So... Reaching her front door, she waited to go in until she'd watched his car pull out of the drive.

As his lights disappeared into the night, hope such as

she'd not felt in so long coursed through her. Marcus was here, living in her town, and she knew, with a certainty that left her breathless, that he had understood why she'd left, had resolved it, and had come to reclaim her. She turned her face up to the moon and the billion stars twinkling to the song of the cicadas, and her heart was as light as the moonbeams falling on her. She wanted to skip, to jump, to burst into song. She couldn't stop smiling. Wrapping her arms around her waist, she hugged herself hard and shimmied, then quietly let herself into the house. Shutting the door behind her, she squatted down to hug and kiss Rusty who'd been waiting for her, then went to bed, unable to stop smiling and eager for morning.

Next morning, it felt strange knowing Marcus was outside somewhere. They hadn't had a chance to say anything other than hello to each other before he and Jack had set off to survey the farm and discuss setting up part of the property as an experimental share farm with the foundation, but when Pearl had smiled shyly at him, Marcus had given her the tiniest wink and words were superfluous.

Pearl was giddy with anticipation the rest of the morning. She was certain that he wanted her as much as ever, and that he was hoping she would feel able to share his new life in Darling Flats. Their relationship still wouldn't work, though, if he'd only quit his corporate city lifestyle for her, but it was obvious he hadn't. She could see how passionate he was about his new project, and he'd told her many times how much he loved being in Darling Flats. He'd made this change as much for himself as he had for her.

The only sad thing was his apparent estrangement from his mother. Perhaps when Linda saw how happy he was in his new life, she'd understand and forgive him for leaving. Despite how dreadfully Linda had treated her at the party, Pearl had grown in the year since that awful night. Running her own business had given her a confidence boost. She thought of Linda and was sure that, were they to meet in the future, she would be able to stand up for herself this time.

And she'd missed her Daddy. So much. More than she'd ever realised it was possible to miss another person. She'd missed his gorgeous face, lovely deep voice, hugs from his big, strong arms, his passionate kisses and sexy loving. She'd missed him dressing her, washing her, playing with her, reading to her, sitting her on his knee and even spanking her. And the more she thought about it, the more she yearned to be his Little girl again.

So, while he was out in the paddocks with Jack, she changed into her shortest skirt, a tight jumper covered with teddy bears, lacy socks and the pink, sparkly runners he'd bought for her. She fastened her hair up in two high pigtails and secured them with ties with dangling red cherries. They were clothes she'd worn about the house before, so her parents wouldn't think anything of the way she'd dressed, but it would be a message for Marcus.

It was lunchtime by the time he and Jack returned to the house animatedly discussing possibilities for the section of land on which they'd settled, and arranging another meeting for later in the week. Mary interrupted long enough to say that lunch was ready and insist Marcus join them. As he came through the door into the kitchen and saw her, he flinched with surprise then grinned, and as Pearl took her seat across the table from him, it was almost like they'd never been apart. He was as relaxed with Jack and Mary as he'd ever been, and he kept glancing across at her the way he used to, silently telling her to be quiet and behave nicely while they had lunch, but she was too excited, too impatient. She fidgeted and tapped the bottom of her fork on the table until Marcus shook his head the tiniest amount and looked sternly at her from under his eyebrows. Then she wanted to giggle, and he squinted his eyes and pursed his lips, and that made her want to giggle more. She tried to swallow it, but choked on her food and had to cough.

"Goodness, Pearl," Mary said. "What are you doing there? Are you all right?"

Pearl caught another pretend stern warning from Marcus and had to press her hand to her mouth to suppress a giggle. "Yes, Mum," she said as casually as she could when she was able to talk. "Something nearly went down the wrong way. That's all."

"So, Marcus," Mary said as they finished eating and cleared the table. "Do you have any plans for the afternoon? You're welcome to spend it here."

"Thanks, Mary," he replied. "But I was going to ask Pearl if she'd like to come for a drive." He looked at Pearl who nodded.

"Shall we go to my place?" Marcus asked after they'd taken their leave and were heading towards town.

Pearl peeked sideways at him and nodded. He grinned and tweaked her pigtail.

"You all shy, little girl?"

Pearl bowed her head and nodded it vigorously, bounced in her seat and looked out her window.

"You are as beguiling as ever. Do you know that?"

Pearl grinned at him and nodded. "And cheeky," he added with a laugh.

Pearl squeezed her hands between her knees and curled up as much as the seat belt would allow, her feet running up and down on the spot. She smiled across at him and rocked her head from side to side.

"Happy?" he asked.

She drummed her feet harder and nodded harder. It felt like her birthday or Christmas except it was the biggest surprise ever because she'd had no idea it was coming.

"You didn't tell me you were coming," she said out loud as she thought it. "I didn't know you had that shop."

"I've only been to town a couple of times. Len has done most of the setting up here, and then I came yesterday for last night's meeting. Are you mad I didn't come and see you?"

She shook her head. "That's good. I was so rushed, and if I had seen you it would have been too hard to spend maybe half an hour with you and then have to dash off. And if you hadn't sent me away like you've done the other times I tried to see you, I didn't want to risk leaving in case you changed your mind." He smiled at her to take any sting out of his words, and she smiled back wondering how she could ever be cross with him. He was so lovely.

"I'm sorry, Daddy," she said, the name slipping out before she realised it was going to. "Oh!" She covered her mouth with her hand and giggled.

Marcus reached out his hand and put it on her leg. "God, I love it when you call me Daddy, baby. I've missed it so much. Am I still your Daddy then? Or at least can I be your Daddy again? I so want to be."

With her hands clasped over the bottom half of her face, Pearl looked at him with big round eyes. "I want it too," she whispered.

As if that said all that needed to be said, they were both silent for the remainder of the journey. After passing through the town, Marcus headed east a short distance before turning into a short driveway leading to an old farmhouse.

"Welcome to Steep Gully Farm, or what's left of it, anyway," he said when they'd pulled up in front of a weatherboard and iron cottage and were out of the car. "Originally, it used to encompass all the land around here." He waved his arm around to give an indication. "Most of the land has been sold off and it's just the house and three acres left. The house, so I'm told, is one of the oldest in the district and it's still in excellent condition. It's obviously been well loved and well maintained. Come on, I'll show you inside. It's not fancy, but it's cosy and comfortable and plenty enough for me."

He held out his hand and Pearl took it as she followed him inside.

"This is the kitchen and the lounge room," he said as he led her through the rooms. "And that's the bathroom, and there are two bedrooms up the hall and my room's over there and there's a sleep-out too. I'll show you my room." They crossed the lounge room and stopped in a doorway. "It's a bit of a mess at the moment, but it'll be better when I've moved in properly. And the other bedrooms," he said leading her up the hall. They stopped in another doorway and Pearl gasped, then looked up at him with wide eyes. He bent and brushed her lips with his, then shrugged. "I brought your things."

Pearl walked into the room, her mouth open in surprise. The bed was made up and over it was the quilt cover with the picture of the tiara-wearing cat. Marcus opened the wardrobe door and Pearl could see some of the clothes he'd given her on hangers, while others were neatly folded in a chest of drawers. Her rug was on the floor, the Shaun the Sheep stuffies were all sitting on the bed, and the room looked for all the world like a little girl's room.

"What do you think?" he asked when Pearl remained speechless. "Do you like it? I thought you might want to spend some time in it. I kind of hoped you would anyway. I've got some other presents. I bought them for you before, but didn't get a chance to give them to you."

Instead of replying, Pearl collapsed on the floor into a cross-legged sitting position, leant her elbows on her knees and rested her chin in her hands. Marcus waited for a moment, but when she still didn't say anything, he sat on the floor with her.

"What is it, baby? Don't you like it?"

"I want Shaun," she said. Marcus reached up and fetched Shaun the Sheep off the bed and handed it to her. She pulled her knees up and hugged the toy, burying her face in it. Marcus made to touch her, but she grunted and pulled away.

"What's the matter, baby?" he asked with a furrowed brow.

"Go away," she muttered.

"Go away? Do you want me to go away?"

She nodded exaggeratedly and edged further away from him so he couldn't see her face.

He grinned and got up.

"All right, then. I guess if you want me to go away, I'll have to go away. I might go into the kitchen and see if I can find some chocolate. You'll be all right here by yourself?"

Scrunched up with her knees as close to her chest as she could get them, and Shaun covering her face, she nodded.

"Okay. I'll go away then."

After he'd gone, Pearl got up and closed the door, then carefully went through the cupboard and all the drawers to see what was there. Each item of clothing was attached to so many wonderful and precious memories. Little skirts and tops she'd worn when they'd gone out together, and the pyjamas with the kissing teddy bears that he'd dressed her in after her bath. She'd never expected to see any of them again, and Daddy had brought them all for her and set up a special room even though he couldn't be certain she would ever come here. Her heart was so full of love for him she was afraid it would burst, and she had to lie on the bed until it stopped beating so fast. He'd given her such a lovely surprise, she wanted to do something special for him too, to show him he really was her Daddy again. It didn't take long to get ready, and then she opened the door, sat on the bed and called out, "Daddy."

Her heart was pounding as she heard him walking down the hall, and then he was at the door. He stopped dead when he saw her. She squirmed. Why wasn't he saying anything? She held Shaun up to cover her mouth, and her movement seemed to snap Marcus out of his trance. He sat next to her on the bed.

"What's up, little girl?" he asked gently, stroking some loose strands of hair off her face. "You're wearing your spanking pj's," he prompted when she didn't answer. "Do you think Daddy should spank your bottom?" She nodded but didn't look at him. "Look at me, baby," he said firmly. She raised her eyes so he could see them. She was trembling, her heart was full and she ached in the hot, damp place he used to play. "Why do you think Daddy should spank you? Have you been a naughty girl?" She nodded. "Come here and tell Daddy," he said pulling her onto his knee and cradling her against his chest. "There, there, baby," he crooned, stroking her hair as she trembled against him. "It's all right, little girl. Daddy's here to take care of you. You've been such a good girl while Daddy was gone, haven't you? You've been so grown up, working hard and going to school. Daddy's very, very proud of you. Do you know that?"

Pressing as hard as she could against his big, strong chest and feeling like she was going to burst, Pearl nodded and shuddered.

"Do you want to not have to be such a big girl all the time?" Marcus went on, speaking gently, stroking her hair and gently rocking her from side to side. "Would you like to just be Daddy's Little girl for a while?" Pearl nodded. "And do you think Daddy should spank your bottom for running away from the party all by yourself and not waiting for Daddy? That was very naughty, wasn't it?"

Pearl's eyes were closed as she let his soft voice and soothing words wash over her. It had been so long since she'd been able to shed her adult persona and be fully a Little girl again. Even though she wanted it so badly, it was hard to suddenly let go after all this time. But there was one sure way Marcus could strip away the last vestiges of her being an adult in control, one place where she was totally his Little girl —across his knee having her bottom spanked.

"Yes, Daddy. I was very naughty," she whispered.

"Stand up next to me then, baby," Marcus said, opening his arms to release her. She wriggled off his lap, keeping her head buried and stood next to him with her feet pigeon-toed and one on top of the other. "Daddy has to undo your flap, baby girl." Pearl slowly shuffled around, pressing her hands to her aching stomach and squeezing her thighs together. What would Daddy think if he knew how she was feeling down there?

Marcus ran his hands over her bottom, squeezing her cheeks. "You were a naughty girl, weren't you? The first time Daddy ever spanked you was for running away from him in the park, wasn't it? And now he's going to spank you for running away from him at the party. I hope you learn your lesson this time. Daddy doesn't want you to run away from him ever again." As he was speaking, he undid the buttons of the flap to expose her bottom and continued rubbing and squeezing it. His hand was big enough to cover a whole cheek, and soon that big hand would be turning those cheeks a deep, deep pink.

"Come on, little girl. Time to put yourself over my knee." Without looking at him, she handed Shaun to him and then lay across his lap. Marcus sat Shaun on the bed, and gazed adoringly at her milky pale bottom framed by her onesie.

"I want you to be a very good girl while Daddy spanks you, and if you are, Daddy has a present for you. Would you like a present?"

Pearl wriggled and nodded. She clutched onto his trouser leg as she felt him lay his left arm across her back. His right hand pushed her onesie out of the way, and stroked her bottom. "Are you ready?" he asked. She nodded. "Say it, baby," he ordered.

"Ready, Daddy," she whispered.

Chapter 30

Marcus

Looking down at Pearl's perfect, pale, round bottom, Marcus felt well-pleased with himself. For the first time in longer than he could remember, he was exactly where he wanted to be and in control of his life and destiny. He had no regrets about leaving Holding Corporation. He'd done his duty and overseen its recovery for the second time in his life, and left it prospering under his brother's capable care. In the time they'd worked together, they'd rekindled their relationship and developed a new liking and respect for each other, and if Ray wanted any help or advice, Marcus was only a phone call away. He understood completely Marcus's need and desire to get away and supported his decision.

His mother, however, was neither understanding nor forgiving. When he'd told her about the multi-million-dollar foundation he'd set up and that he was leaving the company and the city to work in the country, she was furious. Assuming he was using family money, she had demanded he shut it down immediately and return the money, and discovering that, in fact, he'd used money he'd made trading in bitcoin hadn't appeased her. She'd been furious he hadn't offered to invest it in the family business, and told him she was cutting him out of the will and never wanted to see or hear from him again.

It was what he'd expected, but he'd hoped he might be wrong. He didn't want to be estranged from his mother but, more than that, he didn't want his life to be dictated by her. He was going to live the life he wanted, in the way he wanted, with the woman he wanted. And that woman was currently wearing the spanking pj's he'd bought for her and was lying meekly across his knee waiting to be spanked. His woman. His Little girl. She was adorable and she was perfect. He had an enormous erection that was throbbing insistently and uncomfortably, but he was determined to fight temptation to relieve himself yet, although it was taking a herculean effort.

He was tired of being his only release and eager to plunge himself to the hilt in her hot welcoming velvet, but his Little girl had asked him to spank her, had shown she wanted and needed it, and he was going to enjoy this almost as much. As he raised his hand, he sensed there would be a catharsis in it for both of them. He heard her gasp as his hand connected with her soft flesh, but she didn't move. He paused, then smacked her other cheek.

"You okay, baby?" he asked softly, and heard her whisper, "Yes, Daddy." Pulling her to him, he settled into a rhythm, not hard, but relentless, loving how her chubby bottom poking through the flap of her onesie was developing a rosy patch on each cheek.

He paused to feel their warmth. "You're never ever going to run away from Daddy again, are you?"

"No, Daddy. Promise."

"Have you had enough spanking, or do you think Daddy should spank you a little bit harder?"

"A little bit harder, Daddy," was the almost inaudible whisper. Marcus felt like he was about to explode in his trousers. He raised his hand to spank her harder and faster. She began to wriggle and squirm and he had to hold her tighter as she cried out, "Ow, Daddy. Ow. Oh. Please, Daddy. Nuff. I'm sorry. I shan't run away again. Promise. Promise, Daddy."

He could feel her voice breaking and with a last few harder spanks, he stopped, pulled her up onto his lap and wrapped his arms around her, his throat so tight he could scarcely breathe and a tic throbbing near his temple.

"Oh my baby girl," he muttered thickly as she looked up at him with huge, soft, moist doe eyes, and he bent to kiss her gently, savouring the incredible softness of her lips. He could feel all tension leaving her body as she melted against him, and he would have unzipped his chest and snuggled her inside it if it were possible. He moved his mouth from her lips and dropped kisses on her face, her hair, her neck, anywhere he could reach.

"Daddy?" she said in a tiny voice.

"Yes, darling girl?"

"You said I could have a present if I was a good girl for my spanking. Was I good girl?"

"You were a very good girl. Do you want your present?"

Pearl jiggled up and down on his knee, looked up at him with a big grin and bounced her head up and down.

"Come on then, precious girl, stand up so Daddy can button up your flap, then hop into bed and I'll get your present."

Her flap secured, Pearl hopped into the bed with Shaun and watched while Marcus opened a drawer and fetched a bag. He sat on the bed next to her, holding the bag on his lap.

"I bought this for you before the party but didn't get a chance to give it to you," he began. Pearl blushed and held Shaun up in front of her face.

"Naw," Marcus said gently, pushing the plush toy down so he could see her face. "Don't worry, baby. It's forgotten and we won't ever have to talk about it again." He kissed her, then held the bag up. "You don't have to have it if you don't want it," he said seriously. "Daddy won't be offended. Okay?"

"Okay, Daddy," Pearl said seriously despite wriggling with eagerness to see what her present was. Marcus handed her the bag and she opened it, saw what was inside, closed it quickly and shut her eyes tight, then opened them wide with surprise and stared at him. For a moment he couldn't quite read her reaction and held his breath. Then she shimmied with excitement, opened the bag again, reached into it and pulled out a pacifier.

"Is this really for me, Daddy?" she asked.

"It is, my darling. Would you like it?"

She nodded. "Am I allowed to use it?"

"Of course." He took it from her and removed it from its plastic packaging. "Wait there. I'm going to wash it first and then I'll read you a story and you can see if you like it."

She did like it, he could tell. When it was clean and he'd given it to her and started reading a *"Winnie-the-Pooh"* story about a heffalump, she pressed it against her lips. Marcus could see she wanted it but was shy, so he didn't look at her as she poked her tongue out to touch it a few times, then sucked the tip and finally took it all in her mouth and suck-led. Not wanting to embarrass her, he watched her out of the corner of his eye.

When the story was finished, he took her into his

bedroom. Having re-established her as his precious little girl, he was going to reclaim her as his woman. While she waited, he fetched something which he put in his pocket.

"I'm going to undress you," he said. "Is that all right?"

She nodded and didn't move, while he undid her onesie and slipped it off, other than lifting her arms and legs when he wanted her to. He swallowed hard as her perfect breasts were revealed to him after so long. Oh, how he'd missed those soft handfuls with their tasty cherry tips. He massaged each one gently.

"Did you mean what you said about never running away again, Pearl?" he asked. "I shan't make you live in a mansion or have lavish parties or mix with people you don't like. We can stay in this cottage forever if that's what you want. I love you, Pearl. I don't want to live without you. Will you be mine forever?"

"Yes," she replied, tears welling in her eyes. "I love you too, Daddy. I don't want to live without you either. I will live in this cottage with you forever, and will never run away. I hope one day your mother will accept me. I want to be part of your family, if they will have me, as much as I want you to be part of mine."

"I love your folks already, you know that, don't you, baby? They are so warm and welcoming; it's incredibly easy to be part of your family. And even though Mother has been awful, she does love me, and I do believe there's a good chance she will come around once she realises I am deadly serious about living my own life. So, you will be mine forever? Promise?" She nodded. "Will you kneel for me, baby?" She knelt in front him, gazing up with such adoration he could scarcely breathe as he reached into his pocket and took out the diamond collar. "And will you wear this for me when I ask you to, to show you belong only to me?" She nodded, knelt up and lifted her head as high as she could so he could fasten it around her throat. When it was secured, he placed his hand on her head. "Will you do whatever I ask?"

"Yes, Daddy."

"And what will you say if you don't like it or want to stop or I am accidentally hurting you?"

"Barlese," she whispered.

"And will you let me look at you, while I undress?"

"Yes, Daddy."

"Good girl. I'd like you to get on the bed, on your hands and knees with your head resting in your hands, and your legs apart."

Pearl did as she was asked, every intimate part of her exposed to his gaze. He could see her bottom, flushed from its recent spanking, and how wet and swollen she was, how ready to take him inside her. He finished taking off his clothes and pulled on a condom while he gazed hungrily at her, waiting for him like a luscious feast. She shuddered when he placed his finger at the entrance to her tight, wet tunnel, and pressed gently. She was so slick, his finger slid in without any resistance. He felt her relax against him to allow full access to her deepest part, and she rocked gently as he slid his finger out and in. Then he took it out and walked around the bed so she could see him.

"Do you want this, baby?" he asked, closing his hand around his full, hard erection. Her eyes ran hungrily down his beautifully sculptured body, his manly arms, muscled chest, and flat stomach. He moved his hand so she could clearly see what he was offering.

"Yes, Daddy," she said greedily. "I do want it. I do."

"No barlese?"

"No. I don't want barlese. I want you. Please, Daddy."

And she swung around so he could plunge into her, crying out as he filled her to capacity, arching her back as his hand reached around to squeeze her breasts and he bent to gently nip her shoulder. Then he leaned back, grasping her hips and plunging in and out until she was crying out with each new assault. He'd waited too long and suffered too much to take it slow. They had plenty of time for that later. Right now he needed to take her hard and stake his claim. He came with a roar, thrusting deep as his seed pumped out, and he could feel her bucking and contracting under him, crying and moaning with her own desperate need and ecstasy.

Chapter 31

Marcus and Pearl

Marcus walked to meet the bus as it pulled in, then waited by the door for Pearl to alight so he could take her briefcase and help her down the steps.

Once out of the way of the other passengers, he kissed her. "I'm glad you're back," he growled into her ear. "I missed you both." He laid his hand on her gently swollen belly. "I think that will be the last time you go on your own. I don't like it."

"I was fine. Honestly. Look, there's mine," she said pointing as the driver removed her overnight bag from the luggage compartment. "Not that I wouldn't rather go with you, but you couldn't get away, and Ray met me at the bus. And to be honest I think it was good having time alone with your mum, just the two of us. I mean Alan and Ray and Tina and Nick were there last night for dinner as well, but Linda and I had lots of time during the day to do some mother-in-law, daughter-in-law bonding."

"I'm still not certain I fully trust this new version of Mother," Marcus said, collecting her bag and carrying it along with her briefcase to his car. As he opened the door for her and put her bags on the rear seat, he grinned, adding, "Perhaps she's mellowing with age, or being a grandmother, or maybe Alan has talked some sense into her. Who knows? Whatever, I'm not complaining."

"As hard and as prickly as she can be on the outside, she adores you," Pearl said seriously as he got into the driver's seat and started the car. "I think she got quite a fright when you left. I don't think she ever believed you would go – and stay away – but when you did and she realised you were serious, I think it scared her to think she might really lose you. She would never say, but she regrets missing our wedding, as small and unpretentious as it was." She smiled at him. "I don't think she intends missing out on our baby too."

"She's stubborn, though," Marcus said wryly. "I'm not convinced she would have relented without Alan's intervention."

Pearl giggled. "That's true. Alan is so nice, and I think he's good for her. Don't bother coming in," she said as Marcus pulled up outside Reg's shop. "I'll only be a minute. All I've got are the two gold chains I told you were going cheap. I'll just pop them in the safe."

A few minutes later they were headed for home. "So, how do you feel about your family coming for lunch next Sunday. Were you surprised they accepted?"

"Surprised is an understatement! I didn't think Mother would ever come; I didn't think she slummed it out of the city."

Pearl patted his arm. "Alan accepted before she had time to refuse, but I think secretly she was dying for an invitation, but way too proud to ask. She's very curious to see where you're living and have a closer look at what you're doing, and even if she doesn't say so, she's as proud as punch of you and your work. She's seen the stories on TV and in the papers, about how so many people are interested and how well it's going so far."

Arriving at the farmhouse which Marcus had persuaded his landlord to sell to him, they went inside. Marcus put her bags down and looked contentedly around.

"I'm glad they're coming. And Ray and Tina and Nick." He placed his hands tenderly on her belly. "I know we go to the city quite often, but I want the cousins to spend as much time as possible together, so it'll be good if they can come here sometimes too. I think we should build a guest bungalow. What do you think?"

"Oh, Daddy. That's a wonderful idea! I'm glad they're coming, too. And I'm going to invite my folks. And John and Debbie and Tom and Lily. It should be a lovely family day."

"I hope you're right, but you should be prepared for Mother to carry on as though she might catch something nasty from being so close to nature. That's if she doesn't literally faint when she sees the homely cottage her son, his wife and their unborn child live in."

"It's a lovely house," Pearl protested putting her hands on top of his which he'd left resting protectively on her belly. "Besides, we have a trump card here. I reckon she will be trying her hardest to be on her best behaviour."

Marcus grinned and nodded. "Hopefully. She dotes on her grandson, and she never had a girl of her own, just two rowdy boys, so I wouldn't be surprised if she's secretly over the moon at the prospect of a granddaughter. And soon *I* will have two little girls. You will still be my Little girl sometimes, won't you, baby, even when you have to be really grown up most of the time?"

"Of course, Daddy," Pearl responded immediately to his

cue by wriggling up against him. "Your Little girl isn't going anywhere, and she's going to come and play with you whenever she can and you can read her stories in bed and all stuff like that. I want that too, with all my heart. And my mum is going to want to babysit, so we can have playtime then."

"Come and see what I've done while you've been away," he said, taking her hand and leading her out of the kitchen. "Shut your eyes," he told her as they stood before the closed door bearing a sign saying "Office". She scrunched her eyes tight as he opened the door and pulled her gently into the room. "Right, you can open them."

"Oh!" she cried in enchanted wonder as she took it all in. The sign on the door in no way matched the décor of the room, which far from being just a serious, adult room with a desk, chair, computer and files, was also a child's delight.

"Since we made the other room into a nursery, I thought I would make you your own playroom here, and the door can be locked and no one will be interested in seeing my office."

"Oh, thank you, Daddy. It's perfect. You're so clever, and I didn't even know you were doing it!" Pearl said as she opened the drawers and cupboards and found her favourite, Little girl clothes. The pink rug with the white horse standing beneath a giant full moon that they'd bought on their first shopping trip together was on the floor, and a small table held her stuffies and dolls, colouring books and crayons, and the other toys she'd collected or brought from home.

"I'll get a couch to go in here, too, and then we'll have somewhere to put your cushions and to sit and read and whatever."

"I love you, Daddy. You're so clever. I wondered what the others might say or think if they saw these things. But it's our special secret, isn't it, Daddy?"

He took her into his arms being careful not to squash her belly and kissed her. "It is, my precious jewel. It is."

The End

Sneak Peak

Please enjoy this sneak peek at Daddy's Precious Patient, Book Two of the Claimed by Daddy Series.

Chapter 1

L eaning forward over the steering wheel, she squinted out into the tunnel of light created by the head-lights. She hated driving in the country at night. Nocturnal wildlife emerging from the bushes was hard to see until the car was upon it, and animals confused by the unexpected brightness behaved dangerously and unpredictably. Her unruly mind played movies of all the potential disasters: hitting an animal and killing it, not killing it but badly injuring it, crashing her car as she tried to avoid it and killing herself, not killing herself but being trapped, maimed, alone for hours or days or forever.

Her foot eased off the accelerator; she couldn't risk an accident by driving fast in the dark. But being late could be worse. According to the dashboard clock it was 7:20 p.m. She had forty minutes, which should be enough, and arriving early wouldn't get this ordeal over with any quicker anyway.

Anxiety and dread constricted her chest and bloated her stomach. She was terrified. But that was the point of this malicious charade. The fingers of her left hand stopped tapping on the steering wheel and reached across to her handbag on the passenger seat. They would find no ciga-rettes there. She'd stopped smoking eight years ago, but a remnant muscle memory itched in her fingers and they clawed at her bag before admitting it was futile.

She looked at the clock. 7:25 p.m. Switching on the radio, she scanned the channels for any in range. On the first of the only two accessible, a falsetto with a speech impedi-ment over a thrumming drum machine told her life was for 'dancing and trancing'. Trancing? Ugh. Happy music felt too much like another slap across the face or punch to the gut anyway. She tried the other one. A melancholy lady with a tearful twang declared the misery of living with a man was bliss compared to the misery of living without one.

"No," she yelled aloud, banging the off button. Her palms were clammy and her shaking hand slipped as she replaced it on the steering wheel. Pressing a button on the door next to her and lowering the passenger window, she let in a blast of night air, but it was colder than she'd expected. It chilled her lungs and took her breath away. Clamping her mouth tight to quell the chattering of her teeth, she closed the window, turned up the heater and checked the time.

7:30 p.m. In just over half an hour, she would be on her way home. She wouldn't be there longer than ten minutes, and less if possible. Maybe two minutes. She'd obeyed the order to come; she wasn't doing anything else—no matter what. Then it would be over. Until next time. *Please, dear God, don't let there be a next time. I'm not sure I can take any more.*

Outside, the tall trees had given way to low bushes and scrubby country as the road reached the coast. She slowed as she approached a T-junction and, seeing no lights in either direction, turned right and headed north toward the isolated beach to which she'd been summoned. As the road veered even closer to the ocean, the outlines of sand dunes were visible in the light of the rising moon. At least the sky was clear and the moon almost full. She would not be in total darkness, and she'd brought a torch as well as her phone.

She glanced in her rear-view mirror at the bundle in the middle of the seat behind her: a change of clothes, a thick jacket, a warm blanket, and a lunch box with peanut butter sandwiches, an apple, a chocolate bar and a flask of hot chocolate. Her heart ached with anguished longing. He must be frightened, confused and cold. What kind of a monster could be so cruel? And how could that evil have been any part of creating such innocence, sweetness and goodness?

Calculating she was nearing the designated turn-off, she scoured the roadside for a track down to the beach. One disappeared between the dunes, then another, but the one she sought had a marker: a small wooden sign, nailed to a post beside the road, bearing the word 'Covington' in red paint. According to the directions, it was twenty-five kilometres beyond the T-junction, and her odometer told her she had come twenty-three. She slowed the car down to fifty kilometres per hour, then to forty, then thirty as she neared the twenty-five-kilometre mark.

As the car slowed, her heart rate quickened, exacerbating the growing tightness in her chest and belly. What if she couldn't find the meeting place? What if this was another act of cruelty and no sign existed but she was going to spend hours searching for it in the dark? *No. No. No.* She repeated the word over and over, as though it were a magic mantra capable of protecting her from the manifestation of her worst fears. It couldn't be a lie, a trick. Hadn't the last week of loneliness and worry been enough? She must find the sign. She must be waiting when they got there. She had to rescue him. He needed her and she needed him. Desperately. Her battered, broken, crushed heart couldn't take any more. He kept her alive and gave her life meaning. She would take him home and this time keep him safe forever, no matter what.

Covington. The sign appeared out of the darkness, its blood-red paint glimmering in the headlights. Her relieved *Thank God* filled the car as she expelled a stale breath and allowed her grateful lungs to draw in a fresh one. She braked until the car was barely moving and turned off the road onto the track. The wheels slipped on loose sand. *Please don't get bogged.* Inching the car forward and picking out the firmest parts of the track, she followed it as it cut its way between two dunes before curving behind the one on its right. It stopped just above the beach and widened into an open, flat area where visitors, mostly fishers and surfers, could park or turn around.

Facing her car toward the beach, she switched off the engine, closed her eyes and gave herself a second to enjoy a rare sense of achievement – she'd made it this far, and on her own – before bracing herself for the next challenge. Not expecting to be long, she decided to leave everything but the torch in the car rather than risk losing any of her possessions in the sand. Her phone had no reception anyway, so she dropped it with her car keys into her bag, took the torch out and shoved it into her pocket, and stowed her bag under the passenger seat.

The icy wind blasting off the ocean was so strong she struggled to open the door, and the air so cold once she was out she shivered despite her thick jacket, jumper, long warm tights, woolly socks and boots. She switched on her torch and flashed it in each direction. She was alone on an isolated moonlit beach.

Cold joined the fear, anger, and hatred churning through her. Her stomach heaved and, for a moment, she thought she was going to vomit, but she swallowed hard and kept it down. She couldn't fall apart. Not for her sake, she didn't matter, but she had to stay strong until she got him to safety.

Steeling herself against the icy, salty wind stinging her eyes and matting her hair, she trudged across the sand towards the sound of wild waves hitting the shore. This was madness. A new thought revived her panic. Was it a lie, a trick, after all? Had she been lured here to be murdered on this deserted beach? There was no one to come to her rescue, and it might be days, weeks even, before anyone found her body, or her car, hidden as it was from the road.

She paused, wondering if she should leave as fast as she could? Or had the monster been telling the truth? And, if this suffering and misery were punishment, would it be deemed sufficient? Would they be allowed to leave unharmed?

She tucked her hair down into her jacket and pulled the hood over her head, her ears already throbbing from the cold wind drumming into them. She knew she should keep moving to stay warm, but her body was shaking and her legs threatening to collapse as she plonked herself on the sand facing the sea. She pulled her knees up and hugged them to conserve warmth. She should have brought the rug with her, but hadn't and couldn't summon the will to fight her way up the slope to the car to fetch it.

Staring out across the dark ocean split by the silver light of the moon, her eyes searched for anything that wasn't water, her ears strained to hear anything that wasn't the crashing of waves. The sea whipped into a frenzy by the wind was as cold, as violent, and as cruel as her tormentor. Bile rose up and burned her throat and mouth as she shivered on the sand. She closed her eyes tight. *Please, let him be safe. Don't let any harm come to him.*

When she reopened her eyes, a dim shape had appeared behind the waves further down the beach. Her heart leapt.

He was here. In a few moments, he would be ashore and she would bundle him into her car and get him home and they would be safe. For tonight.

She rose to her feet as fast as her frozen muscles and joints could manage, and lumbered towards the object. It seemed to be a small launch moving parallel to the land. She forced her legs into a stilted jog. It was too big to come ashore. It would have to stop and anchor so its passenger could be ferried ashore in a dinghy. Her eyes squinted into the moonlight in case he was already coming, but she couldn't see a second craft. She shone her torch but the beam died a few metres across the waves.

Oblivious to the agony, she pushed her aching legs onward, stumbling on the uneven sand, her lungs burning from exertion and cold air, but she couldn't make up any ground. The boat was as far ahead as ever. She waved her torch to signal her position, but no answering flash reassured her she'd been seen. She laboured on, leaving the car further behind. She wondered if she'd come in on the wrong track. Perhaps she was supposed to take the track after the sign, or two or three or four tracks after. Doubt and panic snarled her insides as she tried to keep going, to keep the boat in sight, to catch up to it.

At last, with no idea how far she'd come or how she could go any further, she saw the boat swing to face the beach and edge closer to shore. Glancing towards the dunes, she spotted what might be a track. So, she had come in at the wrong place. Her tired, frozen face managed to break into a shaky relieved grin and she slowed to a walk. It would take them a few moments to lower a boat and row to shore. She still had to endure the terror of him coming through the waves and then it would be over.

Her gaze returned to the boat the instant it was lit up by a flash so bright it stung her eyes. The accompanying explosion unbalanced her, momentarily knocking the breath from her body and toppling her onto the sand. Scrambling into a kneeling position, she stared in disbelieving horror at the red, yellow and orange flames dancing on the water. The acrid smell of smoke wafted into her nostrils as her mouth opened wide in an anguished scream which rose from her toes, forging itself right up through her body and splitting her face as it burst forth.

She crawled towards the burning boat, ready to fight her way through the freezing, turbulent water to save its precious cargo. Another small explosion stopped her. The boat lilted, its stern dipped, its bow rose, and it disappeared into the black water accompanied by the hissing of doused flames.

It was gone, and she was left staring at an unsympathetic ocean that had already forgotten the boat was ever there. Mesmerised, she watched the waves rushing to the beach, tumbling over each other, spraying her and rushing away. Her jacket afforded some protection from the salt water spraying over her, but her tights were damp and her face burning. She closed her eyes and shut her mind.

Awareness of how cold she was brought her back. It was ridiculous kneeling here, freezing in the dark, and she had no idea why she was. She searched for an explanation. Unable to find one, she stood up and forced her frozen legs towards the dunes. Reaching the edge of the beach, she turned and made her way parallel to the sea until she found a track leading to the road.

Her hands were frozen into fists, her head ached, and her legs were so numb she could only be sure they were still attached to her body because she was moving. She needed help before she got any colder. She would get to the road, flag down a passing motorist and ask for a lift home. Her heart lightened at the thought of home. A niggle told her she was forgetting something, but she was too cold, too tired and her head hurt too much to try and remember. Later would do. First she needed a hot bath and dry clothes to get warm, and she would eat, too, and have a hot drink.

With thoughts of a warm, snug home and a bed to crawl into keeping her occupied and giving her hope, she dragged herself along the last bit of sand and out onto the road. Across from her was another road joining it to form a T-junction. Excellent. There were three directions from which a car could come. That help was bound to arrive any moment was her last thought before her legs crumpled and she pitched forward into a senseless heap.

Daddy's Precious Patient

Polly Carter

Polly Carter has been writing in one form or another most of her life. With more time on her hands after her children had left home, she was finally able to realise her long-held desire to write romance novels.

"I've always loved the idea of being a writer and taking my work with me wherever I go. I hate being stuck in an office, and being able to travel and work at the same time seems like the perfect life. And, of course, I love, love, and love writing about it."

Polly has four children and four grandchildren. She lives in Western Australia where she has spent most of her life. Her other passions include dogs, travel, reading (quantum physics, I know!) and occasionally painting.

You can email her here: PollyCarter@Australiamail.com
Find her on Facebook:
https://www.facebook.com/PollyCarterRomance
Or follow her on Twitter: @Polly_Carter1

Don't miss these exciting titles by Polly Carter and Blushing Books!
Danny's Secret Desire
Rescuing Rudi
The Lawyer's Secret Baby

Claimed By Daddy series

Daddy's Precious Jewel
Daddy's Precious Patient

Blushing Books Newsletter

Please join the Blushing Books newsletter
to receive updates & special promotional offers.
You can also join by using your mobile phone:
Just text BLUSHING to 22828.

Blushing Books

Blushing Books is one of the oldest eBook publishers on the web. We've been running websites that publish spanking and BDSM related romance and erotica since 1999, and we have been selling eBooks since 2003. We hope you'll check out our hundreds of offerings at http://www.blushingbooks.com.